RANGER OF DARKWOOD

RICHARD B. CROWLEY

Cover illustration by Ron Jordan

ISBN-13: 978-1467984119
ISBN-10: 1467984116

This book is dedicated to the women of my life: my sister for surviving our sibling antics; to my wife for having patience during my less than mature adulthood; to my step-daughter for making me proud; and, to my mom for dealing with me throughout it all.

CONTENTS

ACKNOWLEDGMENTS

To my old college friends: Lee, Mark, and Randy whose endless hours of role play games helped me survive the dreary nights at school and help provide the fuel for my imagination that inspired this book.

1 RANGERS' REST INN

A cool spring breeze blew across the well-kept lawns of the Rangers' Rest Inn. Sprawled out on a patch of fresh growth, a young elf rose with great care, but not without many grumbles and groans. Finally elevating himself to a prone position, the victim of a day and a night's drinking binge swayed in a wave of nausea, ending in an attack of vomiting.

Thinking to himself, Nelfindal tried to recall in his two hundred odd years of existence when the last time he had ever suffered from such a terrible hangover. The previous night's festivities were filled with fun and cheer. Definitely one too many cheers! Talking aloud, the elf whispered to a bird perched on a nearby rosalia bush. "All this suffering because that old crusty dwarf, Dwalin thought he could out drink me. Well, he passed out sometime before I did at least."

The tall elf looked around to see where his drunken wandering had taken him. He recognized the rich vegetation of the garden located on the grounds surrounding the inn. The deep green color of the manicured evergreen bushes embraced the elf in its maze of growth designed to give privacy to those reclusive clients. The bushes were well tended to by a venerable groundskeeper and were planted in such a way as to afford the best possible privacy in the open air. The lush growth rose up to a height of three meters and required constant trimming to maintain an even look.

Standing up from the foul remnants of the last evening's food and spirits, the elf carefully made his way to a nearby fountain. Squatting under the unfurled wings of the fountain's statue, the elf looked thoughtfully through his blurry vision at the representation of a spitting dragon. The imposing marble sculpture was a gift from the Iron Hill Dwarves, who were masters at detailed stonework. The animated appearance of the white stone figure extended its graceful neck in an aggressive pose to arriving customers. The tall elf lowered his head into the cool waters of the fountain's basin. The sudden shock of the cold revived him quickly.

Invigorated by the dousing, the elf walked over to a set of large wooden doors, which opened to the inside courtyard of the inn. The inside of the courtyard looked nothing like any other. In the center of the area was a large oak tree with a broad five-meter light brown trunk. The great tree's branches spread out evenly over the open space shading the interior carpet of grass with its many branches and deep golden leaves. The massive boughs were sparse near the first and second floor levels of the inn, but above the third floor the graceful arms of the oak spread thick layers of foliage across the entire courtyard like a natural ceiling.

Nelfindal entered the quiet, shaded interior of the courtyard, where strewn about like driftwood from some great flood were the remnants of the festival's participants. Many of the guests lay on the grass at the base of the tree below the gentle branches while others were sprawled across tables and benches inside the inn itself. Even with the dense roof of leaves above, the great oak allowed its branches to spread apart to allow the warming rays of sunlight to enter the dark interior.

The spring festival was a great success after the inn's first year of operations. The celebration had been planned for many months and the preparations went on for two weeks before the festivities began some two days prior. Many of the people who attended the two-day celebration were by invitation, but by the middle of the first day a few crashers had arrived. The volume of the celebrants was incredible, but the kitchens were well stocked with food and the cellar never came close to running out of spirits. Most of the guests were rangers of the legendary guild of Darkwood; however, there were many common merchants and mercenaries fortunately visiting in the area to participate in the feasting. The two kitchens of the inn ran smoothly for the festival with fresh venison, spring chickens and other assorted delicacies prepared by a short human cook and his young assistants.

The inside of the common room was a sight that caught many people by surprise. The brass lamps hanging on the walls and from the rafters four meters above were crafted by the most talented of elven artists. The elaborate wood tables and benches were also made by master craftsman many of who were from the woodcutters' glade in the elven homeland of Elador. The deep rich ash was carved and polished to a hard shiny surface, which was unmatched by any human sculptors. The lengthy bar at the back end of the common room was intricately shaped from the solid trunk of a birch tree with scenes of wildlife frolicking in the forest. Behind the bar was a large wooden cabinet carved with equal skill, which stored all the mugs needed for several nights of good business. Numerous clay mugs were still resting on the shelves even after the two days of festivities.

The U-shaped common room allowed for many conversations to be unheard and unobserved. This added privacy made the inn the safest meeting place for the secretive rangers of the Darkwood Forest. The walls facing the center alcove of the giant oak tree were lined with stained glass windows, which allowed more light to enter the otherwise windowless common room. During the day the rays of sunlight were captured by the leaded glass and cast a rainbow of colors along the polished floors and tables setting the whole area ablaze with brilliant light.

Weaving his way around and over unconscious forms, Nelfindal slid behind the long polished bar. Searching through his still blurry vision the elf found a bottle of medicine that one of the owners swore to for such emergencies as hangovers. Although the foul smelling and bitter tasting fluid was enough to deter anyone from ever getting drunk, it did offer some reprieve from the pounding headache that seemed forever to follow a night's indulgence. Fortunately, the bottle was full and only a few sips were required.

A faint squeak, sounding as loud as an explosion to those suffering celebrants who retained some consciousness, resonated from the stairs followed by a lame apology by its burly creator. Without turning around the elf immediately recognized the Ergothian warrior and friend, Galtron. The human warrior was a large muscular man who was rarely found far from his deadly battle-axe. Some of the human's closest friends wondered how often he slept with the deadly weapon at his side. Three hundred plus pounds of corded muscle and bone stepped across the squeaky wooden floorboards as much as his large frame would allow. Careful not to disturb the immobile forms by the bar, the human took the unstoppered bottle of cure-all from the tall elf with quiet thanks. With expert and familiar ease the human drained the contents of the bottle and placed it back on the bar with almost ridiculous care so as not to make any undue noise.

Motioning for Galtron to follow, Nelfindal walked out into the fresh air away from the stuffiness of the inn that he always felt confining. The odd pair of human and elf walked silently to a shaded bench under a large aspen, which offered a good view of the town's main road in front of the white marble dragon. The constantly flowing water shot upward from the gaping statue's mouth reminiscent of its real life fire-breathing counterpart.

After taking a few breaths of fresh air the dark-haired human commented, "That was one helluva bash last night. I thought it would never end. Those ranger friends of ours can be just as dangerous with a mug of beer as with any sword."

"It didn't deter you from jumping at some of them last night. You had to be held back from three of them when they tried to `borrow' your axe to cut more wood for the cooking fires," replied the smiling elf.

Smiling at the memory of the look the rangers gave him when he charged, Galtron laughed, "Well it's not a tool to be used for menial tasks like wood chopping. Besides if I remember right you were the one who boasted to our dwarf friend that you could drink twice as much as him."

Remembering how the dwarven ale had affected him, the tall elf rubbed his temples at the reminder of his painful headache then quietly said, "I know and I'm suffering for it now. I'm real glad I didn't try to challenge him in an arm wrestling match instead. I would be trying to figure why I woke up with only one arm."

As the two sat conversing on the night's silly antics of drunken foolishness, the sounds of an active city rose up around them. The clatter of horse hooves along the road in front of the inn attracted the attention of the two recovering fellows long enough for them to realize that it was rather late in the morning.

The sun was already high up in the east horizon and the streets were packed with the usual crowd of traders, merchants and local citizens. Many of the local residents avoided the inn, which was famous for its usual rowdy and dangerous clientele.

Turning towards the busy main street of Cardichen, the muscular human strained his eyes to focus his blurry vision. Galtron turned to his friend and said in a gruff scratchy voice, "It's a beautiful day to begin a journey home. Eh?" The mountain of a human slyly stared out of the corner of his eye at the startled elf.

Nelfindal nodded his head slowly to acknowledge his friend's observation and added slowly, "Yes, it is a nice day to begin a journey. I'm just wondering if it's a good time for me to go back to Elador. There are many people that may not be happy with my return."

The human turned to the tall elf and scowled at him. "Who cares what others think about your return. You stood up against the aristocracy to support the rights of silvar servants. This wouldn't be such a problem if the wealthy bastards thought to treat their servants as something other than property. No one has the right to treat another so poorly," angrily charged the human. Calming himself, he added, "Don't let them bother you so much."

The ranger sighed and slowly replied, "I guess your right. Maybe it is time to stand by my decision and get back control of my life." Thinking about the past events leading to his temporary exile only reinforced the elf's commitment to his declaration.

Realizing the conversation was getting a bit to somber, Galtron loudly challenged, "Hey, are we going to let all these drunken fools take up good profitable space or are we going to clear them out? Let them pay for a room if they want to rest."

Laughing at the human's attempt at sounding like a real businessman, Nelfindal replied, "You can clear out the drunks, I have some preparations for my trip home to take care of. Besides you're better at the bouncing end of the business."

Galtron smiled at the cheery elf and shrugged, "Suit yourself, but you're going to miss all the sour expressions."

"Well, if you put if that way. Let us go do the honors," the elf offered with a devious grin.

Standing up as one the two adventurous companions made their way to the crowded common room to clear out the uninvited participants. After the vagrants were removed to the outside of the inn the two friends began to help their inebriated friends to the comfort of their rooms. It took some doing to move the limp forms of overindulged humans, dwarves and elves from the benches and tables. The few who made it to their rooms the night before started to come down for the midday meal shortly after.

The smell of the lunch preparations wafted through the common room of the inn. After some semblance of order was regained, servants began serving heaping dishes of food and mugs of ale. The faces of many recovering victims frowned at the sight of the pewter flagons that contained the source of their discomfort, but many acknowledged that a little ale would help nullify their ringing headaches. The prepared food appeared in ample time for the awakening customers to eat and continue with their day's recovery. The tasty spiced potatoes and succulent smoked meats were welcomed quietly by the hungry celebrants.

The mood in the inn was very subdued during the meal, but some harsh words were often exchanged when someone was foolish enough to loudly clatter a dish or clumsily slam a mug to a tabletop. Aside from these small disturbances, the sobering visitors ate quietly and with earnest. Fortunately, the cook had anticipated the hearty appetites and kept the food coming. Much like the day before, the food was excellently prepared and the heaping trays never seemed to stop.

The young barmaids that brought out the platters of food were more confident to get close to the recovering group. The night before not one girl was able to walk next to a table without being assaulted by a barrage of overzealous hands. Not that the girls didn't like it, the thought of a crowd of adventurous, handsome and somewhat wealthy bachelors was very appealing to the local unmarried maidens. Most of these ladies dreamt of snaring a wealthy husband who could carry them away from the boredom of the small town. Many of the town inhabitants feared the unknown dangers and horrors that always seemed to lie just outside their town borders.

Later in the afternoon, the inn began to fill up with the usual clientele of visiting merchants, mercenaries and some brave young, local residents. However, tonight observed by only a few curious folk a darkly cloaked figure entered the room. Swiftly taking a seat in a secluded dark corner, the shadowy figure sat quietly without ordering or moving until many minutes later another cloaked figure appeared and sat down. The two strangers shrouded in darkness received only a few curious glances from the most courageous of the night's group. Nonchalantly glancing around the two figures checked to see if anyone was close enough to eavesdrop on their conversation.

After confirming their conversation would be in private the first shadow quietly whispered, "Are you sure this is the place? I haven't seen the one we were sent to find."

After glancing around again, the second shadow commented, "Aye this is the place. The one we were sent for is well known to many in these parts and is said to be a regular here.

It's not hard to miss a tall eldar northerner. They usually flaunt their power and wealth. It's well known that many northern silvars can't stand the high elves."

The first dark figure hissed, "Well, I still don't like the idea of just the two of us sent all the way here just to track this northern scum."

"Hey, if you don't like it go back and explain it to him. Besides all we have to do is follow the eldar's moves and report them back. In the meantime, we wait until he shows up," scolded the second mysterious stranger, but not without receiving a frustrated grunt from his companion. Ending their conversation the two trackers sat quietly. Aside from a barmaid who took their order of elven wine, not one patron or servant paid the secretive pair much attention.

* * * * *

Deep under the inn in a room carved out of solid bedrock, Nelfindal stooped over an unlocked chest made of rich white oak and banded with hardened steel. Inside the chest was his personal traveling gear. Donning the enchanted tan, leather armor and his magical elven cloak, the eldar felt emotionally unprepared for his long overdue trip home. At first glance by anyone other than the elf's closest friends, he would have appeared a slight above impoverished. His soft leather armor looked worn as did the magical cloak that once closely examined constantly changed appearance to match the surrounding surfaces. The ranger's cap resting on his head also looked like it had seen better days. Only by magical means could one discover the fortune that was draped about his body. Such items as the wondrous bow Elenar that disguised itself as a ring on his right index finger, the diamond and mithril medallion of healing that hung around his neck under his leather shirt or the many other items that were well hidden on his person.

After figuring out what to bring on his trip home, Nelfindal closed and locked the last of his many iron bound chests. Upon leaving the magically secured vault, he encountered his silvar friend Lossoth, a well-built elf by many standards, also grabbing a few items of his own out of a chest.

"Well Nelf, were are you headed off to? To wreak havoc on the rest of the elven nations," joked the muscle-endowed elf.

"I'm long overdue to return home to visit some old friends and participate in the spring festival. Unlike you, people don't lock their doors when I show up. Not that you, a respectable ranger yourself, ever caused trouble or anything," cheerfully replied the tall elf.

"What me? Ever cause trouble? Never! I just have fun with those who need education in excitement," boasted the laughing silvar.

"What are you up to? I didn't know you were going anywhere," queried the eldar elf.

"I'm not really. Dwalin wants to practice a new attack technique and thinks I'm the best match available. I think he's still sore about the last time I beat him in wrestling," bragged the muscular elf as he pulled out a gleaming broadsword.

Preoccupied with his search for a strong shield the large silvar continued his foray. Anxious to leave, Nelfindal offered much luck to him in his engagement with the burly dwarf.

Walking down the silent dark corridor that led from the main vault, Nelfindal observed the fine lines marking where one of the secret trap doors was located. A steel door would drop down at each end of the hallway to block off any escape to those trapped between. The instant the doors were sealed shut a raging magical fire would burst up for several minutes until the intruder was dead. It was only tested once and then only charred embers remained indicating the failed break-in attempt.

Climbing up a latter to a hidden door, Nelfindal exited through a well-concealed secret door behind a wine rack into the cellar of the inn. Quietly passing servants like a faint unseen breeze, the elf ascended the stairs leading to the common room. Stopping off at the bar, the elf ordered his usual mug of aged elven wine to warm his insides and raise his already uplifted spirits.

Nelfindal absently scanned the crowded inn sipping his wine, thinking, "I am truly going to miss this place."

* * * * *

Still enshrouded in shadows, the two cloaked figures looked on waiting for their quarry to show. After a few hours, a tall elf stepped into the common room garbed in worn rustic traveling gear. At first, Darius thought he was mistaken by the impoverished appearance of the elf, but there was no doubt in his mind that this was the elusive northern ranger.

Gesturing to the other southern ranger, Raelin, Darius whispered, "I'll wait for him outside and you can follow behind him as he leaves, but remember not to alert him to your presence when you get up." The tracker leader quietly rose and exited the inn to await his target.

After finishing his drink and bidding the barkeep good-bye, Nelfindal walked through the crowded common room and exited the outer doors of the inn. Raelin stood up unobserved by any of the drinking customers or the tall elf and followed silently behind.

Darius waited outside for only a few minutes before Nelfindal stepped out of the inn. The tall ranger walked past the spouting marble dragon and continued on to the main road running through the town. The late afternoon sun rested easily on the western horizon, shedding enough of its light to cast long, deep shadows. In the east, the first signs of twinkling stars were blinking into existence.

The city was very active at this time of the afternoon and it would be some time before the town watch cleared the streets of the many pesky merchants. Shortly after the beginning of the private war between the thieves' guild and the local rangers, the town mayor decreed that all merchants were to stop their business at dusk. This was to prevent any innocent people from becoming victims to the constant violence. Fortunately for many and unknown to most of the common people, there was a tenuous cease-fire. Prior to the truce, many bodies were found in the gutters around town each evening. Many of who were well-known thieves and burglars who happen to fall prey to the policing actions of the local rangers' guild.

Not unlike many cities, the authorities didn't stop the regular night people from carrying on their business. There were still the usual beggars, petty thieves, unaffiliated muggers, and young street urchins roaming the many dark avenues, but most did limit their activities. The local street children had learned to avoid the tall ranger who was one of several secret owners of the Rangers' Rest Inn. He was also one of the people who openly battled the local thieves' guild. The resulting power struggle remained in a stalemate, which no one wished to change.

Many of those who associated with the local underworld knew of the ranger's reputation for surviving difficult odds especially with his unique magical talents. The last thing the guild wanted was for a freelance thief to pick the elf's pocket or a random thug to try to mug him. Such an act would be construed as a declaration of war on the underworld and an end to the already uneasy truce.

Taking the east road out of Cardichen, the eldar elf began his quest home unknowingly followed by the two silvan rangers, who had no intention of letting him get away like other trackers had in the past. Unlike the others that were sent to locate the tall ranger, the two trackers were experts who possessed a great many more resources to aid them. Darius as the tracker leader was next in line to be nominated to the prestigious position of range commander; an honor rarely awarded. The tracker had the ability to summon the magics of nature as some of the most experienced rangers could.

Raelin was an excellent tracker as well, but his expertise was mostly in the area of thievery and assassination. In case, Range Commander Caric gave the word for the two to dispose of the tall elf, Raelin was well prepared with his many poisons and assassination techniques. Until word came from their commander; however, the two were only to follow the northern ranger and track his progress.

While following the eldar ranger, Darius wondered why their range commander was so insistent even fanatical in the search for the northern ranger. It was not well known that before Caric ascended to the rank of range commander that he was the only survivor of a secret mission for the southern high council. During the mission northern rangers ambushed Caric, his commander and several trackers. Though severely wounded, Caric managed to survive the attack and return word of the mission's failure. The council carefully organized several missions to the north to seek out all those responsible. Of the rangers involved only this one eldar elf remained, but the orders were to not terminate him. There had to be a reason for keeping the tall elf alive. Darius thought there had to be either treasure or some magical artifact involved. In the past, several fellow rangers had caught the elf, but died by his hands or with the help of his friends. The eldar was now by himself and unaware that he was being followed. If he did have something of value he didn't show it off to anyone. The whole thing was a mystery.

2 VOYAGE HOME

Nelfindal walked comfortably down the Great East Road, an ancient trading route built by the ancestors of the local human settlers. According to legend, once long ago a great empire existed back when men, elves and even dwarves lived with each other. Those days had past long, long ago. Now, racism spawned dissent between the different races and hatred ran rampant. The past few decades were marked by skirmishes amongst the expanding human settlements and the diverse dwarven colonies. The elven nations stayed to themselves for the most part except when dealing with their Ergothian allies.

The noble Ergothians were the only humans that elves would treat as of equal status. One main reason was that the high humans, as they were called, tended to live well into their third century of existence. It wasn't unusual to see a high human in a elven haven like Elador or married to an elfmaiden.

Still, the elves had closed themselves off so much to the lesser humans that some believed the existence of the elder race was only a myth. The races that did believe in elves were generally hostile to the few they met. Rumors of the great wealth the elven nations possessed was enough to lure the most adventurous human thieves and cutthroats to their borders. Other rumors that formed were that elves slayed all humans who came near their borders, but in fact even the most repugnant were captured and well cared for in sanitary prisons.

The fact was all elves whether silvan, sindar or eldar abhorred killing in any way if it was avoidable. That wasn't to mean that all elves were pacifists, but murder was generally a last resort. The only exceptions to the restraint to killing where those of pure evil nature such as the races of being which thrived on darkness like orcs, trolls, some dragons and the creatures of the hells. It took no second thought on the part of any elf whether or not to slay these monsters.

* * * * *

The first city on the road to the elven homeland was a thriving community called Bethany located on the banks of a great river. No one knew how long the city had been in existence, but most of the citizens believed it was the capital of a once great empire. Every so often a forgotten tomb was discovered when the foundation was excavated for a new building. The contents were often robbed, but the few artifacts that did remain undisturbed were identified as centuries old. The last great empire was known to have been at its high point over ten millennia in the past so it was unlikely that such relics were linked to the fabled nation. It was impossible to convince the local humans that the fabled capital had to have been elsewhere when they were set on believing their city was built atop it. The rumored location gave a bit of glamour to living in the riverside city.

Not unlike many other cities of the times the entire metropolitan area of Bethany was built in levels or tiers for defense. The first or inner tier was the oldest of all the areas. This region was believed to have been the former site of the mythical emperor's castle. The huge structure was supposedly made out of solid marble and furnished with pillars of silver. At the present time, the inner region was host to the ruling duke's manor house and council hall, as well as, the residences of several wealthy merchants.

The second tier was known as the commerce section, which surrounded the first section with many prosperous markets and inns. This area also housed the various public buildings such as the library, town prison and local garrison headquarters. The outer tiers were mixed together so much they were just referred to as the outer city. This was the location of many commoners dwellings, small shops, taverns, and the city garrison barracks.

The east road led straight through the middle of the city and continued on to the banks of the river where one could rent a ferry across. Many of the traveling merchants who showed up in Bethany were from the sailing barges that traveled the length of the large waterway known as the White Flow. Since the young ranger had traveled for quite some time, he decided to stop and get a room for the evening and partake of the social scene of the active human settlement before making his way across the busy waterway.

Along the road into town there were a few dwarves selling their fine steel and worked stone. Their were even a few passing silvan elves who absently nodded in acknowledgment to the proud eldar ranger. Few outsiders knew of the constant rivalry that went on within the elven nation. The eldar with the exception of a few sindar were the only elves allowed any station of power in the elven political hierarchy. Because of this inequity many silvan elves openly detested the eldar, who supposedly possessed all the royal blood.

Unlike the rest of the eldar nobility, Nelfindal was raised in a rustic environment. The silvan ranger who acted as a surrogate father for the orphaned youth instilled the deep sense of morality and equity lacking in most eldar. Unforeseen to the veteran captain were the conflicts these views would have.

The first place the ranger found was more than suitable for an overnight stay. The Black Crow Inn was a modest two story wood and mortared stone structure with a wooden sign hanging over the door exhibiting a mob of flying black birds. The outside face was made of large flagstones and rough-cut cedar wood, which gave the human establishment an appealing rustic look. Stepping through the creaky doors, Nelfindal paused to allow his eyes to adjust to the change in light. The interior of the spacious common room was well lit, but still remained shadowy compared to the sunshine outside.

The elven ranger suddenly realized how thirsty he was and proceeded to walk towards a large counter filled with many clean mugs. A tiny human male stood behind the bar cleaning the pewter cups with a feverish motion. Seeing the tall stranger entering his inn, the owner briskly shuffled around a few tables to the elf's side. The innkeeper who resembled a small scavenger bird himself looked awkward next to the tall frame of the entering eldar ranger.

Rubbing his hands in his apron in a nervous gesture the black haired man asked, "How can I help you, fair elf?"

The ranger responded in the common tongue, "I require only a private room for the evening."

The fidgeting innkeeper escorted the elven boarder to a room on the second floor of the sizable inn and hollered for one of his servants to follow. A frail human boy came running up behind the tall ranger juggling a pitcher full of fresh water and a clean towel. Looking down at the filthy child Nelfindal thought on how he must look from his long trip from Cardichen.

The innkeeper unlocked the door and announced his price for the night's stay. Nelfindal paid the modest price and walked in after the small man child, who placed the towel and pitcher down on a small table and quickly ran out of the room. Closing the door behind him Nelfindal took off some of his gear and wash up in the clear water brought to him by the servant. After cleaning off the trail dust, the ranger left his room and grabbed a cup of wine to wash down the road dust. After finishing his drink, the eldar exited the inn through the empty common room.

The street was crowded with the usual traffic of traveling merchants, farmers and unemployed mercenaries. Squinting through the glaring light of the midday sun the elf questioned himself on his next destination. In such a big settlement there was always something to do. Realizing he wasn't doing much by standing around the young elf began to walk towards the commerce district. After a half hour of weaving his way through the crowded streets the ranger unconsciously thought to look around. It was at that point he noticed his two followers. At first he thought it unlikely that anyone would be tailing him until he recognized the tanned, but otherwise fair complexion of the southern elves.

Immediately, he knew they were following him. The two were very inconspicuous, but the eldar had been tracked by southern rangers before and could easily recognize them. "It was only a matter of time before another group was sent," mumbled the ranger to himself.

The last pair tried to surprise him in a tavern after a night of drinking. The two thought they could overwhelm him when he was drunk. Normally, it was hard to fight when intoxicated, but the abnormal constitution of the elf made it very difficult and expensive to get drunk on human ale. The exchange lasted only a few minutes as one southerner then the other dropped dead from sword wounds. Nelfindal realized that these two weren't going to make such a mistake. Who knew how long they were following him? They must have been very good to avoid detection until now, thought the curious eldar.

The northern ranger observed his predators closely to see if he recognized them. He didn't know either one, but felt like he would soon if he didn't try to lose them. The first one was obviously a very experienced tracker possibly a tracker leader. The leader was well armed and carried himself well. The weapons belt around the southern elf's waist held a short sword and three daggers hung from his chest all of which were well concealed under a dark cloak that opened long enough for the ranger to see the items. The southerner also had a bag, which most likely contained healing herbs by the way the leather was treated. A moderate number of herbs cost a good amount of money in a city like Bethany, but many rangers were experts at locating the medicinal components in the wild and rarely needed to purchase such things.

Unlike the proud ranger, the other follower had the shifty eyes of a thief. He also carried himself confidently, but in a way that unnerved the young eldar. The tall ranger had dealt with many thieves and knew how the best handled themselves. This character was a true expert and knew it. He openly sported a pair of short swords as well, but if he had any daggers they were well hidden. His dark features were enhanced by his deep hood, which was pulled far over his head. Only the shadows of his more pronounced facial features were visible and they tended to give the southerner a look of carved stone. Nelfindal was sure that this one was accustomed to death and killing. The shock of his observation prompted the elf to action and attempt to lose his followers.

The eldar's height gave him a great disadvantage when running from others in a crowd of short humans. Endowed with long blond hair, he glowed like a beacon lantern on the darkest of nights. Seeing the opportunity to escape his shadows, Nelfindal ducked into a dark alley. The dreary place turned out to be a maze of interconnecting roads and paths, which wound around buildings in ever complicated directions.

After an hour of speedy evasion, Nelfindal was confident that he had lost his followers, as well as himself. Still concentrating on the past pursuit, the tall ranger unconsciously walked into a dead end road. Turning around to back track, the elf was suddenly blocked by four street thugs in rags. All of the cutthroats were brandishing crude weapons like a rusty sword or club.

The biggest robber and apparently the leader spoke arrogantly to the trapped elf, "Give us your valuables and maybe we'll let you go elf. If not then you won't leave this alley alive!"

Standing back to size up the situation, Nelfindal haughtily replied, "And who will stop me? You and your friends with those toys? You four look like some brats who haven't had their rags changed in a week! Go home to your mothers."

The insult struck the young cocker like a physical blow. It seemed like he was used to getting what he wanted and from his size it was not surprising. The youngster was not nearly as tall as the ranger, but weighed over twice as much. Feeling the questioning looks of his fellow burglars, the bold youth straightened his shoulders and shouted boldly to the others, "Get the elf scum! Everybody knows they have lots of money!"

With that statement the four youths attacked simultaneously. Jumping back Nelfindal threw a dagger with his left hand at one of attackers' shoulder and drew his sword in the same swift movement with his right hand. The swiftness of the maneuver caught the pressing group off guard and created a moments hesitation. That was all the defending ranger needed as he disabled another thief with a nasty slice to the leg. Seeing the expert strokes of the fine steel the two unharmed thieves retreated from the dangerous twirling blade carrying their wounded friends.

The young leader was the recipient of the thrown dagger. His screams could be heard throughout the area. The keen elven blade still remained in the wounded human as he was carried away. The loss of the dagger was incidental to the valuable lesson the youths had learned. The weapon would help remind them of it, Nelfindal mused to himself.

The confrontation charged the young elf with a surplus of energy. It was long ago, but it seemed like only yesterday when even the three century old elf was just as cocky and inexperienced. By elven standards he was still young in age, but the hardships added much maturity to his otherwise youthful appearance. Since his forced exile, the young eldar had traveled to distant lands and to places never before seen by elves and men alike. The challenges he faced had developed an inner spirit that many thought would be pacified by the real world. Instead, the world had taught Nelfindal to savor life and to take advantage of all its opportunities. However, the biggest lesson of all was that he was master of his own destiny.

The walk to the city market was uneventful after the confrontation in the alley, but the elf's deep thoughts acted as a good distraction until he reached the commerce district. The main market place had scores of tents set up. The entire area was packed with haggling customers and demonstrating salesman. There was a variety of items being sold from all over the known world. Most of the goods being sold were the usual human-made items except for one nearby weapon maker's tent, which flew the banner of the Iron Hills clan of dwarves. The dwarven smiths were renowned for their excellent craftsmanship and metalworking. They also tended to be greedy and difficult to bargain with, but traveling with the gruff dwarf, Dwalin, had led the tall elf to a deep understanding of the dwarven way.

Standing in front of the tent the ranger looked at the weapons on display, but didn't see anything that would set his heart racing. Of course, many of the ornate weapons were crafted to catch a wealthy merchants attention, but nothing of real practicality. Finished with a portly merchant who was showing off his newly purchased, intricately-designed rapier, the middle-aged dwarf trader clambered over to where the ranger stood.

The stout smith was dressed in a brightly striped orange and red satin jacket with soft brown leather breaches. The floppy yellow hat that rested on his broad head boasted a large red plume from some exotic bird. The entire sight almost made Nelfindal chuckle, but one look at the serious business-like expression on the dwarf's face changed his mind. Speaking up to the tall figure the dwarf asked, "What can I help you with elf, friend?"

Hearing the way the merchant hissed the word friend reminded the ranger of the problems going on around the countryside. Speaking in his most authoritative voice, Nelfindal asked, "Your wares are nice, but where are your real goods? I just lost a fine dagger and wish to replace it, but all I see are pretty decorations for some nobles mantelpiece."

Smirking at the observant critic, the dwarf turned around and brought forth an intricately carved wooden case. Opening the locked cabinet, the wary dwarf looked around the market as if he were exposing the hill dwarves vault itself. Seeing no one ready to steal his treasure, the dwarf whispered, "These are my finest creations. I spent weeks forging them into their final form. The steel is magically fire hardened and virtually impervious to breakage. The blades are finely balanced and dangerously sharp."

The callused hands tenderly brought out a pair of excellently crafted throwing daggers. Each had the archaic symbols of dwarven magic carved with a silvery shine into their handles. The tall elf held the light metal of one of the daggers, the feeling of strong magic flowed through his hand. Demonstrating the sharpness of the daggers, the dwarven smith grabbed a heavy bar of ordinary iron and drew the other blade against the edge of it. The dwarf shaved a piece off as if he were whittling soft wood. The ranger examined the daggers' sheaths which were made of hardened leather, treated to last for a long time without rotting.

Thinking to himself Nelfindal concentrated on the ring hanging on his right index finger. The essence of the bow, Elenar, came to life instantly at its master's summons. The elf questioned the magical weapon about the nature of the daggers.

The enchanted bow responded, "The weapons are endowed with very strong magic. The edges are keener than they normally would be."

After hearing this Nelfindal inquired, "how much for the set?" The dwarf grumbled something about months of work and long hours of slaving over hot fires. Then finally offered, "I'll give them to you for a low price of two hundred gold coins a piece, because you appreciate their real value."

"The value of these daggers can't be more than two hundred total. Their good, but not that good," countered the wily elf.

"You wish to haggle, huh? If you want them I can't give them up for no less than one fifty apiece. That is my final offer," challenged the pouting smith.

"Well, I guess I could get away with paying that if I get the wooden case also," countered the ranger.

The dwarf clapped his meaty hands together and cheered, "Done, you won't be dissatisfied."

Taking the money from the elf made the dwarf glow more than before. Nelfindal thought to himself that the price for the daggers was a small fortune to pay, but the quality of the work was excellent.

Upon returning to the Black Crow, Nelfindal immediately went up to his room and packed his new items away. The sounds of customers entering the common room below made the young elf remember how hungry he was. Stowing his gear away in a chest, Nelfindal left his room to go down stairs.

The common room was rather crowded when the eldar entered it. There was an empty table in the middle of the smoky room, which allowed the opportunity to view all the spirited customers. The elf took his seat and soon was waited on by a young human girl with flowing black hair that ended just above her petite bottom. The barmaid was obviously the daughter of the innkeeper, who shared the same raven black tresses and short stature. She smiled shyly at the handsome elf and asked, "What could I bring you fair sir?"

The charming countenance reminded Nelfindal of the elfmaidens in Elador who always looked young and fresh. The tall ranger eagerly replied, "Bring me some dinner for a hearty appetite and a mug of ale. If you have bread and cheese to go along with that I would like some as well."

The young girl curtsied and bounced away trying to imitate the seductive moves she learned from observing the other girls waiting tables. These same motions would have men staring at her lustfully in a few years when she matured, thought the smirking elf.

Soon a melodious tune rang out from the center of the room. The music was played by a delightful young fellow who wasn't half bad at his chosen profession. The night's crowd got into the entertainment and soon the rowdy group was up dancing and singing to the minstrel. The night continued on until the performer begged to be excused to pass out in his room from all the free drinks. The elf agreed with the bard and soon followed his example by turning in for the evening.

The following morning Nelfindal packed his gear and made his way towards the waterfront. After walking the length of the piers to find transportation, he found a small ferry that was carting a few other travelers across the White Flow. Taking a seat near the bow, the elf waited patiently as the craft moved slowly away from the shore. Looking at the withdrawing docks and the flooded shanties built along the river, the ranger realized how high the water table had risen. The shacks built along the heavily traveled trade route were nothing more than well constructed lean-tos many of which rarely survived the thaws.

The tall eldar stared out over the flowing waters and listened to the rhythmic lapping of the intercepted waves which sprayed a fine mist over the barge's bow. The wind blew calmly and refreshed the elf with the smell of blooming trees and blossoming flowers. The harsh commands of the boat's captain rang out over the water as his crew labored to keep the large wooden hull from being carried down stream by the strong deep water currents.

During the slow advancement of the craft, the ranger watched his fellow passengers, all of whom were human, with an almost quizzical expression. The contrasting variations of the race were infinite to the elven eye, some were red haired and fair, others dark and stout. Many of the humans aboard exhibited the traditional tan hair and sunbaked flesh of the southwestern drifters. These nomadic people were found in every corner of the world. Their often distant and unending wandering made them something of a problem to those who settled easily in the many towns and cities of Aragon.

A few looks were directed at the tall elf as he observed his surroundings, but were soon diverted to the closing land. After the short trip the elf and the other passengers reached the opposite bank of the White Flow and disembarked from the craft. At this time of the day, many merchants and farmers were traveling to the city of Bethany. Soon after the ferry had unloaded its cargo of humans, it began to load up for the return trip back.

With occasional glances behind him to see if he had picked up any followers, the eldar relaxed his guard enough to think about his homecoming. It wasn't the first time he had thought about the return trip, but being in such a large settlement of humans had made him much more anxious to walk through the streets of his own city of Galadhon.

The walk down the Great East Road was a delightful trip. The fresh spring air increased the elf's pace. Passing under overhanging tree limbs, Nelfindal pictured himself in the arms of the beautiful mother of the wilderness who protected her elven children from anything that would harm them. The forest was a ranger's best friend and helped him when he needed assistance. This close relationship with nature was the first lesson the eldar had learned from his apprenticeship in Darkwood. The second lesson was to never abuse the rights of the first.

Few humans were allowed into the secret guild of the Darkwood rangers because of their general lack of respect for the wilderness. The few men who were allowed into the legendary society were usually of Ergothian stock. Most of these high men had noble and even royal blood flowing through their veins, which seemed to give them a heightened sense of honor to a great many things.

Few people realized how many rangers existed in the world. The numbers counted into the hundreds and was growing only slightly. The new initiates had to go through a very rigorous training that taught self-reliance and basic survival. The young elves and men learned early to live in the wild with nothing more than their clothes, a spare hunting knife and their wits. If other items were needed then they had to be made from the land. The hardest part for Nelfindal was hunting successfully. It took two weeks to catch his first rabbit until then the elf had to subsist on berries and fruits. After the month long test, the ranger apprentice had learned to live with nature so well that it was the preferred mode of living. Sleeping out under the stars helped his mind think clearly and purified his often troubled heart and soul.

Still reminiscing about the distant past, Nelfindal heard the faint but unmistakable snap of a twig. The noise was followed by the all too familiar clang of metal on metal. The ranger's senses went off in alarm, warning him of the presence of several clumsy humans in hiding. So as not to alert the waiting bandits, the elf drew out his sword in a slow and nonchalant gesture concealed under his generous cloak. After a few moments time the three highwaymen jumped out of their concealment to encircle their victim. The forewarned eldar faked a surprise look and took an apparently shocked and frightened posture.

The lead robber spoke out in a confident voice, "Stop elf! You must pay the toll before you can continue on."

The average sized human wore a battered chain shirt under his woodsman's cloak and like the other two robbers he was brandishing a rusty broadsword which was probably stolen from a unfortunate farmer.

The ranger examined the situation cautiously and searched for a safe way out. The elf spoke out loud in a humble voice, "I carry nothing of real value except a few silvers. If you want, you can have them."

The human robber waived his two men to close in on the apparently defensive victim. The boldness of their approach led the ranger to some daring ideas knowing full well he could handle all of them. Still hiding his sword under his cloak, Nelfindal prepared himself for a sudden leap towards the thief on his right. Just as the ranger was about to charge the approaching human, a figure came down the path towards the confrontation.

The short dark form was humanoid in shape, but walked with an unusually graceful step. The cloaked figure slowly closed in on the staring group, but stopped when it was within a stride's distance. Standing before the three humans and the defending elf, the cloaked figure casually asked, "What do we have here? Three men on one elf? That's not very good odds is it?"

The human robber who spoke before insultingly responded, "Go about your own business and leave us alone. Unless you wish to join the elf." With this challenging statement the human pointed his bent sword blade towards the newcomer. The obvious intent of the move was not lost on the mysterious intruder.

However, the instant the robber moved his sword towards the dark stranger, time seemed to stand still. For the length of a few breathes not a creature moved. Even the birds stopped their joyous singing. The stranger looked distractedly at the sharp edge of the broadsword and spoke out in a clear and commanding tone, "Put down your weapon or I will take it away from you, Now!"

The force of the statement caused even the eldar to lower his blade under its concealment. After a few seconds time the robber and his pair of fellow cutthroats retreated back down the road in a fast run. The stranger turned back to the young ranger and said, "Well now, you can continue your journey home young elf, but do be careful. It is not good to drop your guard these days."

The shock of the statement caught the ranger by surprise. The stranger apparently knew of the his journey home. It was not an obvious determination since very few humans knew the exact whereabouts of Elador. The young ranger questioned the mysterious figure, "How is it that you know of my return home? I do not know you."

The stranger merely responded, "There is much I know about you Nelfindal Goldleaf. You are very well known to many races of Aragon." The closeness of the dark figure made the ranger very nervous as they began to walk down the road.

"Yet, you seem to know much about me personally. How is that?" persisted the tall youth.

"I know many things about many people. You are one of them. Let's just say that you have done me favors before and I am indebted to you."

"This assistance I did for you isn't something you would care to share with me is it?"

"No. There is much I would like to tell you, but it is not permissible. I am only here to see to it that you continue towards your home with great speed. Do not linger to long on your way to Elador," insisted the stranger. "I must go. Remember my words well young elf and journey to the elven homeland with haste."

Nelfindal looked down the path he was walking and wondered what the stranger was trying to say. The young ranger felt embarrassed by the eerie feeling he was experiencing and turned back to apologize to his companion when he noticed the stranger had disappeared. Not a sound had been made when the figure departed. The whole situation was so strange that the elf quickly departed the site of the meeting and started into an easy jog that soon carried him far down the road.

* * * * *

After several days of hard travel, Nelfindal reached a small village of humans. The people of this town were mostly quiet, poor farmers. Their relaxed, rustic life had a pleasant effect on the elf especially after residing in a bustling city for several months. Remembering the first time that he had past through the village of Warren, Nelfindal recalled how the people were shocked by his presence. Many humans thought elves were mythical people and not just another race.

It gave him great joy when the children rushed up to him only to have the parents yelling for him to spare their lives, a few fearing that he was some evil bandit or demon. The children, in all their innocence, had asked for him to help their defenseless parents to stop the evil orcs from raiding their town. The requests struck the kindly heart of the young elf like a physical blow.

Because of the innocent pleadings the ranger promised the young humans he would try. It took several days to convince the village elders that he was sincere in helping them to destroy their orc invaders. The evil creatures had killed many of his own people in past wars and border skirmishes. The thoughts of the torture and carnage the beasts had dealt to the village only boiled his blood even more so and it was this obvious hatred that eventually convinced the people of the town of his seriousness.

The orcs raiding the town constituted a small band of ten young, vicious creatures led by a half-orc captain. By slaughtering a few guards on watch by their forest camp, the young elf had created the illusion of an elven war party attack. Elven rangers fought well without being seen and carefully picked their targets. Orcs were more than familiar with the silent methodical tactics of these fearless warriors and it was a perfect time to demonstrate how well those tactics worked.

By the end of the night, all the orcs were dead and a pyre was built atop a hill to burn the bodies of the grotesque creatures. Since that evening long ago, the people of the village welcomed the once feared stranger. Greeting the elders as he entered the town, Nelfindal mused on how most of the present leaders were those same little children begging him to save their town only decades ago.

The time spent in the small village was always a refreshing break on an otherwise long trip. Many of the villagers had adopted the elf as a friend and family member and shared their hard earned food happily and unselfishly. Now that the village was larger, a town militia had been organized to combat any orcs or bandits who dared to raid it. There were merchants regularly visiting the town to bring news of outside events and more than one local farm boy had gone out to get rich from adventuring in the vast countryside.

After a day of visiting the little town, Nelfindal realized it was time to continue on. The real reason for leaving was not so much the stranger's warnings as it was the homesick feeling he experienced. He promised his adopted families that he would pass by on his return trip. So preoccupied with all the visiting and the final good-byes, however, the elf never once noticed the two visitors following him.

* * * * *

The following day, Nelfindal reached the foothills of a vast range of snow capped mountains. The most difficult part of the journey was always the passage through the Blue Crest Mountains, a range of sharply upthrusting rock that ascended at times up to eight thousand meters. The danger wasn't just the chance of rock slides or avalanches, but the hostile life that inhabited the treacherous range. Not all the creatures living amongst the rocky crags or in the many interconnected valleys were dangerous, but the few that were, were reason enough for travelers to be wary.

After traveling the mountains for centuries, the rangers guild had marked safe paths which helped improve the chance of avoiding the many unnecessary dangers. Many of these paths were well traveled and many merchants had learned to follow them with confidence. However, many of the southern regions of the vast mountain range were often overgrown with large deep green pine trees, which reached to incredible heights and covered some paths so well as to make them invisible. It wasn't unusual for travelers to pass whole camps of soldiers or highwaymen without even a hint to their presence.

The second day into the mountains a caravan of pack horses led by a middle-aged human came clambering out of a heavily wooded gorge almost running into the elf. Recognizing the tall elf as a ranger, the merchant relaxed a little from his original shock of the unexpected encounter. Walking forward to greet the elf, the human grumbled out, "Ho elf! Wh're ya' headed fer?"

Nelfindal replied in the same rough tongue of Ergothian, "Towards the lands of Elador. It's a pilgrimage home that I'm taking."

The other traveler added, "I'm called Marthius. I'm travelin' ta Bethany ta trade silks an' other clothes ta the wealthy nobles there an' maybe ta some in Bandurec."

Standing over a shoulder and a head taller, the elf asked, "How are the lands past the mountains? Is there much orc activity or anything else worth caution?"

"Not much happenin', but back down the trail about five kilometers my pack smelled dragon spore. I didn't see the beast myself, but there was a restlessness in the air. My animals were quite hesitant at first from travelin' further," offered the human uneasily.

The elf thought a while about the prospect of a dragon in the vicinity, then returned to the human's next question.

"How's the way down the west side?" asked the merchant.

"The way is clear all the way back ta Cardichen. Aside from that I don't know of anything along the Great East Road," answered the tall elf.

Done with the pleasantries, the human grumbled thanks and continued on his way, leading his pack of loaded beasts.

After wishing safe journey to the departing human, Nelfindal headed on in his previous direction. The ranger kept a weary eye out for any signs of danger, but after a while his thoughts began to stray as well as his attention. The trackers had lost him back in Bethany and it would be hard to pick up his trail through the well traveled city streets.

If the young ranger had been more alert, he might have realized that he was not the only hiker along the trail. Some hundred meters back, his two extra shadows continued to maintain a close eye on his progress. Even the observant merchant had missed the few signs of the southern trackers. So good were they that even the pack mules dismissed their presence as a mere extension of the overgrown landscape.

After two more days of travel the loud bellowing of a middle-aged dragon was heard by the eldar and his unseen escort. Soon upon hearing the raucous beast, Nelfindal caught sight of the awesome worm. The large creature, as blue as the midday sky, was gliding around in ever descending spirals. Unaffected by the dragon's presence at such a distance, the elf stood his ground awaiting the beast's expected landing.

It wasn't the first time this unusual creature had been encountered by the elf along this path. The first time was a heart stopping event nearly a century ago. The creature was sunning himself on a high rock ledge when the elf walked right underneath him. It wasn't until the creature bellowed out a greeting did the ranger realize his carelessness, luckily it turned out that the creature wanted only to talk and did so quite well.

The dragon, Bolt as he was called by humans, was well versed in the most advanced of languages. Since, their long, entertaining debate the two had become something like friends. It was still hard to think of a twenty-meter long reptile as a friend. Even after so many years of knowing the creature, the physical closeness of the dragon unnerved the ranger somewhat.

The elf's escort caught their breathes at the first sight of the dragon. Raelin whispered to Darius, "Is he mad? That beast is coming right at him."

Still staring at the sight of the gliding blue body of the dragon, Darius responded, "I can't believe the beast has him enchanted. Few great worms have the ability to enchant and most of them are the great fire breathers. He must know the creature or something. I'm more concerned with us. If the beast sees us he might favor two morsels to the one."

As the two southerners secretly watched from their concealment, the dragon landed rather uncomfortably close to the northern elf. The creature lowered itself onto it's haunches and bellowed what could only have been a greeting, but then spoke in such a fair tongue as to shock the hidden trackers.

As Bolt settled himself on the grassy meadow, he greeted the elf the ancient tongue of the elder races. "Welcome eldar child. It's been a while since you have been through my domain. How does the outside world fair."

Still feeling a slight tense at being so close to such a formidable beast as Bolt, Nelfindal greeted the great worm.

"Greetings great worm. The world changes little by our standards, but much has happened since last we meet. Dark forces are emerging in our land. Many clans of orcs have been uniting into small armies and grow in strength as we speak. Many settlements have been attacked and destroyed by the vile beasts."

A resounding snort of derision was the dragon's only response to the news. Even the ancient worm had many unpleasant encounters with the ever unpopular orcs.

Nelfindal continued, "I'm traveling to Elador to be with my brothers in the Spring Awakening Ceremony and to carry news of the growing unrest among the races."

"Many an elf have traveled along the foothills hunting for game. It seems that lately I have been competing with your brothers for the succulent spring venison. It could have been a complicated situation if it weren't for all the deer that survived this mild winter. It seems I may be eating well this year," happily cheered the dragon.

"Well, Bolt, you may be so satiated that you won't be here to greet me on my return trip. I would have looked forward to some wild tales with you as well as a good talk of the old age."

"That may be so. I do look forward to talking with you. If you wish, I could offer you a ride to the foothills at the edge of my domain. The weather has given me much energy and it would be nice to share the day with an intelligent being. This way we could talk and share stories," offered the beast.

"It would be an honor to ride with you Elder Worm, but only if you promise not to try to hunt with me upon your back," uneasily joked the elf.

"Hah! Well spoken! I shall take care of you as my rider. It is a well known fact among dragonkind that elves and other humanoids don't fly well," bellowed the cheery worm.

"True enough," replied the cautious elf.

Leaning forward and lowering a massive foreleg, Bolt allowed Nelfindal to mount. The elf seated himself between two ridges along the armored neck, which afforded only minimal comfort. With a sudden burst of energy, the dragon leaped into the air. The unexpected movement flattened the ranger against the bony plating of the creature nearly knocking him from his already tenuous seat.

With a couple flaps of his great wings, Bolt flew higher and higher above the ground. Soon the beast and his rider were above the clouds, gliding across the cottony puff like a breeze. Unlike many others, Nelfindal wasn't bothered by heights even when an occasional break in the clouds offered a view that made rivers look like so many cracks in a rock. It was only the second time on dragonback, but already the ranger felt at home riding through the cool air.

It was early in the afternoon, a lone elf stood regally with his cloak billowing out like a swirling green and brown cloud. His head rose above an upthrust of granite rock as he stood up to look out towards the distant mountains. Camped out in the foothills surrounding the Blue Crest Mountains, the broad framed ranger stared out towards the western range where he witnessed a brief glimpse of a large bird or other flying creature. From this distance the creature must be quite large, thought the husky silvan. Slowly, the dark speck began to grow, straining his keen elven eyesight, Norin looked at the coming apparition with some astonishment.

It wasn't the first time he had ever seen a dragon this far from the mountains, but this one looked oddly different. Closer now, the shadow of a rider became visible. Scratching his sandy brown head in dismay, the silvan elf speculated on the stability of any individual crazy enough to attempt such a task. Of course, if anybody were around who knew the veteran ranger, they might have said he would, but he never cared for heights even when he summoned his great eagle friends in emergencies.

The last time that occurred was some ten years ago, when the silvan had to face Nuviel. "Was it love?" he wondered or just some enchantment that her father, the arch-mage Glendil, had cast on him. It seemed like centuries ago, yet the physical and emotional scars were still fresh. The confrontation with the enchantress was meant to sway the eldar elfmaiden away from her father's devious persuasions. Instead, the meeting erupted into a struggle for the silvan ranger's life. The beautiful sorceress had the sole intention of turning the ranger captain against his own friends willingly or by magic.

After he heard the magically persuasive offer to switch sides, Norin forcefully refused. Not long after the last syllable of the rejection was uttered his enchantress-lover open up on him with her powerful and deadly assault of black magic. Somehow, he won against her strong magic, but how he won was still a mystery. The last spell she cast seemed to have knocked him unconscious. Was there someone or something that had helped him survive what had to be an otherwise lethal spell?

The druids that healed him said no one had been in the area before they arrived except for his friend, Gwinnevar, the great eagle, who found the crumpled body of the silvan ranger. Next to him was the still smoldering body of his beloved Nuviel. The sight of her destroyed body remained permanently etched in Norin's mind as if to emphasize the intensity of the destructive magic intended for him. Still in the past, Norin only vaguely saw the blue dragon land and the golden haired elf jump from the beast's back.

Offering thanks and granting the creature good hunting Nelfindal strode off towards the reminiscing silvan ranger. Almost as quickly as before, Bolt launched himself into the sky with his strong hindquarters. The powerful wings blew dust and debris about the area creating little torrents of air. The sleek blue body circled the ridge where the elves stood to gain enough height then flew off to rich hunting ranges full of succulent deer.

At the sight of Nelfindal's approaching two meter plus frame, Norin snapped out of his reverie. Taking the younger elf's extended hand in his iron-like grip, Norin greeted his former apprentice with almost paternal excitement. Disengaging himself from the tall elf, Norin humorously commented, "Since when do you get a dragon escort? Most people would worry about being the beast's lunch."

Smiling at the jibe Nelfindal replied, "You always said to me never to turn down a free ride. It would have taken me another week to get here if it weren't for the great worm. Enough with my travel arrangements. How have you been?"

"Well enough, I figured you would be coming this way so I set up camp here. You hungry? I have some smoked venison waiting," offered the excited silvan.

The two old friends talked throughout the entire day about the younger ranger's past encounter with the southern trackers and the intense racial hostilities that were ever growing. Finally, the two turned in for the evening exhausted from their reunion. The younger elf learned early in life to post a guard in the wilderness, but not in the presence of his mentor's enchantments. Nelfindal's spells were potent, but his teacher and friend possessed some powers even some magicians envied. As expected, the night continued on without incident while the two slept under the cool velvety blanket of the western sky. Even in the deep elven trance of sleep the rangers could feel the watchful presence of the scintillating stars.

The following morning was spent breaking camp and heading to the forests of the elven homeland of Elador. After an easy day's travel the two elves reached the edge of the elven forest. Not long after entering the deep green woodland, the two rangers were greeted by a patrol of forest guardians. These hardened warriors defended the land from orcs and other creatures who constantly tried to invade the sacred land of the elves. Many youth dreamed of being accepted into the warriors guild which protected the freedom and peace of all elves.

Nelfindal reminisced on the past when he was one such youth, until he met his companion. Norin was a successful and charismatic Ranger of Darkwood. The rangers were often viewed as something of legends, because of all the secrecy lying about their origin and purpose. Little did humans, dwarves and elves alike know that the rangers were one of the very few obstacles to the growing evil that was forever trying to conquer the free lands of Aragon.

There were many stories of orc raiding parties being decimated within eyesight of small towns and homlets without a sound. The only evidence the rangers left behind was an occasional elven arrow or a glyph used by the guild to identify their presence. Such mysterious events contributed to the cloud of legend surrounding the fable guardians of Aragon.

The rangers were experts at the art of subterfuge and nature manipulation. Upon attaining advanced levels of proficiency, many members learned to channel magic from the very life force of the forests. It was this same magic that fueled the myths and legends about these shadows of the woods.

Soon after being accepted to apprentice with Norin the young elf realized that the rangers played a critical role in the preservation of world peace. A position that was not to be taken lightly. The headquarters of the guild was located in a forest, protected from the most powerful of magical detections. The path into the land proved difficult even to those who knew the way. If one went off the secretly hidden paths, their lives would be in mortal peril. The guardians of Darkwood would tirelessly hunt down the unwanted intruders and see to their inevitable destruction.

Known to only a few people outside of the guild of Darkwood was the existence of another guild of rangers located in the southernmost part of the continent. This community of dark elves, known as the Farghest, strove to gain from twisting nature to their benefit. Many bloody conflicts had occurred between the two opposing guilds. The Darkwood guild fought to maintain peace and practiced humility while the other lived a life of murderous greed. There were many southern elves who were good at heart, but it was the southern guild of rangers who raped all the southerners of any honor.

Nelfindal shivered as he recalled the first time he had encountered a southern ranger. It was one of the closest times he had ever come to death. He was befriended by an silvan tracker known as Caric who led him and his friends into an nearly successful ambush. The young and inexperienced Darkwood ranger was forced to fight the tracker and a range commander while his friends where battling an orc war party. After an exchange of arrows, the young eldar elf luckily killed the range commander with only some wounding to himself. The tracker escaped before Nelfindal could get him, but not after he lightly wounded the fleeing southerner.

Nelfindal's friends had shown up shortly after with the party of orcs still following right behind them. After more combat the group of friends managed to escape to a safe place, notifying the northern guild of the Farghest presence. The report of the incident sparked a reprisal against the elusive southerners. The result of the encounter was the systematic search of every forest and homlet for twenty kilometers for more southern spies. Those suspected were immediately and professionally dealt with. However, the whereabouts of the tracker, Caric, was still unknown to Nelfindal.

Noticing the quiet and distant look on his youthful companion's face, Norin slowed to a halt. "What troubles you? You act like you swallowed a dram of orness?"

Breaking out of his dark memory the younger elf remarked, "Just thinking about the time I went out and encountered those Farghest."

"That was some time ago, you handled the situation quite well. I was certainly impressed to hear my apprentice had exterminated a range commander on only his second mission," recalled the proud Norin.

"Hmm, I guess. Coming back home seems to have awakened a lot of foolish memories; a little taste of the blues," replied Nelfindal.

Encouraging the tall youth, Norin said, "You'll cheer up once the festivities begin. The sight of all those beautiful ladies when you've had a few bottles of wine will change your mood."

"A few bottles? The sight of one elven maiden now would get my attention after being out with the humans for so long," laughed Nelfindal.

"Not so shy anymore, I see. Yes, this will be one wonderful festival. Everybody is looking forward to your return," cheered the silvan.

Nelfindal still couldn't help from being apprehensive about returning to the capital after such a long and controversial absence. Feeling anxious and uncertain about the next few days, the eldar could only respond, "It has been too long."

Norin caught the sadness in the youth's voice, but let the matter drop. It was a topic which those close to the tall ranger left well enough alone.

* * * * *

A dark flowing form flitted in the shadows of the late evening. From a casual glance, the most observant would have mistaken the black silhouette as a trick of the eye, but the talented assassin was no illusion. Raelin moved with a silent step that surprised even a watchful alley cat, which also stalked the lightless alley. The two hunters gazed at each other in silent respect as each acknowledged the other's presence.

The silvan observed the cat's luminescent glare with a smile. Thinking to himself, Raelin imagined how the cat felt every time it pounced on an unsuspecting mouse. The adrenaline began to pump as the thought of the kill was visualized in gory detail.

The sound of soft leather boots on the dirt road nearby was quickly perceived by the sensitive elven ears. The objective of the elven assassin's assignment was moving towards a dilapidated shack which he stood across from. The unsuspecting quarry was a free lance thief, who decided to skirt the local guild's protection fee. The lithe form of a human slipped over the banister which surrounded the front porch of the run-down shanty and opened the remnants of a front door. Before the human had a chance to push the wooden portal a few scant centimeters, a black phantom burst out of the shadows and crashed into the shocked figure throwing it to the floor inside the shack.

Closing the door quietly behind him, Raelin quickly jumped after the tumbling victim in an attempt to grapple with the figure. The slight flash of steel alerted the assassin to the presence of an armed opponent and he barely rolled out of harm's way before the blade cut through the air by his head. The building blood lust enhanced by the close call drove the elf's heart to pounding like a steam driven pump. Unseen to the defensive human was the pleased smile on the silvan intruder's face.

Pulling out a small blackened dagger the assassin attacked the human with the hopeful anticipation of a good fight. The defensive figure evaded the striking blade by rolling into a crouched position. The fear the agile attacker created was incredible and almost overwhelmed the terrified human thief who realized his peril.

Desperately taking the offensive, the agile body of the small human charged the cloaked killer. The carelessness of the maneuver was to obvious for Raelin to take advantage of. The whole idea for the assignment was to forget the stress created from losing the elusive northern ranger. To kill the thief now would be ludicrous. The fun of the job was to stretch out the chase until the climax.

Slowly, the two figures circled sizing each other up. No words were exchanged, because nothing needed to be said. The intention of the unknown intruder was very obvious to the thief. Without any warning the hiss of a thrown dart flew past the silvan elf's ear narrowly missing his right cheek. The missile hit the wall behind the assassin with a thump indicating its solid contact.

Unable to bear the excitement anymore the southerner flew at the dark form of the thief. Striking out at the place were the human's abdomen should have been, Raelin felt the familiar resistance which indicated a good hit. The following groan verified the weapon's contact. The assassin continued his calculated slashes at the bent over form until the loud crash of a collapsed body was heard. The immobile human hardly breathed as his flowing wounds painted the darkened floor with his waning life's blood. Unwilling to let the human live any longer the elf slit the main artery in his victim's neck then began his artistic signature.

The only way others in the profession knew a job was his handy work was by the gruesome display he created with his knife. The silvan assassin was a talented tracker as well as assassin. However, the silvan practiced a morbid hobby of skinning his prey whether deer, rabbits or humans. It took the swift moving Raelin just over half-an-hour to finish the job. The resulting gore was neatly piled into a corner and the skinned corpse was laid out on the building's modest cot. The following day would lead to the discovery of the body and another victim would be added to the long list of the assassin's victims.

* * * * *

After two and a half days of traveling the unmarked paths of the elven forest, the two northern rangers approached the first sight of Galadhon, Elador's capital city. Standing before the beauty of the ancient city, Nelfindal stared in awe at his alienated homeland. The roads leading into and throughout the city were made of hand-cut white marble blocks fitted together with incredible precision. There were some buildings made of the same marble stone in the center of the forest city, but these structures were very few. These white buildings were for either ceremonial functions or for the use by the ruling royal house. In contrast, the city itself seemed to grow from out of a forest of towering gold-leafed valorn trees with suspended walks leading from one tree to another. A crystal blue stream led out of the tree city from a central fountain all the way to the great Nahoa River. The magnificent waterway flowed around the elven city like a stream would divert itself around a large rock, giving the city a natural barrier.

The two elves passed over the main stone bridge where they were greeted by a great green curtain of thick foliage that also served as a barrier wall for the fortified settlement. The gates into the forest city were guarded by a large contingent of elven wardens, the royal guard of Galadhon. The wardens were dressed in the traditional gold and white armor of Elador, which indicated their status as elite guards. Their mithril swords emanated a glow with a pure radiance inherent to the magical metal. About the warriors necks hung green emerald medallions, symbols of their guild and a religiously significant item representing the vitality of life and the blood of low ranking royalty.

The traffic through the gates was heavy with elven craftsman, off-duty forest guardians, elven citizens and the occasional foreign emissary. Most of the visiting ambassadors were tall, bronze-skinned men representing the nearby human settlements, who until recently had rarely dealt with their aloof neighbors. Their brightly colored caravans stood in stark contrast to the rustic appearance of the farmers' carts, which wheeled past them into the welcoming city. The sun shined down on the people entering the elven capital causing a warming tickle on any exposed skin, which hinted to a pleasant summer. A cool breeze blew through the main gates carrying a refreshing scent of fresh forest growth on its currents reminding all that the forest was not far from the ancient city.

Nelfindal felt at ease in the trees of his homeland. Climbing up to a large flet, a platform much like a tree house, the eldar recognized the sign for the Oak Leaf Tavern, a place he had not visited since his last trip to Elador over twenty years ago. This one flet was large enough to allow over a hundred elves to drink and dance among the branches without being knocked off. Unusual for most flets, the tavern had a railing circling the perimeter to prevent any overly indulged elf from falling out of the tree to his death on the ground or on a lower lying flet below. The same ornate brass lamps that were used to decorate the Rangers' Rest Inn hung about the many branches of the crowded open air tavern.

Sitting down at a table the two elves were waited on by a comely young elven maiden who seductively flirted with the two strangers. Speaking in her sweet song of a voice the barmaid asked, "What could I get you two handsome strangers?" The question was followed by an alluring stare, which was directed first to the silvan then to the eldar.

Catching the beautiful sky blue eyes with a return look, Nelfindal teasingly ordered, "We'll each have a bottle of wine and some bread and cheese, if it's no problem."

The enchanting elfmaiden cheerfully responded, "That won't be a problem. I'll just be a moment."

Staring at the shapely hips of the departing barmaid, Norin speculated, "So, how many hearts do you think she's broken? It would almost be worth a king's ransom to just sleep embraced in that bosom!"

Nelfindal enthusiastically agreed, "She is a beauty isn't she. Then again every lady I have seen so far looks great."

After a few moments the entrancing lady returned, but only lingered around long enough to place the servings down and head over to a new customer.

Pouring a glass full and taking a large swig of the tasty red wine, Nelfindal looked around to catch a glimpse of any familiar faces. The tall elf was glad to see the tavern filling up with fellow elves and not humans even though he didn't recognize anybody. The ranger thought it unlikely he would see any of his old friends in the tavern at such an early hour.

After a short while, a bard pulled out his lute and began to play a tender love ballad. Like most elven songs, it ended tragically and there wasn't a dry eye among the audience as the last note drifted off. Building up his confidence, the bard began to sing a happy song, which was a popular tune that many knew the words to. Even the rangers sang with the crowd in there own rich voices.

The bard's voice rang out clearly, almost magically over the level of the audience only spurring the participants on with even greater fervor. Finally, with a short solo on the lute the bard finished the uplifting song. Soon after the second song ended, the performer was swamped with offers of free drinks, which artists like himself could never refuse. As if by request, the sun remained freshly warm as the day wore on and continued until its last rays disappeared over the horizon.

The festive mood at the tavern went on well into the evening. Managing to finally separate themselves from the crowd of drinkers, the two companions left to find lodging. The walkway leading away from the merriment seemed to sway amongst the branches without really moving. Realizing their level of intoxication, both elves commented on the necessity of getting reaccustomed to the effects of the fine elven wine. Stepping onto a flet designed with individual sections for sleeping some hundred meters away, the two searched for the inn keeper. They found the older elf unrolling sleeping mats out for the expected onslaught of drunken boarders. The sindar elf showed them to a unoccupied section where they could sleep during their stay. Ignoring the thought of the outrageous price quoted them, the two celebrants bedded down and swiftly fell into a deep and drunken sleep.

Norin woke up late the next morning only to find his young friend already finishing his morning exercises. Nelfindal noticed his mentor's approach and greeted him, "Well, I think we are the only elves awake in all Elador. Let's go take a walk around town a bit before streets begin to fill up."

"I wish I could, but I have some business to do. I promised I would check in with the royal house upon arrival," said the older elf grudgingly.

Looking at the older elf, Nelfindal joked, "O.K., but will you be around later for the festivities? I would like to meet you for round two in our search to find the best wine around."

Laughing at the thought of another night of drunken clumsiness Norin replied, "Oh definitely, after all, drinking is the second best thing I do."

Nelfindal questioned the other elf, "Now that you've got me wondering, what's the first best?"

The silvan was about to reply when a pretty servant girl brought their breakfast. Norin could only smile and wink at her retreating figure while the eldar laughed at his obvious answer.

* * * * *

After dressing in his best clothing, Nelfindal decided to go visit the Lady Tiluviel. She always welcomed him and it had been a very long time since he had visited her. The ranger's long absence away from the elven homeland kept him out of touch with many of his friends except for Tiluviel. Nelfindal recalled the many letters he had received from the lady over the years. It was with her support that the young elf was able to return home and face the inevitable conflicts which awaited him.

The tree supporting the residence of the Lady was some five meters in diameter and ten times that in height. The branches reached out from the broad trunk holding the multi-level complex like a mother's arms about her child. The light brown wood curved and wove its way around the assembled structure as if guided by some complex plan. The four levels of enclosed flets were occupied by the six wards of Queen Illidrais. At least one of these royal companions was always at the royal lady's side.

The fourth level housed the highest and most significant residence. Unlike the other flets this level was solely for the use of the Lady Tiluviel who was the state advisor to the king and queen as well as head ward. The other flets were shared amongst the other ladies. The design of the tree house was much like the other buildings in the city. The only differences were the rich gold and alabaster decorations, which identified the residence as a royal dwelling.

Nelfindal walked up to the tall lift that would take him up into the tree complex. Before he reached its base, he was confronted by two armed royal guards. The senior of the two requested that the eldar state his business and who he was to see. Having changed into his formal attire, the elf offered a commanding presence. His tall stature was garbed in the gold and white tunic worn by the Eladorian nobility with a flowing white cloak draped over his shoulders.

Standing upright the tall elf addressed the shorter silvan guard, "I have an invitation to see the Lady Tiluviel at my convenience. Do you wish to delay my audience with her?"

The guards seemed unnerved at such a challenge, but realized it was only a proper royal court reply. Stepping back the addressed guard apologetically replied, "Begging forgiveness, the Lady had asked not to be disturbed. She was, however, expecting your arrival, sir."

Nodding his acknowledgment of the proper procedures, the tall elf resumed his walk towards the lift. The eldar ranger pulled the operating lever that activated the magic of the lift to carry him to the top flet. Once at the upper level, Nelfindal was greeted by a young silvan girl, who escorted him to the lady's library. The diminutive servant opened the closed doors and announced his arrival.

The servant backed off as the eldar walked into the bright, comfortable room. The Lady Tiluviel was sitting at a chair writing on a scroll of parchment paper in the delicate script of elvish. After Nelfindal entered the spacious room the elfmaiden greeted the younger elf with a cheerful smile and salutation.

"Welcome home Nelf. How does it feel to be back?" she said.

The ranger seated himself across from the beautiful lady and replied, "It is always great to be back. So how is my big sister these days? Are things going well with you and the husband?"

Speaking in her enchanting voice, Tiluviel said, "My husband told me to say hello when I saw you. He is on a trip to locate some magical device he needs in one of his experiments. As for me, life is going well. The affairs of state continue as usual and all I do is keep them from getting out of hand. It seems that we have more ambassadors visiting this year than ever before. There are humans in the city as well as a contingent of dwarves from the Iron Hills. Both saying that they wish to trade goods with us."

"Sounds to be promising, if the orcs could be restrained from attacking the caravans," added the skeptical ranger.

"Somehow I think that is part of the reason the ambassadors are here. They might be asking for assistance in defeating the growing number of orcs. The disgusting beasts have been getting rather tiresome as of late," the lady added somewhat acidly.

The young elf spoke seriously, "Word from Darkwood is that there is a power that is organizing the various orc clans together. This could prove to be a prelude to all out war with the peaceful nations of Aragon."

"That is our fear also. Enough with the depressing news, how is the inn going?" questioned the smiling Tiluviel.

"The operations are going well. Our idea of a center for information is very successful. The conflict with the thieves' guild in Cardichen has ended in a truce for now, but anything could start a war with them again," added the young eldar.

As the two conversed the sun poured into the chamber from the colored glass windows setting the room aglow with many brilliant colors. Standing up to stretch Tiluviel walked around her desk taking the scroll and placing it in a locked coiffure in the corner of the room. Turning around after locking up the small chest, she spoke to her tall step-brother, "The queen wishes to see you and Norin to discuss an important problem. It seems that our representative to the city of Reah has disappeared."

The news was unexpected at a time of high spirits and celebration, but the ranger was used to surprises appearing at the worst times. Nodding in acknowledgment Nelfindal stood up and slowly walked towards a large window to stare out at the city of trees.

The young ranger commented, "It seems my visit home will be brief, again. I would hate to see what would happen if I tried to move back. I hope it wasn't pressure from those noble merchants that influenced the queen in assigning me for this."

Sensing the sadness in the young ranger the lady walked over to him and placed a gentle hand on his arm. The fair golden hair of the lady captured the sun's light and reflected it like a golden gem. She stood close by her step-brother and whispered,

"It is good to have you back. We all missed you when you were away. You always cheered us up when we were down. Even Norin's dark moods couldn't withstand the assault your cheering gave."

"Forgive my melancholy attitude. I feel that being with the humans for so long has depressed me a little. I heard a bard at the tavern yesterday and it moved me so much that I almost forgot what evil was going on in the world," said the saddened elf.

Sighing abruptly the tall elf turned around and gave his step-sister a gentle kiss on her forehead and quietly made his way out of the confining interior of the tree house. The ivory colored skin of the lady's face wrinkled into a frown. She thought, how many times has the politics of the rich forced those of good heart into unnecessary torment?

Tiluviel stared after her departing step-brother with a sad look. If he only knew of the growing strife that was inflaming the relations between the silvan workers and the eldar leaders. There was much more going on than anybody could have guessed. If tensions got strained anymore there could very easily be a civil war. The thought of elves killing elves on such a scale was never heard of. With that thought the elfmaiden turned to stare out the window and observe the apparently peaceful scene.

On his way down the lift the ranger thought that a good carnival would cheer his dark spirits. After reaching the bottom the eldar made his way to the open grounds which supported the yearly fair. The walk through the city to the fair grounds took the long legged elf only a quarter of an hour.

Nelfindal entered the festive atmosphere and almost immediately his dark mood disappeared. Unconsciously walking towards the archery fields, the tall elf absorbed the feel of all the excitement. Young children ran about playing and screaming with joyous delight. Walking past a magician's tent Nelfindal stopped to observe a human dressed in a brightly colored robe pulling coppers from behind the pointed ears of awestruck elven children. The many brightly colored tents boasted of wondrous sights and mystical feats, which the elf knew to be often phony.

At the other side of the festival were the favorite contests of skill. The archery contests were the most popular amongst the elves, especially the silvan guardians. Nelfindal remembered watching the events as a youth. He had always dreamed of being an archer for the elite guard or some other division of the warriors guild. Now that he was older, he had achieved some small fame from his natural archery skill, which he had developed as a ranger.

In combat his skill was magically enhanced by the special enchantments inherent in his bow Elenar. The thought of his bow awakened the intelligent weapon. The idea of a talking device was ridiculous to Nelfindal when he had first heard someone mention the existence of such things. Until he found Elenar. The bow always seem to help him when he needed it. The biggest fear of the elf was his growing reliance on the artifact's abilities.

Still thinking of his weapon, Nelfindal was disturbed by the familiar voice in his head. "So boss what are you doing standing there. The contest has a bunch of amateurs firing twigs for arrows. I could beat them all even without your skill."

The bowman thought back to Elenar, "The contest is between the participants not their bows. I will participate, but not until the advanced level starts. Be patient."

"Patience you say. I developed the term. Just remember I sat in someone's vault for over two hundred years. You try to sit somewhere by yourself and do nothing for that long."

The ranger ignored his talkative companion, who eventually quieted down once there was no response to its jibes.

After an hour of contesting amateurs, there was an announcement for all experienced bowman to line up on the greens. The eldar elf took a position about half way down the line. The view from this point gave him a chance to weigh the talents of the competition. Some of the other bowman were familiar and they nodded their heads in recognition of the young elf who returned the gesture.

At the referee's signal all the archers nocked their arrows and took aim. Upon utterance of the last command the contestants fired. The sound of some fifty arrows flying through the air whistled like some flock of frightened small birds. The ending thuds indicated that the arrows had hit their marks. Of the fifty odd bowman, only twenty had hit the center region of the targets, which ended the first round.

The second round was started after the arrows were retrieved and the targets moved back ten more meters. Again the hiss of sailing arrows was heard followed by a series of successful thuds. The end of the second round was marked by the elimination of three more contestants, who shook their heads as the results were yelled out. The contest continued until round six where only three archers were left. Reaching this point in the game was easy for Nelfindal. Until this round the need to use the special magic of the bow was unnecessary.

The sixth round saw the elimination of the odd man, which left the eldar ranger and a skinny silvan warrior from the other elven city of Ariadon. The challenging silvan elf inquired into moving the target to a range of two hundred meters. This distance was almost impossible to fire at with accuracy for the normal bowman, but the spectators knew that they were witnesses to two great archers. At this time the crowd was rooting for the eldar though absent from the elven city for a long time by human standards was still well known by many from his last stay in Elador.

This round required each elf to shoot two arrows into a head sized target. The first shot was to be the silvan elf's. Taking careful aim he let loose a well aimed shot that ripped the edge of the target. Nelfindal took his first shot with the same care. Releasing the drawn string, the ranger hit slightly off center. This shot brought out the cheers from the anxious crowd.

The second round of shots was preceded by a description of the prize. The gift was to be presented to the winner by a beautiful elfmaiden. Her presentation caused many to gasp at the sight of her shapely body and comely face. Walking out in front of all the spectators, the young elfmaiden held a fabulously crafted mithril broach. The award announcements ended after some dramatic references were made of the fantastic skills of the two master archers.

The last shot was to be at the same target and at the same distance. The silvan warrior approached the line, took careful aim and then fired. The shot was dead on the center bulls eye. Nelfindal seeing this knew the only way he could improve on the shot was to have the target moved back another thirty meters. After the silvan admitted he couldn't even shoot that far the eldar stood at the line. Taking up his bow, the ranger took careful aim and quietly summoned the magic of the bow. Understanding the need of his master, Elenar enchanted the arrow with true aim.

After the surge of power from the magic was felt, Nelfindal released the silver-tipped arrow. The black shaft flew straight to its target. A moment of time seemed to pass as the crowd held its breath. The resulting thud of metal on cloth resonated across the absolute quiet of the crowded greens. The runners made their way to the target to find the silver arrow tip embedded exactly in the center of the target where the silvan's arrow had been.

The roar from the crowd was almost deafening even in the open air. Nelfindal was congratulated on his expert shot by his opponent and then brisked away by a mob of enthusiastic spectators, which seemed to have grown considerably since the match started. As the contest's winner, the happy elf was presented with the mithril broach and a kiss on his forehead by the fair maiden. Saluting to the euphoric followers in the traditional elven gesture for success, Nelfindal was led away to partake in a victory party in his honor.

The drinking, eating and toasting to the life of elven patrons continued well past reason. Somehow remaining conscious after all the free drinking, Nelfindal managed to stumble back to the inn where sleep waited to embrace him. The elf barely remembered how he got to the distant lodging flet. The last traces of consciousness had completely left the intoxicated youth as soon as his head touch the sleeping mat.

* * * * *

The next day in Galadhon was marked by the Spring Awakening Ceremony. As a religious rite, all elves were expected to participate. The ceremony began in the late morning with an announcement by the Queen, who always promised a perfect day with sunshine and mildly warm weather. It was common belief that the royal lady controlled the weather with amazing facility.

The power of her magic was unmatched by any living elf or human.

That same morning, Nelfindal awoke to the golden rays of the early morning sun. Next to the young ranger was his silvan friend who was finishing his breakfast of bread, cheese and smoked fish. The young ranger raised himself and greeted the older silvan.

"Good morning. How was your meeting the yesterday with the queen?" queried the young eldar.

"It was productive as usual. I saw you win the archery contest. That was some fine bit of shooting you did," proudly complimented the silvan.

"Thanks. I enjoyed the competition. Are you ready for the ceremony today?" asked the eldar.

"Yes, it should be a wonderful ceremony. Hurry up and get dressed so we can get to the Great Oak early," cheerfully ordered Norin.

The young ranger thought of how the ceremony would be starting in a few hours. The Queen would expect everyone to show up for the important occasion. It was while thinking of the queen that Nelfindal noticed the small slip of paper lying next to his mat.

Opening the letter up, the young elf observed the flowing script of the Eldar. Few elves knew the complex, ancient language. Fewer still knew how to write in it. After scanning the note, the elf was shocked to discover who sent it. The signature of the Queen Illidrais was unmistakable. The content of the letter was a summons for a private meeting after the Spring Awakening Ceremony at the royal residence. The post script insisted that the elf's presence was urgently required.

* * * * *

The day long ceremony began with the blessing of the Great Oak, a gigantic and ancient tree with unusually golden leaves. The rite was performed just as the late morning sun's rays hit the reflective leaves, which set the entire region ablaze with a brilliant crimson and golden glow. This religious entity grew in the middle of the woodland city only meters away from the central fountain which it fed itself from.

The celebrants then marched as one to a site several kilometers away called Farmor. This hill of barren white barked trees was the high point of the ceremony. The tomb of a long dead elf by the name of Delfius was buried in the center of the raised land mass. Few elves were ever buried in such a respectful manor, but Delfius was an elf who had given his life for the once young elven nation. This sacrifice saved the lives of countless other elves and insured a long period of peaceful existence. The story behind the heroism was written in long poems and ballads which were sung at all holidays and special ceremonies. Even as the parade marched to the burial mound, the rich sounding elven voices sang in unison the oldest and most famous of the songs, Rona Elar Lo or the Hero Lives On.

The song portrayed a handsome princely eldar who fought a mighty demon delaying it long enough to allow the women and children of the region to escape from its destructive fury. The demon was the general of an army of invading orcs sent to wipe-out the small elven colony and plunder its riches. Fortunately, Delfius had defeated the demon after a long battle, but receiving a mortal wound himself. After seeing the death of their commander the cowardly orcs retreated in fear. The place where Delfius was buried began to sprout the white and gold trees soon after. If one prayed intently on the ground of Farmor, it is said, one could gain the courage and resolve to conquer their own beasts.

The rest of the day was spent by the thousands of elves in meditation around the mound of Farmor. The spring breeze that blew across the wooded forest of Elador carried the sweet scents of blossoming plant life. The atmosphere was that of peace and community. At just before noon the trees of the sacred ground began to sprout new buds and fresh leaves at an unnatural rate. The whole process took the rest of the afternoon. Seeing the fruit of their labor, the meditating community concentrated even harder, which made the trees bloom faster and fuller. Finally, the glade above the hill was in full blossom.

Witnessing the ritual for the first time ever were the human representatives. Their first reaction to the ceremony was that of patient respect for the long ritual until the new growth began to appear. The sight of countless budding leaves taught the ambassadors even more respect for the magical properties of the elven nation. Even the dwarven delegation, who was accustomed to observing the ritual, found it moving.

The ceremony was a marvel to participate in for everyone. For a short period every elf whether silvan, sindar or eldar was linked together in the community effort of life. This year was no less impressive than any other year. Everybody in Galadhon was of the highest spirits throughout the long quiet ceremony. Each participant was dressed in their finest apparel and wore their finest jewelry. Even the most impoverished silvan dressed more richly than a wealthy human merchant.

The amount of richly items on the young ranger's own body was a stark contrast to his first appearance at the city gates. Those who observed him at the ceremony would have guessed him as a very wealthy noble and not a humble Darkwood ranger. Like the rest of his people, Nelfindal was dressed in his best finery of gold and white robes unlike the dust covered leathers he was accustomed to. A ceremonial mithril longknife hung from a gold belt at his side. The tall, golden-haired eldar felt awkward in his fitted mithril chain shirt, a gift left to him from his father. The memory of whom stirred many disturbing emotions. Around his brow rested a headband with a green emerald set in the middle, which identified him as a royal defender as all rangers and royal guardsmen were and a few elite silvan wardens.

The symbolism of the stone color dated back to the beginnings of the elven culture. It was believed that three stones were cast down from the heavens for the elven forefathers. The green emerald for the defenders, the agate for common citizens who tended the needed fields and the diamond for the leaders. Only the royal family was allowed to wear the clear diamond stone of the pure blood. Aside from the immediate royal family members, the pure blooded lady wards were allowed to wear the stones, which identified them as adopted daughters of the royal house.

Nelfindal frowned as he reflected on the symbolism of the stones. The green emerald was the only stone and consequently the only status, which no one was born to. Whether silvan peasant or eldar noble, only those with skill and perseverance could ever earn the status of royal defender and wear the green emerald. Even on such an occasion as this, Prince Orcanth displayed his elaborate emerald headband identifying him as general of the forest guardians.

* * * * *

A little while after the ceremony, Nelfindal marched to the residence of the ruling family, which was located in the largest tree in the forest city. It wasn't known whether the tree was actually one grand oak or a glade of trees magically fused together. Perched amongst the gigantic bows of the wooded entity was the most beautiful residence in the entire elven kingdom. This was the five level complex of Queen Illidrais and her warrior husband, Felastharn.

The Queen was a direct descendant of Farnusthain, who was one of the mightiest leaders in elven history and one of the first colonists of Elador. The queen stood almost as tall as the tallest males, but still maintained a grace none could equal in all of Aragon. Her beauty was so enchanting that few of any race could say no to her requests. Even without her appearance the lady was a strong and charismatic leader. It was true that her husband ran most of the affairs of state, but she had the pure royal blood and power. It was difficult talking to her without thinking of how enchanting she was and how persuasive. Luckily, it wasn't the first time Nelfindal had met her for reasons of state.

After displaying the royal seal stamped on the summons to a royal guard, Nelfindal was escorted by a middle-aged servant up to the council chambers of the ruling couple. The inside of the royal residence was over a millennium old and literally formed out of the living tree entity that supported it. The rooms were furnished with elaborately carved furniture, made the greatest of elven craftsmen centuries before. The walls of the main hallway were covered with golden tapestries naming all the royal bloodlines since the founding of Elador.

For the first time, Nelfindal stopped to read the ancient fabrics. The eldar recognized his family name on one of the worn ancient tapestries. The shock of the sight caught the curious ranger by surprise. He stood staring as his silvan guide patiently waited for him to follow. It wasn't unusual to find one's name on such a tapestry, but the age of the wall hanging dated back to the kingdom's inception. Finally, the servant loudly cleared his throat in an attempt to get the shocked elf's attention. Nelfindal turned to his guide with a startled look and followed the impatient servant still absorbing what he saw.

Expecting a formal audience with the elven rulers, Nelfindal was puzzled to discover that he was being led into the private chambers of the royal lady, herself. Sitting down in a cushioned lounge chair as directed by the hurried servant, the young ranger was left alone with his befuddled thoughts. The young eldar began to feel nervous with such an informal meeting and wondered about the purpose of the secrecy. After many minutes, the queen appeared with a young silvan servant following behind her. It strange, thought Nelfindal, that none of the Queen's lady wards are present.

The young ranger stood up and bowed in greeting to the lady and said, "I came as you requested my lady. What is it that I can do for you?"

After seating herself and motioning for the ranger to do the same, the royal lady replied but in the ancient tongue of the eldar. "I thank you for your swiftness. No one must know what is being said here today. The fact is only a few know what has happened. My husband doesn't even know about this meeting and should not. At least not yet."

Speaking in the same language to avoid from being overheard by the servant the younger elf remarked, "What is it that could be so important as to be kept secret from your spouse and why let me know about it?"

Taking an offered cup of wine from the servant, the royal lady answered, "Our ambassador to a human settlement called Reah has not returned to Elador. She was expected about two days ago and I cannot reach her through any magical means, which can only mean she is in trouble. I chose you because you came highly recommended. The fact is Norin requested you."

Shocked by the queen's familiarity with Norin, Nelfindal wondered how often the silvan had performed secret missions for the royal family. The lady continued on with her explanation of the request, "If my husband discovers this treachery, he would insist on declaring war without a moments hesitation. The relations with the humans are very tenuous right now and anything could ignite this volatile situation. I believe that another force is behind this and wishes for war between the elves and the humans."

The sound of war echoed of the chamber walls like a death toll. Taking a sip of the offered vintage red wine the young elf cleared his mind to think for possible motives for the apparent abduction. Thinking out loud the ranger questioned, "Is it possible that the ambassador ran into a party of orcs or bandits?"

Expecting such a question the lady responded, "No, the guard that protected her was far too large for even three well-armed orc war parties. Besides there have been no orcs sighted in the area. A messenger was sent from the escort telling us of the ambassador's strange disappearance. One morning they found her tent empty. The guards that were posted outside her tent are the best trained warriors we have and they didn't witness anything."

More confused than before the young elf asked, "Is it possible to get to the site of the ambassador's disappearance? It may be possible to locate her from there."

Staring at the young elf the lady commented, "She disappeared only two day's journey from the forest boundary. If you have other means to locate her then that would be so much the better. My magic is weakened by the distance and very strong magic is being used to

hide her location. If she is not found soon, Felastharn may find out and then . . ."

All too familiar with the effects of war, the ranger sighed loudly. The lady stood up ending further questions and said, "You will meet Norin and two of my elite personal guards tomorrow at the Oak Leaf Tavern before sunrise. They will fill you in on any other details. From there you will ride out to the camp site where the mysterious disappearance occurred. I wish you good luck and a speedy success. And try to find out who or what is behind all this."

* * * * *

After leaving the great tree complex, Nelfindal thought about all the recent stirrings in the west. Many orc war parties and bands of trolls had been sighted in increasing regularity. If something was instigating a confrontation between the humans and the elves, they were definitely getting ready to make their own move.

The eldar prepared to spend the rest of the night preparing for the next mornings departure. The tall elf met his teacher and friend at the inn where they were lodging. The silvan elf was returning from the crowded tavern across the way. Smiling to himself, the older ranger began to pack his gear as well. The two elves didn't talk much during their preparations; however, the younger elf wondered what the silvan was smiling about. He knew that it most likely had to do with his usual fling before a mission.

After gathering his gear, Nelfindal positioned himself into the meditative pose that was the elven way of sleep. Crossing his long legs into the traditional sitting position the young ranger concentrated on his past experiences. This method of rest was much better than the human way of dreams, because it allowed an elf to recollect his thoughts to solve present problems that eluded any wakeful solution. It also insured a restful sleep. Recalling a time in the past when he had to track a southern elf who had killed a fellow ranger, Nelfindal remembered how the murderer used a spell to cover his path. To find the assassin, the eldar had cast a spell on the surrounding area and located the otherwise hidden trail.

Nelfindal eventually caught his quarry and challenged him to single combat. The southerner accepted, but tried to cheat his way to victory by using a poisoned blade. One scratch would have killed any normal elf, but Nelfindal's resistance to poisons and disease was far from normal. The eldar took several scratches before the treacherous assassin realized his misfortune. The dark elf tracker eventually died from the point of his own dagger being imbedded in his chest. The poison didn't even have time to effect him before death took his life.

* * * * *

Rousing themselves in the misty early morning, the two elves grabbed their packed gear and left their sleeping chambers. The eldar paid the bill for the room to a sleepy inn keeper and followed his companion to the Oak Leaf Tavern. The usual early morning mist hung majestically below the walkways joining the tree city. As Nelfindal walked across the short distance to the tavern he casually glanced down the thirty meters of open space below him. How many times had he stared down at the ground below in his youth and now he was doing the same except now it was full of nostalgia. It was much different living in the world of humans, many of whom feared any great height.

Walking onto the flet, the rangers were met by two heavily built and well-armed silvan warriors who looked at the rangers with open disgust. It was well known that many members of the warriors' guild disliked rangers, because they received much more respect from the people. The rangers were always considered something of a legendary elite force. Even the most inexperienced novices were regarded better than any warden or forest guardian. And if that weren't enough, thought the two warriors, one is a eldar ranger.

However, after discovering that the leader of the expedition was Captain Norin, a once renowned forest guardian himself, the two royal guards relaxed and grinned with pride. The idea of a eldar ranger being commanded by one of their former guildsman and a silvan seemed to inflate their egos on a grand scale. Nelfindal realized that the trip was going to be very difficult between him and the silvan guards. The young elf never adhered to the prejudices of silvan inferiority like most eldar did. Being raised by his silvan friend and mentor had dispensed all the usual bias from his mind.

The veteran warriors identified themselves in their silvan tongue as Ruiel and Telmin. Ruiel was the senior of the two and also the strongest as was typified by his immense bulk. The commanding silvan wore the green and grey cloak of Elador over his mithril half-plate armor. The broach on his cloak identified him as a squad leader, which was a highly respected rank amongst the wardens and forest guardians. The sword hanging from his waist was obviously a gift from some noble who rewarded him for saving their life or for some other service over and above duty. The value of the sword was far more than what a soldier made in a year. The fine weapon was made of mithril and inlaid with gold along the hilt in the fashion of a spruce tree. Though it looked like a frail ceremonial sword, Nelfindal knew better.

Questioning Elenar, the eldar ranger inquired on its properties. The bow responded, "That piece of tin is nothing compared to what I can do. It only likes to slay orcs and trolls. I could drop that arrogant warrior from two hundred meters away without him even drawing his blade."

Speaking back to the bow, Nelfindal thought, "Calm down, I know your abilities. I just wanted to know how much we could count on the squad leader in case of combat."

The other warrior, Telmin, was a little more subdued than his commander, but exhibited roughly the same mass of rippling muscles. Telmin was equipped much like Ruiel except he didn't possess such a fine weapon. The two standing next to each other made a formidable combination. It was no wonder they were selected to join the rangers in the search, but it was a whole company of these same type of warriors that neglected to observe an abduction right under their sensitive elven noses.

Once the formalities were dispensed with the search party departed the inn. Four elven horses waited anxiously at the gates of the city. The amazing steeds were common amongst wealthier elves, but were rarely seen among any other race. If one was given away it was usually an old gelding of over eighty years in age. Even at that age the elven mount could live another two decades. The creatures were slightly empathic and could respond to the rider without any outward sign of command. This empathy also helped the rider to judge the condition of his mount by simply concentrating on the thought.

The four rescuers rode off at a good pace. Only one person acknowledged their swift movement out of the elven capital. Queen Illidrais looked into a silvery basin full of clear water, on the surface could be seen the four speeding riders flying down the road. She prayed silently to herself that they could accomplish the task set forth before her husband found out. Even though she was the royal ruler, her warrior husband had a way of stirring the fire in every elven heart. It would only be a matter of letting the word spread of the abduction and a resolution for action would be demanded by the elven people. She had more reason than anybody to want action, but it was over six centuries since the elven people went to war and peace was paramount to any personal motives and desires. Even when a royal mother is concerned over her child.

* * * * *

The small band of elves had a day or less to get to the camp and then had to pick up the missing ambassador's trail. Talking to Norin, Nelfindal estimated that they had from a week to ten days to find the missing emissary before word got back to Elador.

The brief conversation with Norin attracted the attention of the two soldiers. The looks the two gave the eldar ranger made

71

him nervous and he wondered what would happen if they were sent after him. They looked like two hungry wolves staring at a lonely calf. Nelfindal hoped they wouldn't pounce on him like the wolves would with their prey. Trying to break the tension, the young elf asked, "How long have you two been in the guard?"

Ruiel was the first to answer, "It takes a strong and resourceful elf about two hundred years to attain the position of squad leader and another one hundred to be nominated as a company commander. My nomination for company commander will be coming up next year maybe sooner with this louse-up. I know the wimp in charge of the ambassador's escort, he's a real dunghead. If I were in charge there wouldn't have been a mishap like this."

The young ranger knew that if there was any sorcery involved there would have been nothing the silvan could have done to stop it. Nelfindal looked at the other questioned warrior.

Seeing the ranger's inquisitive look, the burly Telmin responded, "This is my forty-ninth year since I entered the guard. I have a long way to go to even reach the rank of squad leader."

Ruiel looked over at his warrior companion and said, "Don't worry, lad. After this, we'll both get promotions."

The four riders found nothing more to talk about as the day wore on and slid into their own little worlds of thought. At the midday break, Norin walked up to Nelfindal who sat quietly by himself and tossed him a wafer of par-la, an elven journeyman bread. The distracted eldar caught it in mid-air and nibbled on it absently.

Norin leaned up against a tree by the moody elf and quietly said, "You shouldn't let those two bother you with their foolish antics. Not many understand you as well as I do."

Staring sharply at his friend for having such keen perception, the younger elf slowly softened his stare and distantly said, "Its hard to deal with being away from home for so long and then returning to such harassment. If I had only accepted my place in society as many have done. I would have set them in their place and told them they should treat me with the respect of a noble born."

Observing the intense frustration in the youth, Norin soothingly remarked, "If you had said anything to them, I would be pulling them off of you. Let them vent their hatred out and in time they will realize that you are quite different. You are of noble blood, but you have the good heart of a silvan commoner. Don't try to change. If you do I'll pop you on that golden cap you call a head."

The seriousness of the statement was lost in the look displayed by its speaker and the laughter that soon followed.

Across the grass the two warriors sat wondering what the two were laughing so hard about, but dismissed the idea of trying to guess the thoughts of rangers. Telmin looked at the squad leader and gruffly said, "Are all rangers so mad or is it a trick to befuddle normal people?"

Agreeing with the speculating warrior, Ruiel grumbled, "Humm, who knows. I'm just glad they keep to themselves."

3 BETHANY

The third day in Bethany was marked by the arrival of the message from Caric. Eating lunch in the Black Crow Inn, the two elves quietly read the letter. The range commander was displeased to find that the two trackers had lost the eldar ranger, but admitted it wasn't easy to enter Elador unchallenged, as long as the two knew where to pick up the northerner's trail. In the message the range commander ordered the two trackers to return to the border of Elador and to await the eventual return of the eldar. The spies in Elador had informed the range commander that the ranger was not well-liked by the majority of the noble born living in Galadhon. His dislike for the maltreatment of the silvan servants in Elador was well-known. The powerful and influential eldar merchants would inevitably force the ranger to take another leave of the elven city. When he did leave, the trackers should be waiting for him.

The orders also advised the two southerners to make attempts at luring the eldar northerner to a wooded glen a few kilometers southeast from the border of Elador where a company of armed southern warriors would be waiting to capture him. The need for the northern elf to be captured alive was strictly expressed in the letter. If any unnecessary harm came to him there would be hell to pay to all who failed to obey.

Reading this final sentence, Raelin snickered in open disgust. "Why can't we just kill the northern scum and get it over with?" "You know as well as I do that orders are orders. If you want to experience the wrath of the range commander, then go ahead and kill the elf," said the equally upset Darius. Finished with his lunch, Darius raised himself to leave.

Looking at the sour mood of his companion, Raelin responded, "Well, I had my fun this week. The other night's job went very good. Not ideally, but the little pest did put up a decent fight."

The tracker leader frowned at his fellow southerner and wondered how he would react if he were allowed to kill the northern ranger. Most likely the fool would be happy for weeks with the head of one of his greatest challenges hanging over a fireplace mantle. Shaking his head Darius left to go pack his gear. The ranger thought how capturing the elf could actually be fulfilling. Why not torture his mind instead of his body? The recently lost smile and springy step returned to the silvan tracker at this new perspective.

The following day was marked by the departure of the two southerners from the bustling city of Bethany. Retracing their previous days' steps, the two trackers marched down the Great East Road towards the range of the Blue Crest Mountains. The day was much clearer and milder than the stormy day when the two boarded the ferry to the city. The rains from the spring storm created an explosion of blossoming vegetation, which displayed a variety of colors and scents. Passing a few merchants along the road the southern elves concentrated on the future confrontation with the Darkwood ranger.

The combined force of a company of silvan warriors and the two expert trackers should prove adequate enough to catch the slippery eldar, thought the tracker leader.

The empty road continued on for several kilometers without a sign of life. Talking aloud the southern assassin spoke, "The day is bright and cheery. It almost gives one the energy to go on a hunt."

Darius turned to his partner and responded with a small grin, "You wouldn't be thinking of hunting alone would you?"

The assassin turned to look at his smiling companion and quickly took off at a run into the forest. The tracker leader followed the nimble assassin's lead and also raced into the dense foliage of the forest. Raelin had played this same game with the tracker leader many times. The two would chase each other around until they found other prey to play with. This day was no different. However, the race only lasted a short while. After a half-hour of cat and mouse play the two ran into a small camp of human bandits. The brigands were squabbling over some treasures they had stolen from a recently attacked caravan when the trackers jumped into their camp.

The adrenaline that coursed through the southerners blood was brought to new levels when they viewed the five armed humans. Charging out into the campsite, Raelin drew his two longknives. The sight of the blood crazed elf brought the human thieves out of their petty argument. The closest victim fell quickly as he swung out with a broadsword. The clumsy weapon was easily avoided and two enchanted steel blades dug deeply in the exposed abdomen of the gurgling corpse.

Darius followed his enthusiastic companion into the melee with no less excitement. The ranger brandished only one weapon unlike his engrossed partner. The deadly edge of his longknife sparked as the blade made contact with an upraised mace that was used by one of the two parrying adversaries he fought. The speed and skill of the tracker leader proved to be too much for the thieves and one fell limply to the ground with a slashed groin shortly before his friend lost his life to the whirling steel of the same elven blade. The suddenness of the attack seemingly continued without end as the surviving pair of humans faced off against the intruding elves. The four circled each other. The two thieves were obviously unaccustomed to fighting elves who smiled menacingly at their human quarry. The threat in those small expressions was enough to convey all the evil that was intended to fall upon the brigands. With a sudden explosive move Raelin leaped at his self-appointed prey and deftly slashed at an unprotected throat. The resulting spray of blood covered the elf in its crimson shower, which only heightened his euphoria. The assassin proceeded to dismember the corpse before it fell to the ground. The surviving defender stared in utter horror as the grinning elf left behind a pile of surgically dissected body parts.

Caught up in the almost religious act of murder, Darius stepped toward the gawking human. The combined sight of the approaching elf and the bloody remains of his fellow brigand was too much for the last living thief. Unable to handle the thought of the excruciating horrors which awaited him, the human impaled himself on his long broadsword. The look of disappointment on the face of the southern ranger was enough to freeze any heart. Before the last signs of life disappeared from the suicidal thief, Darius smoothly executed a fine stroke of his long bladed knife severing the dying human's head from his shoulders. The bloody mop bounced off into the brush surrounding the encampment.

Turning to the disgruntled tracker leader, Raelin bellowed, "Good shot! I never saw such a fine roll. His head must have been perfectly round to go so far."

Still caught up in the thrill of the fight Darius replied, "I had to redeem myself. No one ever steals my kills! Not even my victims."

Kicking the headless corpse which lay before him, Darius added, "It was a good shot wasn't it?"

The assassin smugly complimented, "The best I have seen in a long time. But you have to give me credit for my artistic display of swordsmanship." The dark southerner looked down at the neatly stacked pile of human debris that surrounded his feet. The severed limbs of the dead human lie before him like some evil sacrifice.

"You did top my swing. That execution was unquestionably impressive," responded the tracker. Turning around to head back to the road Darius added, "Let us leave this mess and continue on our journey. It is not good to be distracted so."

The two journeying elves left the carnage, which they had created. The whole gruesome sight would have appalled even some of the most experienced warriors. To the two elves, it was just another day of work or as Raelin viewed it in his own warped mind, another day of relaxation. The journey to the mountain range was silent and uneventful. The tension of the failed chase with the young eldar was released on the band of highwaymen. The trip through the mountains took longer than usual because of the detour away from the dragon's hunting grounds, but was otherwise speedy.

Passing the majestic peaks of the Blue Crest Mountains was breath taking even to the distracted southern elves. Raelin had to admit that the view through the range was impressive. After several days of hard travel the elves reached the foothills of the mountains. The low lying hills that preceded the forest of Elador were mostly barren of life. Even deer were not found along the desolate rock faces. After the foothills were traversed the incredible forest of Elador became visible. "Here", whispered Darius, "here we will wait for our prey."

* * * * *

The makeshift campsite was swiftly cleared and the four elves continued their journey. Norin thought they were making good time and shared the thought with the others, who agreed. After mounting the rested animals, the group moved into a easy run.

Another seven hours of hard riding brought the group of riders to the encampment of the royal caravan. After their lathered mounts were taken from them by some servants, the group was taken to a moderately sized tent where they were greeted by the company commander. The commander was a short, well-built sindar warrior with a nervous look on his face.

"It is good to have some experts to help solve this dilemma. We have no trackers or rangers ourselves, but we searched the surrounding region carefully," said the distraught leader.

Taking his lead from the disturbed sindar, Norin questioned, "Has anyone been in or around the tent since the disappearance?"

Calming himself the elf replied, "Only two guards who have had some experience in tracking, but lack real expertise such as yourselves. Our company magician could only detect the essence of some enchantment, but has no ability to locate the ambassador."

The newcomers quickly ate and drank an offered repast refreshing themselves after the long ride. After the short dinner the four investigators went to examine the tent and the surrounding area. The two warriors stood back from the rangers as they performed their careful study of the ground around the tent. Finding nothing the two rangers entered the canvas structure.

The first observation of the interior and its furnishings raised a few questions. The most obvious question was why the belongings inside were left untouched, even an unlocked chest of gold was left behind. There was great wealth in everything viewed, it was no wonder the queen had sent the group. The ambassador was obviously one of high nobility and very important to the royal family. It was also quite obvious that the abductors were only after the ambassador.

Out of sight of the other elves, the two rangers began their secret enchantments. The surge of power coursed through their bodies with every movement and with each syllable of incantation. The information they sought was searched for on levels unfathomable to ordinary beings. This continued for almost an hour as every avenue of magical investigation was probed.

Outside the tent the awaiting crowd of royal guards stood wondering as to the nature of the search inside. At the end of the hour the two rangers reappeared. Impatiently, the company commander questioned them on their findings. "Well, what have you found? Was there someone who enchanted her away or something more horrible?" asked the anxious sindar elf.

Thinking to himself, Nelfindal shivered at the power that was used to hide the tracks of the kidnapper. It took the combined talents of the two elves to discover the whereabouts of the missing emissary. Realizing that the silvan captain was too preoccupied with his thoughts to respond, Nelfindal answered thoughtfully, "The ambassador's location is roughly known. She was taken by a magician of some great power. It is possible that it was a human mage, but I know of no human with so much power at his disposal. One confusing point, however, is the discovery of half-orc footprints hidden by the spell."

At mention of orcs in the center of the camp, even half-orcs, caused the surrounding guards to swear oaths to numerous deities. For an orc to enter a camp of elite elven warriors was unheard of. Coming out of his thoughtful meditation, Norin remarked, "We should hurry to find the ambassador before anything happens to her. If she is in the company of orcs anything could happen to her."

With the urgency in his voice, Norin quieted the shouting guards. The two accompanying warriors followed the two rangers to some fresh steeds and prepared to head off after the intruders. Ruiel ordered the sindar leader to speak of this to no one and to relay this to his own men. The commander didn't question the subordinate officer and promised to stall the return to Elador to delay the discovery of the situation as long as possible. With the completion of their final preparations the group departed at a fast pace. After a few moments the dust settled and the race to rescue the emissary had begun.

The direction of the abducted ambassador was towards a mountain range known as the Black Hills. The desolate area around the region was the ideal home for an evil race of creatures known as orcs. The grotesque beasts were the product of some dark sorcery that corrupted a species of odd apelike animals. The resulting mutation led to an animal that looked much like a hairless ape with oversized incisors and a massive humped back. The orcs intelligence was generally comparable to a human child at best, but there were many known to progress to the level of a low mage.

The evil creatures tended to be very violent and were even known to be cannibalistic to their own. However, their favorite prey were the fair elves, because of this the conflict between the two was more than territorial; it was a matter of survival. The elves stood for everything that was good and kind while the orcs stood for everything vile and evil. Only death resulted when the two encountered each other.

The history of the two race's constant warring led to many great stories of bloody and vicious battles. Unfortunate to many other races on Aragon, orcs weren't just particular to the elves. Many humans fell prey to the feared war parties, which destroyed entire villages without so much as a second thought. For all their limited intelligence, the nasty creatures compensated for it in cunning and patience. The worst trait about orcs was their close relationship with demons and their need for a violent and evil leader. A thought which never left the minds of the four riders as they raced to locate the enslaved emissary.

* * * * *

The meager campsite was lit by a small smokeless fire. The combination of darkness and heavy foliage concealed the stray beams of light from where Nelfindal sat on night watch, but he knew it still burned. The trip to their present campsite was uneventful, but the group knew they were being followed and the anticipation of an ambush grew as they moved closer to the mountains. Earlier in the evening Norin had consulted with Nelfindal on the proper precautions to take. It was well understood that the search party had been under surveillance and should take precautions in case of attack. It wasn't the first time any of the group had expected a fight and definitely not the last.

Half-way through the young ranger's first watch, the attack occurred. The party of orcs was well organized and hit the campsite from different directions. Fortunately, this type of maneuver was prepared for. The rangers had set up several traps, which were immediately set off by the unsuspecting attackers. One such trap was a pit located behind the eldar ranger's hiding spot, which was revealed when two sneaking orcs stumbled over its covering of branches and leaves. The young elf immediately cast a spell to create a wall of vines and roots over the top of the pit sealing the flailing victims inside. On the other side of the camp the sound of clashing steel rang out followed by the screams of wounded and dying invaders. The shrill cries could be heard even through the dense forest undergrowth.

The young ranger decided that it was his turn to attack. Stepping out of his natural shielding of foliage, the golden-haired elf engaged his first opponent. His first assailant was a half-orc of rather large size wearing a coat of rusty chain mail. This warrior proved to be more than what the elf was prepared to encounter, but instead of engaging the creature in sword play the eldar summoned his magical abilities. The resulting bolt of lightning emanated from his extended hand and lit up the entire area with light. The eyes of his target flashed with horror just before they burst into flame. The sizzling body was thrown back some five meters where it landed, smoldering and unmoving.

The flash of light emanated from his left side. Knowing that Nelfindal had begun his fireworks on the orcs spurred the older elf on. Thinking to himself, the ranger captain smiled at the effect such an attack had on those who had never witnessed the eldar's magic before. The youth had a way of shattering any attackers' moral with his magical demonstrations. Almost getting his head shaved by an axe, Norin returned to his present engagement with two half-orc warriors. The two human-like creatures were simultaneously swinging battle axes at the ranger, but hadn't landed any hits on his agile body.

Throughout the intense engagement, the voice of his enchanted sword, Nimnar, screamed with incredible fury. Trying to control the chaotic urges the sword exerted on his will, Norin fought with a subdued vigor. The elf parried an axe strike, which cleaved the cumbersome weapon in two leaving the attacking orc wide open. Without hesitation the veteran ranger cut the orc down with the fiery blade, which cut through armor, tissue and bone with equal ease. The taste of flesh drove the chaotic sword on even more, making the control only that much more difficult.

Seeing his companion go down, the second orc managed a lucky strike on the upper arm of the defending ranger. The minor wound sent a searing pain through the silvan elf. It hadn't occur to him at first, but Norin now knew that the orc weapons were magically made to inflict more damage elves. The anger building up in the elf broke his only barrier to controlling his domineering weapon. Screaming with victory the enchanted blade moved of its own and sliced the orc into three flaming pieces. The rush from the flowing power of the sword pulled Norin to the next group of attackers. His normally fair visage changed dramatically as the ancient power of the sword took over his mind and body. The sight of the snarling elf terrorized all the orcs who looked upon his face; many of whom turned and ran in horror.

The two silvan warriors fought on as more and more orcs appeared. The royal guards played themselves off as decoys for the ambush. Already, many dead orcs lay strewn about the campsite. The blinding flash of light from the tall eldar flared behind the defending warriors, helping them get a good look at their attackers. The grotesque beasts appeared to be coming from all directions. The quick flashes of light illuminated the area so much that the two soldiers where able to see into the thick forest. The reflection of over two dozen eyes came glowing back to them, illustrating the number of orcs attacking.

It was difficult to defend against such a large force and it showed on the pair of warriors. Ruiel had a small gash across his head, but was otherwise uninjured. His companion was not so lucky. The young Telmin had been hit by a crossbow bolt in the left side of his abdomen and was bleeding quite badly. The youth still fought valiantly, but was weakening from the loss of blood and what must have been a poisoned weapon.

Another lightning bolt flashed directly behind the strong squad leader. It wasn't until he heard the eldar's furious cry did the veteran soldier realize his companion had dropped to the ground unconscious. The mortally wounded silvan was replaced by a sword wielding Nelfindal. Aside from his obvious dislike for the sword, the young ranger fought with a vengeance and many more orcs laid dead on the ground.

After what seemed like days of fighting, the last orcs fled the camp. The carnage around the forest was unfathomable. Hacked up orc limbs and smoldering remains lay everywhere. However, the victory was not complete. Laying in the arms of Ruiel was the dead body of Telmin. Unable to heal the wounded elf in time, Nelfindal only whispered the ritualistic prayers of final passage. The living spent moments in silence to honor the memory of their dead comrade. Breaking the deathly silence that seemed to have spread throughout the forest, the silvan warrior swore, "The death of our brother in arms will be avenged by a hundred orc deaths. Never will I rest until I have revenge for this outrage!"

After burying the body of their dead comrade in a glade of early spring grass and young birch saplings, the group proceeded to burn the remains of the dead orcs. The two orcs who had been trapped in the pit snare were questioned by the rangers then given over to the silvan warrior for swift execution. The information gathered from the orcs was valuable in explaining who and what was behind the abduction and ambush attempt. It seemed that a new power was growing in the midwestern region of Aragon. The magician who apparently kidnapped the elven ambassador was only a servant of a much more powerful and greater evil. From the babbling prisoners Norin was able to deduce that the leader of the growing army of orcs was a giant black human named Lord Romulus. The ambitious human was a formidable knight seeking to be the king of the region south of Elador. If given the time he would muster enough orcs to assault the elven kingdom.

The location of this human conqueror was known to be in the mountain range appropriately known as Devil's Horn. Stories of the dark, evil place were often told to scare young children of all races. It was said that from this place evil magicians would summon demons without the need of magical portals. It was sort of a natural doorway to the hells below.

Thinking aloud Nelfindal said, "If this human had been living in the castle or temple for some time, he could have many demons at his disposal assuming he had magical control. It was possible that the lady ambassador is a sacrifice for a powerful demon or devil."

Norin uneasily interjected his thoughts. "If so, the best time to sacrifice her would be during the full moon in eight days. That leaves very little time to find her and escape back home before the caravan arrives."

The three discussed the legends regarding the location of the unholy place. Recalling the childhood stories told to them, the small group worked out a crude map with prominent landmarks to guide their way into the valley. None of the group questioned the validity of the map, hoping it would lead them to the sacrificial tower spoken of in their childhood stories.

After discussing plans to get to the demon temple, the three elves quickly packed their gear and rode off towards the entrance to valley leading to Devil's Horn. From the map the valley sat in the center of the mountain range they were approaching. As they rode out of the dense vegetation, the elves noticed an obvious and sudden change from forest to mountains. It was as if the forest stopped itself from getting to close to the sharp spires of the range. This oddity only added to the already tense and unwelcome feeling the three riders felt as they rode up to the beginning of the first rise.

The elves stopped shortly after riding up rocky incline as they realized how rough and unsure the footing was.

Looking around Ruiel remarked, "this range is too rough to ride up on. The horses will have to be left behind so we can make better time."

4 SEARCH PARTY

A day after the orc attack, the elves led by Norin searched for a cave, which was supposed to be the entrance to the valley where the temple was located. After half a day of frantically searching the mountain side, Nelfindal stumbled upon a concealed opening into the darkness of the mountain's interior. At first the group thought it was just a fissure create by some long ago earth quake,but after closer examination the opening showed signs of some travel.

With the sun setting leaving very little light to look for any other caves, the group entered the jagged opening. The elves were very glad they had magical sources of light else they would have been lost in the utter blackness of the underground even with the use of their elven eyesight. As the three elves moved down the tunnel the odd sensation of loneliness haunted them as it did many others who traveled the dark depths of the earth. The dark cave was definitely the entrance to a long winding tunnel that continued down for hundreds of meters before branching off into three other dank tunnels.

Realizing the necessity for speed the two rangers cast spells to search for the quickest path. After many long minutes of concentration, the way was felt more than shown to them and they continued down the far left tunnel. The pulling sensation felt by the spell tugged at them incessantly and at times the two rangers were asked to slow down by their winded warrior companion.

After only a few hours of traveling the dusty underground maze, the rescuers smelled a peculiar odor. At first it was very faint and unidentifiable, but as the group marched on, the smell became more pronounced. Finally, Norin identified the sulfurous scent as the smell of forge exhaust. Following the smokey trail, the three elves nearly ran into a large mountain troll working a huge bellows. If it weren't for the glow of the forge fires the trip would have been very short.

Quickly hiding behind a row of large barrels filled with a smelly liquid, Nelfindal and his companions observed several orc smiths forging raw tempered steel still glowing cherry red into nasty sword blades. The troll was only one of many other trolls which helped the orc smiths forge the many weapons. Ruiel squinted his eyes through the burning haze past the grimy bodies towards a rack of dark bladed swords.

Norin looked around and noticed that the forges were in an immense underground cavern. The ceiling of the rocky chamber rose past the limits of his watery elven eyes though it was obvious that a chimney rested at its peak. The black sooty smoke rose slowly out of the furnace disappearing into the heights, adding to the deepening haze. Along the opposite side of the large chamber were rows and rows of forged weapons. The glistening reflection of thousands of swords, axes and other implements of war were visible even in the shadowy cave. Stacked along the elves' side of the monstrous chamber were countless barrels of black murky water and huge mounds of coal. Feeding the forge with the dark rock were several huge mountain and cave trolls whose large muscular arms strained with each burdensome load.

Silently watching, the three decided to continue for fear of being seen. The sight of the forged weapons brought many fears to the mind of Nelfindal who understood the ravages of war more than many of his people. Finding a smokey tunnel close by the three dark shadows disappeared into it. The party stopped to recheck their position some hundred meters away when Nelfindal whispered, "We have major war preparations going on here. I think we should hurry and find out as much as possible about their tactics and likely targets before we leave."

Nodding agreement the other two elves motioned to continue. After an hour of avoiding orc guards and wandering smiths, the three stopped to take a rest in a dark abandoned section of the underground complex. The room they were in was off from the usual path used by the smiths and their henchmen, which allowed for quiet undisturbed conversation.

Taking a sip from his waterskin, Ruiel commented, "I'm concerned as to our defenses in Elador. The number of weapons back there was incredible. There must be thousands of warriors to build that big of an arsenal for. I wouldn't want to accidentally walk into their barracks right now. Are you sure this is the right way?"

Norin chewed on his lower lip and slowly answered, "The spells we cast tell us this is the fastest way. It could be possible the shortest way is straight through the middle of the main garrison. Or it could mean an untraveled portion of this maze."

"The thought of having to go through a thousand or more orcs makes me a little bit skeptical about following you around," replied the silvan warrior uneasy. Emphasizing his anxiety the burly elf sarcastically said, "So, we just walk where we will and hope the orcs don't mind our intrusion?"

Everyone knew the remark was uncalled for, but the two rangers were just as worried at the thought of a possible encounter. After a short break the three got up and continued on their previous path even more cautious than before. Their footfalls were so quiet that once the three passed a resting orc guard who wasn't even aware of their presence. Several times the small group came close to encountering a party of marching orcs, but each time the disgusting beasts seemed not to notice them.

After another day's travel underground the three exhausted explorers eventually emerged out of the tunnels into a long cave. At the other end of the cave was a large crack allowing the early morning light to illuminate its interior. The three checked the dusty floor for fresh signs of passage before relaxing. After finding the area clear the tired travelers dropped roughly to the ground. Each member of the group knew the weariness they felt was largely due to the stale air of confinement created by the underground maze of tunnels and not by physical exertion.

A large valley could be seen from the entrance of the cave. As they rested in the early morning sun for a short spell, the three elves looked upon the valley. About thirty meters below them, a layer of thick clouds shielded the valley floor from view. At the far end of the valley some twelve kilometers away rose what appeared to be a black island amongst the sea of clouds. It was too distant for the three to tell exactly what it was, but they agreed it didn't look too promising. Feeling somewhat refreshed the group resumed their search out of the cave and into the valley.

Staring closer at the shape of the valley and its blanket of clouds, Nelfindal noticed countless bands of swirling iridescence. The whole mass of mist seemed to be moving with a life of its own. The sight of the phenomena drew the curious ranger on down the small path, which led into the layer of mist. Walking down the path, Nelfindal thought he had seen a leathery winged creature flitting about in the misty void. But the creature didn't look like any bird he had ever seen. The tall eldar stared at the area where the dark shape seemed to have been for many moments, but he finally moved on thinking it was a trick of the eye.

"What's the matter?" questioned Norin as he walked up behind his former student.

"Uh? Oh, nothing. I thought I saw something. It was probably a large bird or bat flying around in the clouds," replied the doubtful elf. The young eldar shook his head to banish his worrisome thoughts and followed the others into the deep misty covering, which shielded the valley from view.

Entering the mist was quite possibly one of the most unusual sensations the three elves had ever experienced. The expectation of thick, heavy dampness one encountered when entering a cloud was not forthcoming. In fact, as they slowly entered the mist a strange tingling shot through their bodies as each part entered the strange iridescence. It was as if thousands of tiny needles lightly pricked at every portion of their bodies. Even the other senses were affected differently. The smell of burning incense was overwhelming and burned the sinuses with each inhalation. The eyes watered as a wash of colored light set the visual spectrum ablaze creating much disorientation. The worst was the cries and shrills of pain and laughter heard throughout the cloudy mist. The screams of countless voices were heard even after the three emerged abruptly out of the mist about thirty meters down the path.

The entire experience left the three dumbfounded and neither spoke a word for many moments afterward. Each battled his own nightmarish thoughts as they continued down the path trying to act as if nothing had happened. Trying to regain control over the situation each concentrated on the path they followed.

About another forty meters below the cloud layer was the lush and dark valley floor. The small trail the elves were on led into a dank jungle forest smelling of rot and decay. The ground was very moist and the path, which they were on was barely visible. At points the path disappeared completely, overrun by thorny vegetation. The usual signs of forest life were nonexistent in the thick vegetation. It was as if all the plants left no room for animals to survive.

After about two kilometers along the floor of the valley the path broke off into two branches, one going left in a northwesterly direction and the other going right southeasterly. Taking the left path, the older ranger checked to see if the trail was regularly travelled. The look on the silvan ranger's face wasn't promising.

Norin looked at his companions and said, "This path is well used by orcs and trolls. The small footprints are unmistakably orcs, but their are two sets of large prints. The one set definitely belongs to wild mountain trolls, but the other set is booted. It appears that there are a lot of black trolls in the area. Their feet are steel shod and the prints are deep. They must be heavily armored and well armed to sink into the dirt this far."

Thinking of how rare the black trolls were in these regions brought a few questions to mind. Nelfindal was the first to speak up. "That would mean that whoever is the commanding power over this army is using the black trolls as elite forces, which means we might have to face them to rescue the lady. If we survive I think I'll retire and become a farmer, its a safer job," offered the eldar.

Smirking at the sarcastic eldar, Ruiel remarked, "If we do this right, they won't even know we were here. We sneak in then sneak out."

Knowing the logic was right, but failing to see how it would work in reality, Norin added, "If we had a magician to defeat all of their early warning spells, we could dance on their roof and kick them in the rear without them seeing us. Be realistic, their mage was powerful enough to teleport himself and another to the camp site then return with a struggling victim and was never seen or heard. Our chances aren't good with this one."

The tone of Norin's voice shot down what ever rebuttal the proud warrior had prepared, but the flushness in his sculpted face was enough to display his anger.

Nelfindal saw the need to break the tension with a well motivated challenge, "If we don't rescue the ambassador and escape with word of this growing army then many lives will be lost due to our failure. I don't know about you two grumbling mud boars, but I'm going to take a good shot at what I was sent to do."

The response from the two silvans was a firm nod of agreement. The three determined elves continued with their riginal mission and whatever unexpected dangers laying in wait. However, none of the alert party observed the single glowing red eye, which hovered only meters away. The words of the elves appeared to spark a small sign of recognition, but just as quickly disappeared. Slowly the eerie beacon moved after the forms of the elves, carefully pacing itself with their progress.

* * * * *

The trail through the dense foliage of the forest became even more eerily quiet the deeper the elven group marched. The ight from the stars was so feint that even with his keen elven nightvision, Ruiel was almost blind. The warrior thought silently to himself, "These blasted rangers are probably suffering from the darkness like me," but he knew better than to believe that mere blindness could stop these adept rangers.

As Ruiel reprimanded himself about the rangers abilities, a trong hand grabbed him by the arm and pulled him down to the ground. The move was done with such ferocity that the warrior almost cried out until he heard the soft voice of Nelfindal telling him to remain silent. The guardsman knew immediately that his companions had sensed something out of the ordinary. Staring out into the darkness all the silvan warrior could see was the darker shadow of Nelfindal squatting in the underbrush next to him.

After what seemed like an eternity of waiting, a faint gurgling could be heard followed by the voice of Norin signaling that all was clear. When Ruiel and Nelfindal met up with the ranger captain, the corpse of an orc sentry was laying at his feet with what was assumed to be a slit throat. Norin leaned in close to his two companions and whispered, "there are sentries all throughout this area. Stay low and quiet. We almost walked on top of this one and he was ready to give us away until I found him."

Several times along their hike the two darkwood rangers avoided the almost invisible forms of other orc sentries. The two elves had boasted of smelling the creatures before sighting them and it might have been true for all the burly warrior knew.

Ruiel whispered to himself, "Give me a good fight anytime instead of this blasted sneaking around."

The eldar was close to the silvan warrior when he made the statement and he laughed inwardly, thinking about how the stress of infiltrating the occupied land was building up in all of them. To get his mind off the tension, Nelfindal summoned the spirit of his bow to keep him company in the eternal silence and darkness.

Awakening from his dormancy the fire bow said, "the sense of powerful magic is building in the air. It may pose a problem if you intend to go up against it."

The empathy between the weapon and its master exchanged every bit of emotion created. There was never any misunderstanding between the two. This time was no different. The bow was quite adept at typing the power of magic and the realm that it was drawn from. The power had to be immense to be detected by Elenar from such a distance. It only made Nelfindal more nervous, but it did help to understand his enemy in greater detail. Feeling a little insecure the young elf drew his broadsword.

The action caught the attention of Norin who was also growing very nervous. The passage into the dark valley was far too easy, thought the silvan ranger. The orc ambush that seemed years ago was a failure though several orcs escaped. The news of their continued existence should have set the entire army on alert, but there was only a few poorly hidden sentries. It was another trap they were headed for; Norin was sure of it. The question was who or what was waiting for them and when were they going to show themselves?

It was over an hour before the silvan ranger's question was answered. The small group of elves entered a large clearing of grass. At the far end was a pavilion with several other small tents set up. The scene looked much like one of the fairs the humans had for festivals or special events. Many of the small tents looked much like the booths in Bethany's merchant district. The only difference was the lack of activity. No townsmen walked about looking at any merchants' wares nor were there any merchants haggling with customers or selling merchandise.

The only sign of life was two distant horsemen. The black silhouettes slowly trotted towards the elven party. After a few minutes a pair of darkly clad knights came into view. The image of the fully armored knights was an impressive display. The armor was made of a unique alloy that was much like black steel, but gave a shiny reflection that no lacquer could have. It wasn't until the two apparitions approached closer did the three notice that the armor was made out of some enchanted metal.

Drawing his enchanted sword, Nimnar, Norin noticed a brief flash of magic behind him as the elf replaced his sword with the fire bow, Elenar. Just off to his right he saw Ruiel draw his mithril sword. The mounted opponents had a slight advantage on horseback, but there were ways around such things, thought the thinking ranger. It wasn't until the slowly walking horses came within some fifty meters did the first effects of demon spore touch them. It hadn't occurred to Norin that these two black entities could be demons. It should have been obvious. The armor they wore was too unique to be made by mortal hands. Now, it made the situation a bit more perilous. The power of the creatures was not just physical, but magical as well.

The cold deathlike voice of one of the unearthly beings shattered the anticipation Ruiel had for the conflict. The first creature spoke with an almost tiresome sense of command, "Drop your weapons or your deaths will be slow and agonizing."

The impact of the command was almost unbearable, but the silvan warrior resisted its magical pull. The two rangers were also fighting the magic with apparent signs of straining, ending with similar results. The silence lasted for many long minutes before a sound was heard. It was the young eldar who first spoke to the dark minions after the magical command.

"Otherwise a swift demise, so you can prey upon our souls? The pleasure of sending you vile scum back to your own realm will be very satisfying," awkwardly challenged Nelfindal. Following the insult, the ranger quickly took aim and released a silver-tipped arrow. The black shaft shattered as it hit the creature's breast plate and dropped to the ground, smoldering.

The attack only angered the two demon knights. They spurred their anxious mounts into a charge right towards the waiting elves. Before the creatures came within twenty meters the first horse dropped in a flaming ball of burning flesh and singed fur as another silver-tipped arrow was released striking the mount's chest. Seconds later, the second horse struck a magically summoned chest high stone wall. The resulting collision shattered the creatures front legs and broke its neck. The two demons were shot from the saddles of their mounts, but rolled out of the falls and moved to engage the loathsome elves as if nothing had happened.

The first demon engaged the silvan warrior with an unbridled ferocity, which only a demon could possess. The shock of the first sword strike against the elf's shield rang through his body with an intensity, which seemed to almost shatter the royal guardsman's shield arm. The strong warrior used all his experience and mercenary tricks to just keep from getting hit. The black sword of the meresch demon whirled blindly at the dogging silvan target time and time again. The blurring attack put the warrior in many awkward situations, but his experience barely saved him each time.

At the same time, the second beast went to engage the eldar elf who had shot him. Before the demon approached the elf a cube of flame rose up engulfing the two. After a few moments the flames had disappeared and Nelfindal lay unconscious on the ground at the feet of the silvan ranger who quickly moved to defend his crumpled body. Across the top of the young elf's head was a nasty gash, which bled profusely from a deep sword wound.

Norin fought with a vengeance rarely seen by anyone. His barrage of blurred sword strikes was too fast for any mortal eyes to follow. The once confident demon was on the defensive as his opponent left minor nicks on the otherwise unscratchable armor. The humming of the glowing Nimnar was heard clearly by those close enough to witness the fight. In the back of Norin's mind was the same commanding voice. The persistent plea whispered for the elf to let go and give into the sword's will. Determined to not allow the enchanted sword to take complete control, the silvan ranger fought quickly and with fervor.

While the other demon was defending against the humming blade, the second meresch still continued to offer a problem to Ruiel. His demon was far stronger than even the soldier's own remarkable strength and was incredibly fast. There were several flowing gashes on the muscular body of the silvan warrior and the signs of exhaustion were growing quite apparent. The incredible pace the demon set was difficult to maintain. All Ruiel could do was block with a combination of shield and sword parries. The royal guardsman knew he had to make a move soon or fall prey to the untiring beast.

From nearby the sound of clashing swords was heard. Nelfindal couldn't remember what exactly had happened, but he did recall summoning the power of the bow, Elenar, to engulf the demon and himself in flame. Luckily the effects of normal and magical fires were nullified by the magical bow. The flaw with the ranger's attack was that the demon was also immune to the fire. Before he could parry the extra-planar creature, it swiftly struck out with its sword. The attack would have cleaved off the elf's head if it weren't for his quick reflexes. Fortunately, the young eldar ducked just before the blade struck him fully. However bad the cut, the concussion from the magical properties of the sword knocked the young ranger down. Nelfindal's blurred eyesight barely allowed for the vision of Norin who was engaged in an apparently winning battle with the demon. The creature looked in sad shape as the silvan ranger forced it to take the defensive. After a few more sword strikes the creature was struck down and disappeared in a wisp of black smoke, which was carried away by an unseen breeze.

Meanwhile, the silvan warrior was evaluating his dilemma and decided to take a chance and strike back at the pressing abhoration. Dodging a weak blow by the demon knight, Ruiel swung at a luckily critical moment when the creature left its neck exposed. The resulting strike thrusted the enchanted mithril blade up and into the head of the quivering beast. Lamely drawing back the silver blade, the royal guard slowly dropped to his knees as the figure before him vanished similarly. Still bleeding from numerous wounds Ruiel remained conscious long enough to see the eldar run over to attend to his injuries. Falling into a wave of unconsciousness, the silvan elf slumped forward. Shortly after his collapse the big warrior felt his body surge with a healing power. The powerful magic stopped his bleeding and mended torn tissue.

After healing the wounded silvan warrior, Nelfindal worked on his own bleeding forehead. Running a herb filled hand across the gash and chanting sacred words, the elf began to feel the healing properties begin to work and the bleeding stop. The three recovering elves sat resting as the day wore on. Norin had received only a few minor gashes, but looked no better off than his two companions. The fight drained him of his will as he controlled his battle crazed sword as well as the demon sickness which effected them all.

* * * * *

The moon continued waxing as its power was drawn to begin the sacrificial preparations. Leaning over the still unrobed form of the unconscious elfmaiden, Zagros chanted slowly and quietly the binding spell that would insure a proper effect. The creature being bound to the magician's master was the strongest of its type. To many, it would have been considered an arch-devil, but few knew the real power of demons. The evil entities had a uncanny habit of playing themselves off as weak around mortals just before they stole their souls, but others didn't resort to such petty deceptions.

The demon being summoned in the next fourteen hours was one of those beings who needed no deception. Mericademius was a mighty devil beyond the vale of demonkind. In terms the mage had to explain to his master, Romulus, the creature was the equivalent to an evil demi-god. It controlled vast armies of demons and could easily have taken over the continent if it had free access to the mortal world. The binding spell would prevent the creature from gaining unlimited access between the hells below and the upper plane of Aragon. The spell also limited the powers the creature could summon to its aid.

The mage worked industrially to insure all the proper steps would be taken when he began the ritual. While the wizened mage double checked his work, a giant dark shadow entered the room. Zagros knew of only one person who could have gotten past his demon guards without question, the master.

Lord Romulus entered the cluttered study, his seven foot stature rising above the dwarfed image of the crouching magician. The dark warlord was an immense black human of indeterminate age who boasted an inhuman strength and surprisingly agile mind.

Speaking in his deep rumbling bass of a voice, Romulus inquired, "How are the preparations going? Will they be ready in time?"

Even after months of close work with the giant human, Zagros was unnerved by the commanding presence of his master. Zagros immediately replied, "I'm double checking the steps and precautions now. When the moon reaches its zenith you will have another ally to your side." The human mage never stopped from performing his work, but could feel the anticipation the large knight felt. It was shared equally with the power hungry magician who looked forward to questioning the powerful demon lord on matters of science and magic to increase his already formidable resources.

Satisfied with the short magician's response, Romulus continued on with his reason for interrupting the spellcaster. "Did you send those demon knights out to guard the west path as I commanded?" bellowed the commander. Waiting patiently as Zagros finished sketching a glyph across the ambassador's stomach, the knight leader listened for the expected response.

Finally looking up from his work the magician answered, "Yes, they were sent some hours ago and I expect they should provide much more of a defense than those orcs were. And as ordered, the cowards were slowly executed in front of the rest of the troops." The memory of the difficult and dangerous summoning briefly reminded Zagros of his future attempt. The demon lord was many more times powerful than the two meresch type demons who were the next strongest creatures. The meresch were a powerful, but stupid breed that proved to be quite good at basic defensive jobs.

Although, the last report the mage had from his floating sentries was the dangerous skill the three intruders had. At first Zagros thought of mentioning his minions report to his dark lord, but thought it somehow trivial. The meresch would dispose of them swiftly enough. Few mortals could defeat demons in combat and the two summoned beasts were very strong.

Seeing no further need for conversation, the dark warrior left after his expected answer, leaving the small human to work alone undisturbed. The attempt to bind the demon lord, Mericademius, was going to take all the resources the magician could muster. The knight could only stand back and make sure there was no interference. After the beast was bound to him, thought Romulus, he could exert his mighty military strength across the land. The first to fall would be the accursed elves. They would prove to be the most difficult adversaries. After their destruction the rest of the races would fall without challenge and Romulus would rule all of Aragon.

* * * * *

After a couple hours of rest and some added magical healing the three elves managed to rejuvenate their strength. The medallion of healing hanging around Nelfindal's neck surged with power one last time before the three continued their search. Thinking back to the fight only hours ago, the young ranger remembered how close the now healthy warrior was to dying at the sword point of his opponent. The numerous gashes had taken time to clot and heal even through magic. The deep gash across the eldar's own head was still healing. The injury would leave no scar as typical with elven metabolism, but the vivid image of the attack still remained.

The day wore on as the three continued their march towards the opposite end of the valley. After a couple hours of hiking through dense undergrowth the party walked into a large clearing void of vegetation. At the north end of the open ground was a large dark stone structure with a tall round tower rising from the rear of its roof. The tower's height disappeared into the swirling mass of multi-colored clouds like a giant spear thrust into a ghostly animal, the surrounding mist taking on a blood red hue. The whole scene gave an eerie feeling of foreboding evil.

As if that weren't enough, the surrounding area leading to the main doors of the ominous structure was watched by a company of armored black trolls. As typical of trolls, the tall dark skinned beasts carelessly guarded the main doors leading into the temple. Moving quietly and with the stealth of experienced infiltrators, the group of elves sneaked their way past the lazy sentries. Sneaking past sleeping guards and around regions of heavily guarded terrain, the group of rescuers made their way through the unsuspecting enemy lines. Their unnoticed passage eventually led them to the large, dark entry way, which beckoned them to enter.

Norin ended the trek towards the dark temple-like structure with its six meter tall obsidian pillars with a silent wave of his hand. The mysterious stone columns showed signs of wear, but the images of demons and other horrifying monsters were still barely visible. Just before the silvan ranger reached the pair of brass doors, a loud roar reverberated off the stone walls. The silvan elf turned to his right only to face the visage of a large black troll, which was hiding in the shadows.

The body of the beast was well over three meters tall and armored from head to toe. The vile creature brandished a large war mattock, which it swung around in a wide intimidating arc. Before the creature could strike the ranger, a black shafted arrow struck it in the neck exploding in a ball of flame. The concussion of the blast was strong enough for the close silvan ranger to be thrown off-balance. After the smoke cleared the charred remains of a headless body were all that was left of the attacking troll.

The blast echoed throughout the surrounding area alerting the armed guards who lazily watched over the entryway. However, the next several seconds demonstrated the speed with which the defending group of bulky beasts could organize. Before Nelfindal and his companions could reflect on the repercussions of the eldar's maneuver, about a dozen heavily armed trolls came sprinting toward them. The massive legs of the anxious soldiers worked like steam driven pumps pushing the heavy weight of their armored bodies.

Seeing the opportunity to escape the three elves slipped into the open portal and the darkness within. Norin and Ruiel quickly threw their bodies against the massive door. The groan of burdened hinges echoed off the interior walls with a deathly wail. Only seconds before the black trolls reached the top of the stairs, the wood bracing was slid into place sealing the entrance from attack.

Soon after the doors were securely locked, the sound of several mailed fists were dully heard striking the outer surface. The rhythm echoed the panting elves' heartbeats from the close escape.

It was Ruiel who first broke the silence. "Are you mad?! You could have gotten us killed with that bow of yours! You probably alerted every orc and troll within a hundred kilometers of this place!"

The tall eldar looked directly at the silvan warrior with a stare as cold as ice and deadly menace in his voice. "Had I not killed the damnable beast with my first shot, our good friend here would have been picking up his head from the bottom of the stairs," seethed Nelfindal.

The sincere look on the tall ranger's face was not lost on the royal guardsman. Calming himself down, Ruiel replied, "We better get moving so no one has time to prepare for us."

"I'm afraid they may have been waiting for us for some time," replied Norin, "demons and black trolls aren't just left around to guard something unless there is the anticipation of assault."

"Norin is correct. Both creatures only do what they are told to do if there is a promise of a good fight and much reward," added Nelfindal.

"Well, in that case, let us continue and find the ambassador before they realize we have gotten this far," charged Norin.

The inside of the temple was more foreboding than the outside depicted. Along the inside walls were murals showing demons and devils performing murderous acts of carnage. The graphic detail of the paintings was a disgusting site to the normally peaceful elves, who abhorred unnecessary killing. Even the veteran warrior, Ruiel, was taken aback by the horrible sight. The warrior thought to himself that no sane person would ever paint such abominable scenes.

Passing the gruesome artistry, the three elves walked down a wide foyer that led into a dark inner chamber. The inside chamber was mostly enshrouded in shadow. The ceiling rose up to heights of some seven meters or more. The actual distance was hard to tell with the smoky fog that clung to the rafters. The three rescuers continued their trek towards the far end of the room. The closer they got to the back wall, the more they were able to see. As they silently made their way across the rocky floor of what seemed like a chapel, the shape of a large stone alter became discernible in the darkness. On the rough, worn surface sat a rather wicked looking knife. It appeared to be a sacrificial dagger by its ornate style.

Off to the right and left of the altar were rows of dark sculpted pillars of demonic visages rising up to a height of some five meters. Behind the two rows of columns were several doors apparently leading into adjoining rooms. Deciding to examine the doors the group, led by Norin, checked the closest door to the altar some ten meters away. The door to this room had a large iron lock on its front, but it wasn't locked.

Slowly opening the large wooden door the silvan ranger peaked in to see if it was occupied. Shortly after opening the door, a darkly robed human came charging out flailing a mace at the ranger's head. The blow completely missed and careened off the door jam splintering the wood frame and dragging its wielder out of the room. The obvious lack of proficiency with the mace soon led to the cleric's demise as he was run through by the swift thrust of a mithril blade.

The body slowly slid off the shiny blade as the last breath escaped from a pair of ruptured lungs. The silvan warrior cleaned the crimson blood off the sword using the robes of the now dead human with the casualness of a veteran soldier. The brief look of satisfaction glimmered in the silvan's eyes, but was soon replaced by the professional indifference that was forever etched onto the fair elven face.

Grimacing slightly at the suicidal charge Ruiel remarked, "Stupid fool, we might have spared him if he hadn't charged out carelessly. Let's hurry and find the ambassador."

Searching the cleric's room didn't give any hints to the missing emissary's location. The impatient warrior tromped of to the next room and kicked in the door to the dissatisfaction of his quiet companions. Ruiel walked swiftly into the chamber awaiting any foolish adversary to challenge him. To his dismay the room was completely empty and he turned around to voice his apologies to the two staring rangers.

"I'm sorry about that. I'm just anxious to get this over. This place gives me the jitters," childishly apologized the large soldier.

Norin sympathized, "We are all anxious to get back, but we have to be patient. If we run into more demons like those other two we fought, we are going to have to be very careful." Looking around at his two listeners, Norin received nods of agreement. Following the conversation the three went across the large chamber to the middle door, which was locked securely.

Speaking in a overly philosophical tone Nelfindal commented, "If its locked then its hiding something valuable."

The young eldar moved the older elves aside and proceeded to pull out a small packet filled with several slim strips of metal. Nelfindal took two long pliable rods and carefully bent them at odd angles. The tall elf followed by sticking the lockpicks into the mechanism and worked a while at moving the tumblers. The rewarding click quietly rang out into the silence. The young ranger pushed the door handle and warily entered the next room. This chamber was well lit unlike the other chambers. At the far end of the room was a large stone staircase leading up, unlike the other chambers this room was well lit by torches hanging on the walls.

The three elves walked towards the large staircase that beckoned to them. Along the walls of the room were several large stone statues of armored warriors brandishing a variety of vicious weapons. Looking over at the marble sculptures, Nelfindal felt an odd sort of tenseness in their appearance. With Norin leading the group the elves stepped onto the first step of the large stairway. The action caused a complex chain reaction, which was marked by the sudden attack of six animated stone warriors. The creatures moved with a speed that could only have been magical. Ruiel was the last in line and met the first creature head on. Fortunately, the large silvan had been anticipating some form of an attack.

Slicing at the hardened body of his first assailant, a sudden realization manifested itself in the veteran warrior's mind. How do you kill something, which isn't alive? As he worked out this confusing dilemma, his mithril blade chipped out a sizeable chunk of the creature's mid-section, which only slowed the aggressor down. As if that weren't enough, Ruiel had to parry a pike attack to avoid being skewered by another attacker.

Nelfindal dodged a blur of swinging flails as two statues attacked him from the opposite side. The ferocity of the attacks were almost overwhelming, but the eldar ranger was no novice to combat. After rolling off to the side the young elf drew one of his magical daggers from his calf and tossed it at the head of the first attacker. The magical blade sank deeply into the center of the creatures forehead. The force of the magically enhanced throw shattered the head into a fury of stone chips. The rest of the body dropped to the ground and broke into many more countless pieces.

Following the actions of his companions, Norin hacked at the swinging form of his initial aggressor. The fine blade of Nimnar neatly sliced off an arm of the animated warrior, leaving the weapon arm still attached. A second stone being swung at Norin with a nasty looking flail. The weapon grazed the side of the silvan ranger's head leaving a bloody gash, which bled profusely and threatened to blind him. The ranger swung again at the one-armed opponent and chipped a large chunk from its head.

The usual blood lust of Nimnar wasn't excited when the elf hit the stone bodies of the non-living creatures. The only sound from the enchanted sword was the solid ringing of the blade as it chipped the blindingly fast rock warriors. The one armed warrior eventually dropped as the elf chipped the last bit of head it had left. The flail wielder continued its swinging even as the other warrior dropped into a cloud of chipped stone and dust.

Ruiel found the stone guardians to be a difficult challenge, but not overwhelming. The pike armed attacker had dropped sometime after the first strike of the mithril blade, but the other creature posed a greater problem because it wielded two maces simultaneously. The double attack was a new dilemma, which confused the veteran soldier. The stone warrior attacked with a parry-bash-swing technique that was hard to counter. Until the warrior realized that the creature's legs were unguarded and could be easily broken. Instead of swinging at the head and mid-section, Ruiel swung at the left leg when it was time for the bash stroke. The sound of shattering rock was the reward for the elf's maneuver. The creature lost balance and fell backward onto Nelfindal's last opponent. The two fell in a heap of broken rock and flailing limbs.   After the last attacking stone warrior fell the three slightly wounded rescuers continued up to the second floor of the temple. The room at the top of the stairs was also well lit by flaming torches hanging from steel sconces on the walls. Along the stone walls were two doors of solid wood, which were bound with iron bands to strengthen them. The decision to take the farthest door was resolved quickly when the three heard the clatter of boots from below. Nelfindal was the first to the door and quickly ran through to the next room. The connecting chamber was very dark and ended some six meters away at a large wood panel. Thinking fast, Norin and Nelfindal searched for a secret door. After a few moments the resounding click of a locking mechanism sounded and the panel smoothly swung inward just before the sound of large, booted feet became louder.

Norin took the lead with the young eldar following the group last to close the door. The group remained silent to listen for their pursuers. After a few long moments, the sound of the search party faded away leaving the three to examine their good fortune. The secret chamber they stood in was well lit by a dozen magical globes, which gave off an eerie blue light. The walls of the long room were covered with the heads of many strange creatures. Some of the creatures were recognizable, but mostly from legend. The feathered head of a griffin, the sharp horned head of a unicorn, and even a small dragon skull.

Also along the walls were many exotic weapons designed by many different and unknown races. Long polearms, exotic bows, swords and every other possible instrument of death conceivable. Much like the walls, the floor was crammed with many treasures. Along the length of the chamber were large iron bound locked chests. Ruiel was the first to think of ransacking the enemy's treasure, but silently agreed with the others that the time wasn't right. The ambassador needed to be found first and returned safely.

The deep scuff marks of iron shod boots were found everywhere in the room, apparently made by a large armored figure. Looking more carefully at the pattern of the markings, Norin noticed that the scuff marks disappeared through a wall. With this new discovery the search for another secret door was begun. The second secret door took far much longer than the first one had. It was Ruiel who accidentally bumped the head of the griffon that eventually led to the location of a hidden lever.

The soft grating sound of rock on rock reverberated off the walls of the chamber. The three elves walked into the dark, adjoining room, which was the wide circular base of the black tower. The spire was over twelve meters in diameter and had a staircase, which wound around its inside edge up to the first level some thirty meters up. The floor on the ground level was void of any furniture or signs of travel except for the unusually large and deep scuff marks made from the same iron shod boots found in the treasure room. The elven group quietly began their trek up the long staircase, which ascended into the darkness above.

5 SUMMONING

The wiry mage finished his carefully checked preparations and began to take the unconscious form of the ambassador up to the roof of the tower. The long trek up the spiraling staircase was good exercise to the cramped body of the anxious magician. The weight of the elfmaiden was incredibly light even though she was a good two meters tall. The enchanting elfmaiden was obviously a eldar from what Zagros new of elves. Her fair silver hair and amber eyes proved that the lady was also of a pure blooded line. This was the reason she was selected as the sacrifice. Romulus' spies were sent out across the continent to search for a suitable victim. It was only after a couple of weeks of searching local, well-populated cities when word was sent of a visiting emissary to the city of Reah.

It was only after kidnapping the ambassador, that the mage found her to be a member of the royal elven family. How she was related to the ruling family was unknown to the curious human, but such things mattered little. The gift of any elfmaiden was the best any demon could ever hope for. The spirit of such a sacrifice would be enough to satisfy Mericademius for quite some time.

The mage finally reaching the top of the stairs where an otherwise empty chamber was located. In the center of the barren room was a strange looking pyramid shaped apparatus. The point of the device stood four meters tall and was made of a dark brown wood. The mysterious looking object was the only way to travel to the roof lying above. Since no mortal could enter or exit the mist without magical assistance, the pyramid acted as a doorway to and from the cloud covered rooftop.

Zagros depressed the four glyphs on the center pedestal in a preset sequential order. The resulting flash of the device's magic was sudden and bright followed by the strange prickly feeling of distant demon spore. After adjusting his eyes to the strange light, the mage stared out into the blood red mist which surrounded the top of the ebony tower. Thinking to himself Zagros thought about the amount of power being summoned to his side in the next few hours for the binding enchantment. No living mage had ever dreamed of accumulating so much power by himself.

The power was a gift from several other demons the mage had encountered in his time. By tricking the evil beasts into revealing their secrets, Zagros had cheated his way into vast amounts of magical power. The human found that the demons drew their strength from an unlimited source known as the Well of Souls. By taking another's soul through a secret ritual, a demon was able to add to his power much like added wood to a fire. And Zagros learned how to steal this power from his demonic victims. He would feed them whatever sacrifices they wanted and then he would steel their essences away and add to his own formidable magic. Along the way he learned of many things, most of all was the true name of the arch-devil, Mericademius. The demon lord ruled an entire level or vale of the hells. It was just after learning of this important information that Zagros began his work to trap Mericademius with the assistance of Romulus.

The preparations took many months of study and many long hours of conversing with lesser demons for information. The practice received from summoning the lesser beings allowed the mage to gain confidence in summoning more powerful creatures. The high point of Zagros' time was the successful summons of the two meresch demons. The creatures were easy to coerce into working for the dark lord who the mage know pledged allegiance to. The promise of elven souls was more than any demon could dream of.

Distracted by his thoughts, the magician walked over to the large sacrificial pentagram painted on the tower's roof and placed the nude sacrifice in its center. The silent body drew the attention of the mage for only a brief moment. Had he been like any normal human with the same basic physical drives, the mage would have been moved by the almost angelic beauty of the elf. Unfortunately for her, Zagros no longer enjoyed any physical pleasures and the sight of anything considered beautiful had the effect of scratching a brick wall.

Shaken from his thoughts of the forthcoming summoning, the mage didn't notice the dark shadow standing meters away from him. From the far end of the cloud covered rooftop came the familiar deep voice of the armored general. Romulus stood over the bent form of the mage as he carefully lowered the limp body down to the cool stone and stepped over to his own protective circle.

Garbed in his enchanted armor the black warrior offered, "You should have asked for me to carry the sacrifice. It is not good to tire yourself so."

Startled by the unexpected presence of his master, the jumpy spellcaster quickly spun around to face the leering knight. Knowing a response was expected, Zagros thought his words out carefully so as not to offend the proud warrior, "I needed to have the lady close to me before the demon received her. It is an honor to be so close to a royal blood."

Satisfied with the grumbled acknowledgement his master gave him, the magician turned to gather his magical components from a bag, which he had spilled over part of his elaborately drawn protective circle during his shock. Collecting as much of the material as possible, Zagros didn't notice the small patch of powder covering his protective circle.

Standing off towards the very edge of the tower, the burly conqueror touched his large two-handed sword. The metal seemed to have a life of its own as it was caressed by the calloused hand. A large cloak flowed down off Romulus' broad shoulders and billowed out behind him, snapping in the breezy air. His large helm was shaped like that of a winged dragon, its wings covering the sides of the large warrior's face. The black headgear gave the general a sinister and frightening appearance to all who saw him. The presence of the mighty ruler was his most powerful weapon and he spent much time mastering its terrifying effects on others.

Fear was a powerful adversary when not understood, thought the giant leader and his half-demon blood gave him an instinctive understanding of its various uses. Zagros had never guessed that the unnaturally strong and powerful warrior was part demon spawn, but the secret wouldn't be hidden from Mericademius. In fact, fear was the demon lord's best weapon not just its powerful magic. Luckily, demon fear had been nullified in the past by Romulus' diluted blood.

Sighing with anticipation, the large warrior thought how the time was moving too slowly, but soon the evil demon lord would be summoned and bound to service to the half-human warrior. Patience, thought Romulus, the need for patience was paramount for such summonings. The demon lord would fight the summoning magic until the very last moment before making his appearance.

* * * * *

Zagros stood in his circle of protection and began the lengthy series of incantations that would open a rift to the domain of evil. Taking his magical components from his little bag, the frail human began to sprinkle the assorted items into the air around him. A tingling of power flowed through the mage at levels never felt before by the human. The silent form of the elven lady began to shift as her comatose state began to deteriorate. Slowly, the magic began to build causing the cloudy mass around the tower to swirl in its bloody embrace. The clouds themselves were only an extension of the hells housing all the demonic beasts, but the tower that rose into its depths was the bridge binding the hells with the material plane of Aragon. The swirling of the mist began to increase as the magical pull of summoning excited the dark powers binding it.

The powerful form of Romulus stood close by the magician to share in the powerful protective enchantments, which were caressing their mortal bodies. The strong tingling of demon spore became much more pronounced as the two realms were brought together. The essence of countless demons hung closely around the tower's edge. As the rhythm of the chanting picked up in tempo the name of the summoned demon lord was spoken once then twice. Each time the name was pronounced the mist seemed to stop its chaotic dance. After several more attempts at summoning, the unseen wind driving the mist stopped suddenly. At the far end of the tower roof a wall of black fog flowed onto the rooftop like a shadowy serpent. The coiling shadow appeared to resist whatever unseen hand drew it out. Slowly the forming mist took shape gathering itself into a large cloud of the deepest black. Before long the tall, hideous form and angry visage of Mericademius appeared.

The demon lord was like no other hellish creature. The beast stood over four meters in height and displayed a pair of leathery wings, which fanned out to each side. The massive muscular arms flexed easily as each meaty paw held a vicious weapon of death. In the left clawed hand was a massive flog of nine tails that quivered with a life of its own, each strand was well over six meters long and tipped with ebony black steel hooks. In the right fist was a flaming sword with a two meter black steel blade, which was barbed by the hilt and hooked like a giant scimitar at its tip. Two small scaled tails swung absently behind the smooth hindquarters of the arch-demon.

The effects of the demon fear hit Zagros at the first sight of the creature, but the mage was too well prepared for the fear to have it hamper him. The concentration needed to control the demon lord was enough to keep his mind off the fear. Romulus was alarmed to discover that he felt his first ever twinge of fear. The effect more shocked him than anything. He thought he was immune to fear, but realized his half-human side did handicap him a little. The mighty warrior realized that such a creature commanded armies of demons who could match even his incredible fighting skills.

* * * * *

The rescue party reached what seemed like the end of an eternity. The last room was empty except for a strange pyramid shaped object in the center. Norin cursed himself for not realizing the possibility that the mage could have gone somewhere else to do the sacrifice. The three were about to leave the room when the first effects of demon spore hit them. It was so strong that Ruiel turned completely around swinging his sword to find the source, but nothing appeared.

It was Norin who first spoke, "The strength of this demon spore could only be from a creature beyond the vale of demonkind. This creature is very close by, either below us or above us."

Thinking along the same line of thought as his former teacher, Nelfindal speculated, "The summoning could be taking place on the roof. The only question is how do we get up there and what do we do when we get there? The thought of fighting demons doesn't agree with my better judgement."

Ruiel spoke quickly before the older ranger could comment, "We were sent to rescue a lady and not necessarily fight a demon. We could take her and leave the beast to those who are summoning it. I'm sure it won't care to help them once we take her back."

The idea was enough to get the other two elves thinking. It was Nelfindal who began looking at the pyramid shaped transporter. The three quickly figured that whoever was up on the roof used the device to get there. It was Norin who inspected the glyphs on the center pedestal.

Speaking distantly Norin said, "I think that we have to press the glyphs in some order to transport us upstairs."

With his observation the silvan ranger pressed the glyphs in a random order and waited, but nothing happened. Trying again in a different order, Norin succeeded in transporting the three to the receiving platform above. The flash of the transporter's magic surprised not only Romulus and the mage Zagros, but the demon lord as well. The three elves stared at the huge demon lord then at the large armored warrior leader who stood over the entranced form of the magician and finally at the now squirming body of the half-conscious elfmaiden.

* * * * *

Standing atop his observation platform, the range commander looked down at the elaborate training grounds built for the final testing of apprenticing rangers. The one hundred square meter wall area was sectioned off into quadrants. The first section was an obstacle course with many physical challenges to overcome. This was designed to demonstrate the athletic abilities of the individual by having the initiate scale high walls and cross deep mud pits. The next two areas were actually linked together to create one large forested area. The object of this region was to test the tracking skills of the apprentices who took the test. Many of the tracks were meant to mislead the tracker and lead him astray, but an experienced ranger would not be so easily fooled. The actual set of tracks led to the next section. This last section was a walled in open arena, which currently housed several captured orcs. The beasts were equipped with only crude clubs to challenge the tested apprentice ranger.

The last section was where all the attention was centered on. Around the edge of the enclosure were all the initiated rangers and their instructors. The newest recruit had easily made it to the fighting arena where he encountered four confused, but anxious orcs. The initiate was well-known amongst the other apprentices as an excellent bowman. Caric thought to himself on how the missile weapon was too limited to specialize in. The range commander was a swordsman himself and frowned on anyone who concentrated on any missile weapon. The weapons were designed by cowards, thought the silvan leader.

Caric looked down intently at the ensuing conflict. The young elf had downed one orc with a well placed shot into the creatures chest. The other three fanned out to surround the nervous youth. Taking his time the initiate picked his next target and fired another arrow. The accuracy of the shot was excellent and immediately took the life of another beast. The bow took too long to reload, however. After the second creature dropped to the ground the other two orcs charged the unprepared elf from opposite sides. Trying vainly to shoot an orc the initiate managed to break his bowstring. The first orc raised his club only to catch a foot from the young elf in the stomach, which toppled the aggressor into a heap.

The second attacking orc was more successful in his charge. The fire-hardened wood of the its club met soundly with the unprotected skull of the young defending elf. The following blows soon brought death to the defeated recruit in short order. The orc backed off from the corpse of the dead apprentice. The defiant creature raised its bloody weapon and bellowed a war cry in its rough, guttural language. The beast's challenge was returned with a black shafted arrow, which plunged itself deep into the creature's back. Standing immobile for a moments time, the confused orc curiously looked at the protruding arrowhead sticking out of its chest, then fell dead into the dirt.

Glancing at the anticipated failure of the bowman apprentice, Caric turned to his lieutenants and questioned aloud, "Will they never learn not to emphasize on such toys? Let us try to teach the art of warfare with good steel and not with flimsy twigs."

Stepping down from the observation platform, the husky form of the range commander walked back to his tent. His long, powerful strides made it difficult for many of his officers to keep up. Caric liked the idea of keeping his soldiers working hard to maintain his pace. Walking was not the only thing his warriors had difficulty equalling Caric in.

Turning around to face his jogging officers Caric added, "I want you instructors to teach these recruits to develop other defenses and not to emphasize on one weapon alone. Let them see the body of the dead initiate to prove your point."

Turning swiftly into his tent, Caric thought how his legion of warriors and trained trackers were turning out. Some of the best rangers in the guild were educated under his tutelage and maintained relatively high status in the political scene in the capital city of Terrilon. Many northerners thought the southern guild was a separate entity even a bit too roguish for the political scene. In fact, many of the members of the ruling general council were strong supporters of the southern rangers guild. It would only be a matter of time before the guild achieved power over the entire general council. The thought of the increased power that Caric would gain from such an accomplishment made him smile broadly.

Talking aloud to himself, Caric said, "With the capture of the eldar ranger, the council will have to give me command of the guild. How wondrous that will be! Ah, you will soon be my guest Nelfindal and my ticket to power."

6 MEET THE MORTALS

The bright flash of magic emanated from the transporter platform some four meters from the circle of magical protection. The mage, Zagros, was too busy concentrating on controlling the demon lord to pay any attention to the intruders. Romulus was the first to act to the intrusion by drawing his enchanted blade, but he still remained within the protective confines of the magician's spells.

Mericademius looked upon the assorted group of mortal beings with open contempt, which only increased the strain of control already taxing for the magician. The demon lord realized that there was little or no protection on the elves behalf, but the mighty demon also discovered a flaw in the magical circle protecting the knight and his mage. A few glyphs were covered with carelessly spilled components, which the anxious mage missed in his haste. The realization of the poor protections on the elves and the humans made the angered beast move into action. Taking his hooked flog, the demon lord struck out at the closest unprotected target.

The steel hooks dug deeply into Ruiel's flesh as the evil creature pulled on its weapon. The silvan warrior nearly lost consciousness from the incredible pain, which streaked through his body. The royal guardsman struck out blindly at the tails of the whip, severing several snagged strands, but unable to cut all those attached. The muscular elf strained against the powerful pull of the enchanted flog. Through the searing pain of the burrowing hooks, Ruiel heard the hiss of a bow and the resounding thud that sounded like a successful hit, but the incessant pulling continued. The warrior made another attempt at cutting the last strands, which held him. Lifting his mithril blade the elf dropped it on the few remaining strands. The whiplash effect of the disconnection threw the delirious warrior down to the ground followed by a sharp crack in his shoulder.

The first shot fired at the demon hit the evil beast in the sinewed shoulder of its whip arm, but did apparently no damage. The usual blast of fire was nullified by the fire demon like water on a fish. The arrow did manage to get the attention of the beast, but didn't slow down its pull on the whip.

It was at this point that the creature first spoke to the attentive audience in his booming voice, "Well mortals, in a few minutes time I will be savoring all of your souls in the solitude of my own domain. This puny mage cannot hold me forever. His will is already weakening."

It was Romulus who first noticed the pale look on his mage's sweaty brow. The magician looked about ready to pass out from the obvious strain. If the mage lost control the beast would be able to attack all of them without any restraint. If that weren't bad enough the creature could summon help if the need arose. Realizing the seriousness of the situation the half-human leader stepped out of the magical protection of the weakening Zagros.

The action attracted the silvan ranger's attention, but the giant knight ignored the challenging look he received. Instead, the knight stepped forward to confront the arrogant demon. The creature looked at the approaching figure a bit curiously.

Mericademius stared at the tall dark human form that approached him. The lord of many armies and the slayer of many powerful rival demons sensed the slight spore of demonkind on the human and laughed in a booming voice, which rocked the stone tower. Speaking in his deep bass, the demon questioned, "And what do we have here? A demon bastard? I didn't know a human woman could survive the rape of a demon. Well child do you even know your evil sire?"

Romulus expected the irritating questions that were the demon's customary speech. Standing upright the dark lord responded, "Aye, I knew who my sire was and slew the worthless slug as was befitting his station. I originally summoned you to have you as an ally, but now I will destroy you and send you back to your plague infested home. Your arrogance nauseates me." Expecting a reprisal, the half-human brought up his sword just in time to parry off a blur of attacks from the demon lord.

It was at the same time that the high pitched scream of the mage, Zagros, was heard. The scream sounded as if the human was run through with a hot knife. Norin turned around in time enough to see the flaming body drop forward. The magic the magician was using against the demon lord seemed to have been turned back on him with a little demon sorcery to add to his quick demise.

The silvan ranger went over to Nelfindal who was trying to help the mortally injured silvan warrior. The pale form of the once strong warrior was only a dry husk of flesh and bones with only a little life remaining. Like a faint candle in a cool breeze the last signs of life were whisked away from the royal guard. The blackened marks from the whip's tails hung from his body still quivering with a life of their own as every drop of elven blood was drained from the royal guard. The sight repulsed the two elves and sparked an inner fire that began to blaze into an infernal of vengeful hatred. As one the two stood up and quickly stepped towards the battling pair of demon lord and half-human.

The battle with the demon lord was draining and the fire the creature immolated licked at the hairs on the knight's arms even under the protection of his armor. The enchanted sword was the only thing protecting him from the powerful and deadly strokes of the two meter blade of Mericademius. Already the magical sword was chipped and the dark general's armor was dented or punctured in many places, exhibiting numerous bleeding gashes and nasty bruises. Out of the corner of his right eye Romulus could see the two rangers walking silently towards the engagement. The shorter of the two had drawn a sword while the other held a longbow. Thinking to himself, Romulus laughed at the futility of such an attempt of aggression. The scrawny elves were nothing compared to him and his opponent and would quickly perish.

It was Norin who first engaged the demon lord by screaming a war cry at the creature. The attention of the beast was diverted to the silvan ranger long enough for the mighty demon lord to realize a horrible twist of fate. In ages past, a group of powerful elven mages, with the aid of master smiths, created a sword with the sole purpose of destroying creatures of the lower planes.

It was centuries since demonkind had heard of the whereabouts of the holy sword. Most thought it lost and Mericademius was one such being. Now, the mighty weapon stood only meters away from him. Its blade sang a tune of impending doom, which few creatures ever heard so clearly. Sensing the presence of a mighty adversary, the sword hummed with intense excitement.

Ignoring the dark human long enough to size up the new challenger, Mericademius decided not to chance underestimating the new opponent. With one great leap the Lord of the Fifth Hell engaged the smaller aggressor leaving the dark half-human staring after the mighty demon lord some five meters away. To the beast's shock his elven opponent took an offensive move and engaged the demon lord head on. The connection of sword on sword shook through both creatures with equal power knocking both back several meters. The impact was so great that it threw Norin against the ground knocking the wind from his lungs.

Romulus saw that he had the chance to escape and quickly moved to the transporter. Stepping over towards the magical platform the giant warrior was blocked by the tall elf armed only with an unloaded longbow in his left hand. Thinking how easy it would be to cut down the defenseless elf the knight charged the eldar ranger. The gleaming black sword was raised for a vicious chopping strike, but the action was never finished. The young elven ranger stood back and hastily raised his empty right hand towards the oncoming giant. The flash that emanated from the extended arm struck the knight in the chest with enough force to throw him to the ground. The previously marred armor protecting the warrior's chest was melted through in several spots and left serious scorch marks on his exposed skin.

Slowly lifting himself up the knight raised his hands in the universal sign of peace. It wasn't the first time he had ever fought an elf and knew that many avoided killing their opponents when possible. It was a weakness, which led to the deaths of many elves in the past, thought the injured warrior.

The effect of the poorly summoned lightning bolt was much weaker than the young ranger expected, but it served its purpose. The knight was stopped from escaping to mobilize his armies. Amazingly, the giant man stood up as if nothing had happened and held out his hands in the sign of truce. Under normal circumstances Nelfindal would have obliged the human with a demand for surrender, but this was a different situation. The elf thought to himself about the wicked deaths of Telmin and Ruiel. The young ranger knew these deaths were the human's fault and yet it was the way of the elves to show mercy to all.

The essence of the magical bow, Elenar, came to life as the troubled young ranger debated over the matter. "The damned fool of a human just tried to kill you! What are you doing second-thinking about his welfare? Just fry the bastard! Let me call up a cube of fire to toast him as you watch the man burn to death," screamed the vengeful weapon.

Responding to the overly enthusiastic sentience, Nelfindal thought, "I will not let him escape. He captured a royal blood and chose to sacrifice her to that vileness. I will not let him be forgiven so easily!"

"Good, then let me cook him in a hotter fire than he would ever find in hell!" gleefully offered the intelligent bow.

"No! I will handle him myself!" commanded the determined elf aloud.

The thought that this one man would rage war on Elador and all the peaceful human settlements living nearby if he lived fed the flame of the eldar's resolve. The young ranger made up his mind and knew what he had to do. The young elf concentrated on summoning as much power as he could for one last chance at stopping the hated general.

The tall warrior saw the mixed expressions of confusion and hatred in the tall elf's face, but couldn't figure what he was going to do next. The internal debate seemed to have reached a climax when the tall eldar screamed out in his native tongue, which the mighty warrior couldn't understand. Seeing an opportunity to calm the unpredictable ranger, the half-human decided to talk his way to freedom.

Speaking in his best diplomatic voice, but not dropping his sword Romulus spoke in the rough language of westronese, "Peace brother! I wish no harm I only want to leave this dreary place and return home. Please have mercy!"

Romulus thought to himself on how he would slaughter the elf as soon as he lowered his defenses, then flee to safety amongst his awaiting armies. The thought of the elf dropping his guard and relaxing his defenses was somehow funny to the devious mind of the dark knight. If the elf could have seen through the dark helmet he would have seen the devious smile on the knight's face.

The giant commander stood towering over the form of the eldar elf and extended his gloved hand with the palm out towards the outstretched hand of the young ranger to top off his deceptive performance. His other meaty hand tightly held the ebony blade that was preparing to pierce the chest of the unknowing elf with a single quick thrust. There was no way for the tall half-human leader to expect the result of the conflicting emotions in Nelfindal. The thought had never crossed Romulus' mind that the elf would ever strike out as he did at that moment. The only hint was the tingling of power which everyone on the roof felt, even the mighty Mericademius felt the unusually large amount of summoned magic. The result was a bright blue flash, which shot forth from the outstretched hand of the avenging eldar.

The older ranger was completely unaware of his friend's mysterious summoning, so engrossed in his battle with the demon's insane barrage of attacks. Norin barely blocked the blows of the mighty demon blade with only a few counter strikes himself, but it wasn't until the blade of Nimnar had tasted the rich demon blood that the real power of the weapon was demonstrated. The silvan elf left a large and nasty gash along the side of the constantly regenerating demon. The sword screamed out loud enough for even Mericademius to hear the excited tone of the holy sword. The blood lust of the enchanted weapon took over Norin who freely let himself be controlled by the glowing sword, seeing no other way to defeat the much greater opponent. The speed of the attacks doubled as the laen and mithril blade wove an intricate pattern of magic and metal.

The fury of the attacks took the demon lord by surprise and for the first time in his many millennia of existence, Mericademius felt fear. The demon lord didn't feel ordinary fear, but the gut wrenching terror that he himself had created countless times in his innocent victims; the fear one exhibits just before certain death. The blade took pieces of the evil creature's existence away with every cut and scratch. Mericademius' very essence was stolen away with every nick and gash of the mighty weapon, leaving the evil lord weaker with each hit. The strength of the magical blade ripped his very being, which the beast had taken for granted for too long.

The affect of the sword's control over Norin was obvious. The fair features disappeared and were replaced by a visage that was almost frightening to look at even for the wounded demon. With each strike and thrust the silvan ranger became even more aggressive as the sight of victory came ever closer. In the back of his mind Norin reminded himself that he shouldn't let the sword take total control over his mind and body, but for now he needed it.

At the same time, the insane laughter of the sword's joy could be heard in the silvan's mind. The ranger captain knew his own limitations and realized that he could never defeat his demonic opponent without help. The ranger was wounded himself in several places, but Nimnar refused to let him slow. With each successful hit on the weakening defender, the elf strained to regain some control. Even the painfully bleeding injuries on the silvan elf couldn't break through the incredible power, which the sword now commanded over him.

The second blast of lightning rang out over the edges of the tower and shook the very foundations, which supported it. Unknowingly, the young ranger had harnessed the incredible magical power, which the powerful mage Zagros had summoned. In that short fleeting moment, nature's awesome destruction was skillfully demonstrated. The charge created by Nelfindal's magic struck the armored body with a force unseen for centuries. The deadly blast shot forth literally vaporizing metal, bone and tissue into dust.

The strength of the spell carried the bolt out over the valley ripping through the vast misty ceiling like a divine beacon. Many kilometers away, the forming army of orcs and trolls stood as quiet observers of the brilliant flash and resounding percussion that signaled the end of their imperialist leader.

The partially melted sword and the darkly scorched area around the location of the demon/human was the only reminder that life had existed around it. Staring in bewilderment at the destruction he had caused, Nelfindal turned blankly to look towards the awestruck form of the ambassador. Snapping out of his shock the elf quickly walked over to help the naked, shivering form of the eldar maiden. The ranger removed his own cloak to wrap the firm, but weakened body of the confused emissary. After seeing to the confused elf maiden, Nelfindal turned to check on his fighting companion.

Norin was fending off several dangerously close blows of the demon's sword. The festering wounds on the silvan seemed to only increase the speed and ferocity of the already blindingly fast attacks. After only a few more exchanges, the silvan ranger drove his enchanted weapon deep into the chest of the dying demon. The resulting flash of black smoke was immediately consumed by the blade of his sword. For a brief moment the blade took on a blindingly bright white glow along its length. The look of ferocity disappeared from the silvan ranger's face and he slowly collapsed to his knees.

Not knowing whether to go to his former master or to stand guard over the recovering maiden, Nelfindal just remained where he knelt. After Norin regained his composure, he painfully stood up. After a few moments of disorientation, the bloody silvan ranger walked over to the clinging forms of his apprentice and the conscious ambassador.

The lady quietly spoke to her two rescuers, "I thank you for saving my life. I don't know what would have happened if you two hadn't arrived in time."

Nodding in humble thanks, Nelfindal spoke out in a painful voice, "It is not us you should thank, but the two brave warriors who gave up their lives for you. We don't deserve any credit for your rescue compared to them."

The lady looked over at the shriveled form of the once large and healthy Ruiel. A shadow passed over her face at the thought of the two sacrificed lives, which were given up to save her. Tears began to flow freely as she hugged the eldar ranger for comfort. Nelfindal looked over to his friend, Norin, and the two allowed themselves to mourn the deaths of their fallen comrades.

It seemed like an eternity before the three left the top of the tower. It took some time to heal the infected wounds caused by the demon lord, but Norin recovered well enough to travel. Once inside the tower the elves quickly climbed down from the heights to the treasure room level. In one of the rooms on the second floor of the temple they found the remains of the ambassador's clothes. The group cautiously made their way back to the secret treasury room where they could rest undisturbed. It wasn't until the group sat down to eat and rest themselves did they plan the return trip back to Elador.

It was the lady who spoke first with a rather embarrassed tone. "This may sound strange, but what are your names? Mine is Nickoleta, but after all this you can call me Niki, for short."

Thinking about the quickest route out of the valley, the two rescuers were taken off guard by the question and it was Norin who recovered first, "Uh? Oh, my name is Norin and this young fellow, here, is Nelfindal. Queen Illidrais sent us to find you in hopes of preventing a war with the humans. It appears the King would have gotten a little upset if he knew of this."

The silvan smirking ruefully and added, "She would never have guessed this. A whole army of orcs and trolls only a week's ride away from our borders!"

Shaking off his childish shock, Nelfindal asked, "What happened when you disappeared from the camp?"

The ambassador shivered with the thought of the past events and replied, "The night after we set up camp, I was resting in my tent when a flash emanated from behind me. Before I got a chance to scream out for help, an ugly half-orc punched me into unconsciousness. The next thing I remember is staring up at a large black human who mentioned something about how I was ideal for the beast. I can only assume he meant that demon you killed, Norin."

The memory of the battle came back to him and Norin lowered his head in shame of letting his sword take control as it had. Before the silvan could say anything the lady continued with her story.

"The mage cast a very powerful sleep spell on me so I would remain somewhere between consciousness and a strange dreamlike state until the proper time. The first thing I remember clearly is staring up at Nelfindal's face as he covered me up in his cloak." The look the enchanting lady gave the young ranger caused the eldar to blush from ear to ear.

Quickly the young ranger explained, "You had no clothes and I figured you would be cold. Besides, I think the demon lord as staring at you a little too hard." The defensive ranger stumbled over the last words as if he lost his tongue. The obviously innocent attitude towards the lady made her smile girlishly, a sight that was very appealing to the young ranger.

Not paying much attention to the looks the two eldars ave to each other, Norin said, "I'm glad we got here in time at least. I would hate to have to defend Elador against a horde of orcs, trolls, and demons. We should consider ourselves very lucky."

The thought of what had almost happened brought the group back to their present situation. Nelfindal slowly offered, "The ugly beasts are probably expecting their leader to visit them with news of the summoning. My guess is that we should vacate this place as fast as possible or we'll run into a nation of our worst nightmares after stepping out of the door."

The other two agreed and prepared to leave the confines of the temple. The three made their way down the rock strewn stairs where the prior fight with the stone creatures had occurred. Their quiet and frightening walk through the temple was punctuated only by the screeching of a startled bat. The battle on the tower roof apparently scared off the temple guards who were all to familiar with the dangers of uncontrolled demons.

The company of trolls which guarded the front of the temple were nowhere in sight and the usual scouts had also quickly departed. The path out of the valley was poorly guarded. However, a few orcs were encountered along the way to the caves, but they were quickly dispatched by the two rangers. The fiery demonstration from the tower's roof apparently unnerved the detestable creatures causing them to leave the now leaderless army.

The hike back to the cave was uneventful until the three approached the misty vale covering the valley. The brilliant iridescence swirled around the path like a cloudy watchman. The color of the mist took on an unusual pale blue that contrasted sharply with the rest of the haze. Norin walked forward with an odd look on his face. A look the tall eldar had not seen before the battle on the tower roof. The fair features of the silvan's face took on an almost frightening appearance. The usually calm and sober eyes became almost insane with hatred as the ranger captain held out the humming blade of Nimnar.

As Norin approached the transparent guardian, the pale blue changed to the normal white of the surrounding mist. All signs of the odd apparition disappeared as if the image was an illusion. Norin continued on through the cloud holding the sword up high, its brilliance acting as a beacon for the two eldars following closely behind. Before long the three emerged from the vale of mist, the only hint of how perilous their passage could have been was the high pitched scream that emanated from the area about the path. The same pale blue appeared briefly behind them, quivered in the light of the still upraised sword and vanished as before.

After a couple days of hard travel through the dreary underground system of caverns and avoiding the many hundreds of armed orc warriors, the escaping elves chanced a rest in a small cave looking out over the great plains surrounding the Black Hills. Nelfindal took watch as the others fell into an exhausted fit of sleep. As much as he tried to stay alert, the young eldar soon followed his companions into a dreamless state of unconsciousness. It was only after the sound of a distant whinny that the tall ranger realized he had been asleep for a few hours.

Raising himself to take a look for the source of the equine sound, Nelfindal was caught by an absolutely stunning sight. The young elf walked out of the cave's mouth leaving his slumbering friends behind still completely exhausted. About a hundred meters away were the three steeds, which carried the rescuers to the mountains. However, it was not the sight of the horses, which caught the awestruck ranger's attention. Standing only meters away was a fabulously brilliant white tiger. The giant feline was over meter and a half at the shoulder and stood protectively over the grazing herd. Seeing the dumbfounded elf, the creature began to shimmer and change. With in seconds, the strange elf encountered outside of Bethany stood before the eldar.

The lithe form of the changeling walked forward towards the still form of Nelfindal, who could only look on in disbelief. The familiar stranger looked deeply into the ranger's eyes and smiled.

"We meet again Nelfindal Goldleaf. I see you made it home safely," said the mysterious figure.

"Who are you?" inquired the recovering eldar.

The changeling walked past the tall elf and into the cave where he took a seat across from the still forms of Norin and Niki. Looking down at the lady in an almost fatherly expression, the dark elf whispered, "She is beautiful isn't she? What do you think my friend? Is she not what you find perfect?"

Nelfindal looked at her peaceful slumber, which expressed everything the young elf wished he could enjoy. He stared back at his perceptive visitor with countless questions on his mind, but only one question came to mind. "Who are you and what do you want here?" stammered the youth.

"Hmmm, well, I guess you are just as young and impatient as your father was." replied the stranger. "Before you say anything, the answer is: yes, I did know your father. He was a very formidable figure and a great leader of his people."

"That is what I was always told, but why did he leave me?" questioned the angry youth.

"A question I cannot answer. But, enough with this. I am not here to discuss passed issues of little importance. I am here to tell you of your possible future. One filled with great pain for you and those you love. If you prove victorious in overcoming the many obstacles that face you, the land of Aragon will be united together. If not, then all is lost and nothing will remain. A dark force is attempting to drain the land of its life and only you can help."

Nelfindal listened to the mysterious stranger with some skepticism, but remained otherwise attentive. It was hard for the youth to believe that he was to save all of Aragon, yet this changeling seemed to add credibility to the statement. Something about this strange and obviously powerful creature seemed to make everything true to the disbelieving elf.

"Your father was to take on the responsibility, but the evil power behind this destruction got to him before I did. Beware, there is evil all around and you must trust your true friends for help. It may be this trust that will inevitably save everything. In evil, there is no trust or friendship. There are only alliances of convenience. My time here runs short, make your way back to Elador quickly. Watch your back at all times and know your friends."

Following his last statement, the stranger walked to the mouth of the cave and changed back into the snowy white tiger. The clear blue eyes of the great feline looked back at Nelfindal and winked at him then ran out of the cave with a speed which defied nature. Even after Nelfindal recovered from the shock of the speedy exit, the creature's presence was still felt, but the image of the speaker disappeared from his mind's eye. It was impossible to recall what the stranger looked like or even appeared to look like, but the memory of his words hung in his mind like an open book before him.

After an hour or so, the others awoke only to find the young ranger in deep thought. Seeing the distressed look on his face, Niki inquired, "Are you all right? You seem noticeably upset."

Nelfindal looked back at the lovely face and recalled the odd

statement, which the faceless visitor had made. He did find her very attractive and unquestionable perfect. It was after a few moments that the youth began to blush realizing that he had been staring at the lovely visage far longer than he should have.

The young lady turned away from the blushing ranger with a small flushness of her own. Trying to change the subject, Niki offered, "We better get going and find some way to catch up with the caravan before we get to far behind them."

Climbing down from the steep mountainside, the three caught sight of the grazing horses, which remained where they were left over a week ago. The three steeds were comfortably munching on the fresh, new spring growth that grew in abundance in the low lying pastures around the bottom of the hills. The mounts were anxious to be ridden and proved to be a valuable mode of transportation. The otherwise long trip to meet up with the slowly advancing escort would only take about two days of hard travel.

The first sight of the royal caravan was the loaded wagons that trailed behind the main company of elite guardsmen. The sight of the arriving riders created a stirring of confusion until the company commander recognized the ambassador and the rescuing rangers. When word spread through the caravan that the rangers had returned with the ambassador, a joyous roar rose up. The shouts and cheers that rang out over the fields were directed at the valiant rangers. When the returning group met with the commander at the front of the caravan, the escorting warriors began to sing out the Song of Heroism, an ancient ballad about the sacrificing of lives for the peace of elven life. The song was known to be sung for only those worthy of the very highest of honors.

The open display of gratitude and respect caught the two rangers off guard. Norin looked uneasily at his companion who only shook his head in humble disbelief. Leaning closely to Norin, Nelfindal awkwardly replied, "I feel guilty about the reception they're giving us. With the sacrifice the other two gave and all."

Nodding his agreement, Norin added, "It is embarrassing. We did what was asked of us. They make it out as if we were the conquerors of the whole nation of orcs."

The song continued on for a while and finally ceased. However, the congratulations and praise continued for some time after the singing stopped. The looks on the faces of the individual guards was that of incredible pride in their fellow countrymen. A look, which many had thought gone with the civil disruptions going on in the homeland.

Ambassador Nickoleta guided her energetic mount over towards the quiet rangers and happily said, "Don't get all modest for what you did. You both deserve it. I couldn't thank you as much as they just did. However, if you ever need anything, please ask. After all, I owe you my life."

Nelfindal uneasily replied, "We thank you my lady, but we were sent to rescue you and we did. If it were any other way maybe we would take you up on your generous offer. Please, don't feel obligated. It was our duty."

The conversation dropped off from there as the ride home sparked a new excitement for everybody. Soon the two rangers were riding in the point position by the request of the company commander to scout out the area for any hostile beings. The two didn't see the lady following their last talk until the royal escort entered Galadhon. Word was eventually sent ahead by a swift mounted courier of the impending arrival of the envoy.

* * * * *

The sight of the returning entourage brought many citizens to the streets. The royal guard proudly escorted the lady and the rest of the caravan to the royal house in the center of the city. The two rangers managed to escape from the enthusiastic crowd and head towards the Oak Leaf Tavern. After finding a stable to rest their horses in, the two elves climbed the stairs to the large flet above. The tavern was empty of customers at the time, but the barkeeper was present and was working hard to clean the place before his rowdy patrons returned from the parade below. Seeing the look on the faces of his two travel worn customers, the silvan barkeeper quickly brought over two bottles of wine and a pair of glasses.

Glancing over the wooden banister that kept the drunk customers from falling out of the tree, the silvan sighed and said, "I see you two don't wish to fight with the crowds down there. Good thinking on your part. That mob is going to get very rowdy after a while. I only hope my tavern survives. Have you heard the rumors that the Princess Nickoleta was kidnapped?"

It was Nelfindal who choked on his drink and quickly responded to his friend, "The ambassador is one of the Princesses? I didn't realize that!"

Norin noticed the shocked look on his young friend's face and said, "That's what you get for leaving home for so long. She's younger than you so you wouldn't remember her very well. Why is it such a shock. After all, that's why the Queen sent us and kept it quiet. If the King found out that one of his daughters had been taken prisoner by humans, all the human diplomats in the nation would have been pronounced as spies and exiled from Elador."

Understanding the logic, Nelfindal replied, "It was just that she didn't seem like what I perceived as a princess. I knew she was of royal blood, but I would never have guessed she was the oldest daughter of the Royal family."

The sound of the young eldar's last statement made the silvan ranger wonder at the real reason for the younger elf's shock. Nelfindal actually appeared upset at the revelation that he had saved a princess. Norin wondered at the many possible excuses for the tall youth's reaction, but soon gave up speculating after the first boisterous customers walked into the tavern. After the two elves had polished off their fourth bottle of elven wine, neither remembered to care about the past week's events or of kidnapped princesses.

* * * * *

The days after the unexpected announcement of the ambassador's heritage were filled with a persistent dreariness. Nelfindal felt angry and disturbed by the news that the lady he saved was the princess. Most if not all of the male population of Elador would have killed to get the chance to save the enchanting Princess Nickoleta.

"And here I am walking around, unhappy with the prospect. Why did she have to affect me so?" silently questioned the tall eldar.

Since the day of the homecoming, Nelfindal made a daily trip to the mound of Farmor where citizens of all classes went. The holy ground was said to have recuperative powers for those of troubled spirit. Nelfindal was very religious, but found no relief in meditating on the sacred land.

As done on each of his daily visits, Nelfindal asked, "Why do those who created the planes of existence allow for one to fall so easily for another? It shouldn't have happened as it did. Not for one like her. Or to one such as I."

On the fifth day of visiting Farmor, Nelfindal ran into the young princess who was also meditating on the sacred ground. Silently walking past the still form of the entranced elfmaiden so as not to disturb her, Nelfindal was startled by her sweet voice, calling out his name.

"Greetings Nelfindal. It has been a while since last we speak. How are you?" cheerfully asked the young princess.

Trapped by the situation, the ranger responded, "I am well and yourself?"

"Doing well enough. My mother and father wanted to thank you and Norin for saving me, but you two mysteriously disappeared."

"You must understand that the two of us don't like crowds much and besides it was you everybody wanted to see." replied the evasive elf.

"Perhaps, but there are very few real heroes for these people and it would have helped things here at home. Especially, when they realized a eldar and a silvan worked together," added the princess.

Embarrassed with the title of hero, the tall elf quickly changed the conversation and asked, "So, what are you doing here?"

"My communing with the land was necessary to ease my disrupted spirit. That human wizard had caused a disharmony in me and I have been trying to come to terms with it," replied the distressed Niki.

"The deaths of my companions and other distressing matters have sent me here. It hasn't seemed to help me that much."

"That is a shame, but I understand it is difficult to mourn those that have given their lives. I have been praying for the two spirits to be taken to the high place and to rest in the embrace of the Forest Mother," added Niki.

"It is soothing to know that they will be treated well, thank you. Has your father decided what to do about the current situation with the leaderless army in the Black Hills?" asked the tall eldar.

"My father is convening a council to discuss the matter. I believe you and Norin are to be there, as well as representatives from many other nations of Northern Aragon. I will be there to discuss the trade agreements, which I negotiated with the city of Reah," said the princess as she stood up next to the ranger.

The close presence of the princess made the ranger uncharacteristically nervous. Trying to pull himself together, Nelfindal began to walk down the hill with Nickoleta at his side. Not knowing what to say the tall ranger commented, "It is good to be back home after so long."

"Yes, I heard you have been away for a long time, because of some disagreements with some of the lower nobility. The royal house shares your sentiments about the current injustices afforded the silvan population," sincerely added the princess.

"And what about you, princess? Do you agree with my views or those of the local nobility?" skeptically questioned the doubting elf.

"Rest assured, Nelfindal, that I hold your beliefs to heart. I am a priestess of the White Tree. I cannot view others anyway other than equal. However, I think I'll exclude orcs from that from now on," impishly grinned the beautiful princess.

The unladylike expression made by the princess made the ranger laugh. The gesture eased the tensions between the two eldar bringing the rest of the conversation to a very informal level. It was no longer royal lady and noble, but two friends lightly conversing. Nelfindal and Nickoleta walked towards the shaded embrace of the Great White Oak near the center of the city. The view brought a lightness to the hearts of the two eldars who hadn't seen the sight for some time. The temptation to hold hands was unbearable, but neither hinted to the shared feeling. There were many people in the park surrounding the great tree and the show of affection would send ripples of controversy throughout the capital. Instead, the two played the part of friendly, but impartial acquaintances like no actors could.

As they walked silently under the low lying branches, Nelfindal remembered that he was to meet Norin back at the tavern. Looking into the pale blue eyes of the Princess Nickoleta, Nelfindal changed his attitude to a more proper tone and begged the princess' leave to go meet his former teacher.

"Forgive me, but I must leave. Norin waits for me on the other side of town and I am already late," begged the ranger.

"I'm sure he will still be sitting around at the Oak Leaf Tavern when you get their," replied the lady.

Nelfindal questioned the lady's knowledge of their favorite watering hole. "How is it you know of our `meeting' place."

"The whereabouts of the great heroes is known to everyone. Besides, I wish to keep track of my friends' welfare." The princess smiled at the tall youth setting his heart racing.

Realizing the need to leave before something embarrassing happened, Nelfindal bowed formally to the ivory skinned princess. His blond hair fell off to the side of his head hiding his sidelong glances to see if anyone was around.

Taking his lead, Nickoleta offered her hand which the ranger quickly took to his lips. The speed of the golden haired ranger's departure left the lady wondering as to whether she dreamed the delightful walk or not. Rubbing her hand over the area where the ranger had kissed her soft tingling skin, the princess confirmed that she had not dreamed the encounter.

Walking back to the tavern where Norin waited patiently, Nelfindal tried to decipher the scrambled thoughts that were inundating his mind. The complex emotions he had for the eldest daughter to the royal family were clear and yet unclear. There were too many people in the capital city that would make an issue of the once exiled ranger and the princess courting.

"But who cares about what others think," mumbled the elf to himself. "Why can't I just tell her how I feel and stop hiding from the truth?"

"Because there are many in the nation who don't agree with your thinking," whispered the empathic Elenar. The bow sent visual impressions of the elf's past persecution by the lower elven nobility and the possibility of being permanently exiled out of Elador.

"They would never force me out for the rest of my life. The social tremors would die down after a while then everything would return to normal," countered the hurt eldar.

"They would to protect the nation from a civil war. The country is already on the verge of a major uprising. Open your eyes and look. The princess is the most available lady in Galadhon. She is at the age of marriage and there is an army of suitors just waiting for a chance at her hand," hissed Elenar.

"I see your point, but can't you sense how I feel for her? Can't you tell that I may be in love with her?" thought the ranger.

"Yes, that is why I'm telling you all this. If you didn't love her you wouldn't argue the point so well. I'm letting you discover your feelings for yourself," soothed the intelligent weapon.

"I appreciate your good intentions, but a relationship with her still only complicates matters. Someday, I will let her know how I truly feel, but for now I must wait," conceded the young eldar.

After walking the streets in silence for a few more minutes, Nelfindal entered the Oak Leaf Tavern. Norin sat in a bright section of the open air bar and smiled as he saw the tall youth approaching.

"Well, it's about time you got here. I thought you had forgotten about our luncheon date," cheerfully prodded the silvan ranger.

"How could I forget. Besides this tavern has the greatest wine I've ever tasted," said the slowly cheering eldar.

"I saw Tiluviel earlier and she wished for us to stop by later this afternoon to talk with her about some ideas for the council meeting tomorrow," said the silvan.

"Is the council meeting tomorrow already? I've been so busy I forgot. Any more news on those armies in the Black Hills?" questioned the eldar.

"Only a little. It seems some of the clans have headed back to their holes, but there is still a large number of battle-hungry orcs sitting around. It is posing a problem with the new trade agreements the humans and the dwarves are proposing," added the frowning ranger captain.

"Well, we will have to see what these ambassadors have to offer in return for our trade and our protection," challenged the young elf. The food and wine came out soon after the youth sat down and ended any further attempts at conversation. The two ate heartily and drank with equal vigor.

Unnoticed by the pair of preoccupied rangers was a lone eldar merchant who carefully took note of their entire conversation. Garilin sat quietly sipping on a small glass of elven red wine and thought about the troublesome young eldar sitting only meters away.

"Why is everybody else so interested in this young ranger?" questioned the wealthy trader to himself. "What threat could he pose to my friends in the south? Whatever it is must be very important by the gold offered for his head not that I need that as incentive for this one."

The short eldar stared on at the two friends as he went over the details of their conversation and the slight nuances of the younger ranger's personality. The best way to know people was by observing them closely in a relaxed atmosphere. This young eldar ranger was more than he appeared that much was for sure, but Garilin wondered how much more. Since making contact with the assassin, Raelin, the trader was curious on how much the Darkwood ranger was really worth to the council leaders in Terrilon.

* * * * *

After finishing their meal the two rangers left the tavern and made their way towards the lady Tiluviel's residence. The walk to visit the eldar's step-sister was a refreshing trip under the broad boughs of large aspens and valorn trees. Still observing the two rangers from a safe distance, Garilin took note of their destination. Already, the plans to get the young eldar out of the capital city were forming. Garilin snickered to himself on the ease of having the ranger exiled again. The last time took some doing.

Many years ago, Garilin and Nelfindal's father had crossed paths on the general council, which the ruling family convened for important matters. The elder Goldleaf was a wise and powerful man who was also a resourceful ranger, unknown to his son. The patron of the Goldleaf family had devoted his entire life to the elimination of the southern guild of rangers and expanding the safety of the Eladorian people. Because of this self-appointed quest, the elder Goldleaf had created many enemies.

The price on the councilman's head was almost a king's fortune to the then young Garilin. It took several years to weave the elaborate web of deception and gain the older ranger's confidence, but in the end it was well worth it. At a critical time, the snare was set and the famous Farifane Goldleaf was trapped. The arranged battle with the former ranger lord resulted in the deaths of over two dozen southern guild members and the death of Farifane Goldleaf, himself. Many wondered as to how the elder eldar died, but only a select few knew.

All those involved with the assassination thought the royal name was dead, but it was Garilin who discovered some years later that the Goldleaf name was continued by Nelfindal. The young eldar was secretly raised by one of Farifane's closest friends, a ranger captain named Norin Whitethorne. The silvan ranger raised the youth and initiated him into the elite guild of Darkwood in hopes that he would follow in his father's footsteps. After several decades in the secret forest of Darkwood, Nelfindal returned to Elador to claim his name. It was sometime after this that Garilin moved to eliminate another Goldleaf.

Still young and naive, Nelfindal wasn't aware of the growing unrest between the lower-classed silvans and the upper-classed eldar. By working with a few other elves, the wealthy eldar established the rumors of that some individuals were the cause behind the civil uprisings among the silvan elves. By leading the young ranger to a planned riot and coercing him to appear as a supporter was easy. The fact was the youth did most of the work. One of the plotters began the ruse by beating a silvan slave of his. This act ignited the sense of honor Nelfindal was raised to believe in and drove him on to striking the slave's owner. By striking out at the eldar master, the foolish youth created the perfect picture of a rebel leader inciting a revolt.

The result was the temporary exile of the young ranger. Garilin and his fellow compatriots wished a permanent exile, but the name of Goldleaf was to well established in the royal house. Instead, the devious Garilin plotted yet another snare to trap a ranger. However, this one didn't work out so well. The young Nelfindal had foiled the attempt by killing the range commander assigned the task and wounding a tracker leader who assisted.

Since that first attempt on the young ranger's life, many others had failed.

Garilin sighed loudly then whispered to himself, "You are the luckiest elf alive, Nelfindal Goldleaf, but not for long. I underestimated you once, but never again."

* * * * *

The rangers walked off the lift of the tree house and entered the reception area of the Lady Tiluviel. This room much like the rest of the complex was formed from the branches of the tree and the walls that connected them were created from the magic of the priestesses of the white tree. The bark of the trees stretched out from one branch to another much like a bats wing had skin stretched across the finger bones. The priestesses were very talented manipulators of nature, shaping the living wood into intricate dwellings. With the exception of the Royal House, the lady wards' dwelling was considered the finest building in Galadhon.

A young serving girl stepped forward and greeted the waiting visitors. Motioning the two guests to follow her, the young servant guided the two elves to the private study of the Lady Tiluviel. Entering the bright room, the enchanting form of the lady ward came to meet the two newcomers with greater enthusiasm towards her step-brother.

"I'm so very glad you could come," welcomed the fair lady in the westron tongue. After giving a big hug to Nelfindal, she turned to her other guest, a short stout figure who stood confidently behind the eldar maiden.

"We are always happy to help in state affairs," replied Nelfindal with a broad smile directed at Tiluviel.

The lady looked at her stocky guest. "I would like you to meet the ambassador of Krelusch and member of the dwarven royal family, Grolesh Stoneheart," formally announced Tiluviel.

The grey bearded dwarf bowed low and greeted the two respectful rangers in an barely accented silvan tongue, "Greetings rangers of Darkwood. From my King I offer salutations and thanks for your guild's fabulous work at keeping our mining caravans safe from the scourge of orcs."

"It is our duty to protect the peaceful nations of Aragon and our dwarven friends to the north," humbly replied Norin.

Tiluviel made motion for the three guests to be seated in the plush upholstered chairs that faced her desk. After everybody was seated the lady began the meeting with her melodic voice. "Ambassador Grolesh has been talking with me about the possibility of increasing the number of caravans to Elador. The only problem is the fear of this massing army of orcs down south in the Black Hills."

"My people wish to share their bountiful surplus of mithril and gold ore. It is well known that no race except for the elves has the talent to work these metals as well as the dwarves," smiled the ambassador, who like many of his countrymen wore a large braid of gold around his neck where the symbol of his family hung. The code of arms for the royal family was a mithril hammer over a mithril anvil set with a flawless diamond between. The entire necklace was worth a fortune and many dwarves had been known to starve to the death before selling such family heirlooms.

"There are a good number of elven smiths who would relish the thought of more mithril and gold. And I'm sure they would also wish to share forging secrets with your craftsmen to nhance the current level of metalworking," said the grinning Nelfindal.

"As for the orcs in the Black Hills, I think we could handle them and possibly even avoid them entirely. As you said my lady, they are located south of Elador, but the dwarven caravans would be coming in from the north. The northern routes are very safe," added the silvan ranger.

"This maybe true, but we would like to increase the level of protection already maintained. There are more than just orcs on the roads these days. No offense to our human neighbors, but there are a great many human bandits around the whole region of northern Elador," countered the middle-aged dwarf.

Standing up, Nelfindal walked over to a large map of Elador and all the neighboring nations. The young ranger pointed to the large Nahoa River that wound its way down from the eastern Iron Hills to southern Elador. The tall elf turned to make sure he had everyone's attention.

"We could arrange an escort to the source of the Nahoa River and ride this all the way to the Galadhon tributary. This way we would avoid the long and dangerous overland routes. Once inside Elador, there would be no worries of highwaymen or orcs," speculated the young eldar.

"You do have a point there young elf. The only problem is that we would have to make boats to handle the load. Another problem is to find some dwarves who aren't afraid of water, a rare commodity in my people," challenged the dwarven ambassador.

"We could arrange for our river merchants to sail upstream to your future port and pick the goods there. This way no dwarf has to be forced to sail," offered the Lady Tiluviel.

"That would work. We may have a solution as of yet," the dwarf said cheerfully, but skeptically added, "Tomorrow we shall see if the humans are willing to trade their goods in such an agreeable manor."

The four continued with the details of the trade agreements and finally worked out a plan that satisfied both sides. The grisly dwarven ambassador proved to be quite enjoyable when the work was going well. After the conference the two rangers and their new dwarven friend left together and made their way down the lift.

On the way down the lift, Norin offered, "Ambassador would you like to savor the taste of some of Elador's finest wines?"

The biggest smile the silvan had ever seen on a dwarven face opened up between the cracked features. "I would be honored in a way only a fellow drinker could understand," bellowed the grinning dwarf.

"Then let us be off to a bar that offers some of the strongest and tastiest wine in Galadhon. My friend, here, and I have visited this one particular establishment often. It is called the Oak Leaf Tavern," boasted the silvan ranger.

"It may not serve dwarven spirits, but I'm willing to bet that the wine could still curl your whiskers in the right way," joked the tall eldar.

The lift reached the bottom of the tree with a soft thud. The three conversing figures slowly walked off the magical elevator and continued down the path to the tavern.

"All this talk, yet you two move as if you were talking about pulled teeth. I wish to see this fine place before I wake up from this wonderful dream you have created. You make this tavern out like it is heaven itself," teased the ambassador.

The three burst out in laughter and picked up their pace to a point where the dwarven emissary had to almost run to keep up. The long graceful strides of the two taller elves proved to be trialsome for many shorter people, but the anxious dwarf kept up the quick stride with a smile. The ambassador thought to himself on how much he liked the energetic elves. "Almost like young dwarves they are," mumbled Grolesh.

* * * * *

The day of the council meeting was a dreary one. The sky was filled with heavy spring clouds, which eventually dropped large amounts of rain on the elven capital city. Dressed in their finest clothing, the two rangers quickly made their way to the royal house near the center of the city. Nelfindal used some minor spells to ward off the attack of the large raindrops that would have marred their fine white and gold apparel. After several minutes of running, the two elves reached the Royal House where the meeting was to take place. The rangers had to wait many minutes before the lift returned to the ground level where they stood patiently under a waterproof canopy.

Nelfindal and Norin remained silent on the way up the lift to the lowest level of the tree complex. It was not unusual for the city to be rained on, but the weather was the worst the elves had experienced inside the borders of the elven homeland in years. If the weather was this bad, it usually indicated a very distracted queen. It wasn't going to be a good meeting, thought Norin.

The rangers stepped off the lift into a large foyer magically shaped from the branches of the massive tree house. The entrance led to the council chambers, which was renowned for being the largest single room in all of Elador. Nelfindal walked past a pair of mithril doors large enough to allow a full grown mountain troll through. After entering the council chamber Nelfindal was shocked by the number of people in attendance. There were representatives from every guild in Elador and from every settlement that directly or indirectly dealt with the normally isolated elven nation. There were even several dwarven ambassadors from the diverse western clans of Aragon, who rarely congregated together for anything short of war.

After finding a place to sit the tall youth studied his surroundings. Each passing moment added to the growing number of attendants to the spacious council chambers. The room was large enough to hold a few hundred people with room to sit for all. The rafters above the center of the floor were over ten meters high and were not just wooden beams, but the white branches of the tree complex itself. The mighty bows supported the upper levels as well as the vast council chamber, which measured a good thirty meters across. The oval shaped chamber allowed for even the quietest of voices to be carried to all the listeners.

The majority of those in attendance were elven merchants and craftsmen. Being gone from home for so long left the estranged Nelfindal wondering as to the identities of the different noble lords many of whom he knew he should recognize. Even if he had recognized all of the elven attendants, there would remain the two score human and dwarven dignitaries to recall. Fortunately, the rangers were left to talk amongst themselves with no interruption.

Seeing the questioning look on his companion's face, Norin turned to Nelfindal. "Why such a confused look? This is a momentous occasion when all the representatives of northern

Aragon meet to develop the long overdue trade agreements," said the excited silvan.

"It's just that I hadn't realized that there were so many people in the world. Each person here represents a larger group of people. Even the other elves here stand for a guild or group of workers. Its overwhelming," said the awed elf.

"Your father used to help head these meetings before you were even a thought in his mind. That was one elf that could bring order to even the most heated of meetings," declared Norin.

"I forgot that he held some position with the council. I wish I knew more about him. Did you know him well? Was he really so powerful and important as some have said?" asked Nelfindal.

"More than we'll ever know, but let us not dwell on that. Look the Royal Family is entering," replied Norin, avoiding the subject about his long dead friend. The silvan ranger knew that his younger companion tried very hard to discover any information about his father, which Norin thought he was unprepared for.

When everybody was in the council chambers, the large silver doors were closed and locked as was dictated by custom. After the chimes of the magical lock rang out over the crowd signaling that the chamber was secure, the Royal procession began to make its way into the large domed council room. At the sight of the gold and white banner of Elador, everyone stood in respect to the ruling royal family. The younger and more distant members of the royal family were the first to enter dressed in their finest robes with strands of gold woven into the white fabric. Following directly behind them were the members of the immediate members of the ruling family.

Leaning over to his younger companion, Norin identified the members of the ruling family. "The first one walking in is Prince Talthaison, a captain of the elite guard and youngest member of the family. Behind him is Prince Melphais dressed in the blue robes which identify him as the guildmaster of Necron. And the lady next to him dressed in the gold and white robes is the youngest daughter, Princess Elladrana."

As each prince walked out, the chambers were filled with the sound of fine music and the applause of the congregation. When the Princess Elladrana appeared next to her brother, Prince Melphais, the applause grew louder at her beauty. Although not quit a century old, the young princess already showed signs of taking after her mother's enchanting appearance.

Nelfindal stared at the entering procession and asked, "What of the Princess Nickoleta?"

"There she is, next to her older brother, Orcanth, who is the General of the forest guardians. Look at how beautiful she is. She definitely takes after her mother," said the smirking silvan who followed the observation with a jab of his elbow.

The young eldar was overwhelmed at the beauty of the eldest royal daughter. The princess was dressed from head to toe in a snugly fit golden dress that shimmered as she walked. The design of the garment was obviously made to accentuate her tall shapely figure. The effect was well noted by all the council members as the resounding applause began to falter as the audience stared in awe. Next to the Princess Nickoleta, Prince Orcanth walked confidently in his complimentary white robes, highlighted by his silver hair. His large frame boasted the same formidable strength his father, the king, was known for. At his side was a fabulously crafted mithril sword inlaid with many fine cut jewels.

Following the last of their children, King Felastharn and Queen Illidrais entered the chambers. The royal couple were dressed in their courtly robes of gold and white with the white diamonds of their status woven into the long cloaks that dragged behind them. If anyone was stunned by the beauty of Princess Nickoleta, the were completely dumbfounded with the beautiful of the queen. Her long platinum hair matched her daughter's as did her still youthful appearance, but her overwhelming presence added to her beauty a hundred times over.

Nelfindal stared at the queen's appearance and felt a deep sense of concern. Even though, elves didn't normally age, the royal mother looked more tired than usual, a fact very few would have noticed or even admitted. After three and a half millennia, she still looked incredible beautiful. King Felastharn himself also looked as if he were as young as ever except for the same tired look. Apparently, the royal couple shared some disturbing news that drained them both.

Following behind the main procession were the royal lady wards led by the Lady Tiluviel, who was garbed completely in white. Nelfindal's step-sister stepped forward to a marble podium after the royal family was comfortably seated.

Tapping a silver chime with a small mallet, Tiluviel announced, "the council is now in session. Those wishing to speak are free to take the floor as in accordance of the law." Her clear, sing-song voice rang out clearly across the large expanse of the council chambers. After the announcement, everybody seated themselves.

The Lady Tiluviel turned to the royal family and curtsied to the King and Queen and walked off to stand at their side. King Felastharn looked around the chambers and spoke out in his deep, clear voice. "I wish to start off this meeting by thanking the ambassadors of the northern and southern human settlements and thanking the dwarven ambassadors from the Iron Hills and beyond for coming all this way to discuss the universal trade agreements."

The red-haired Grolesh stood up slowly and replied, "As a representative of the various dwarven colonies and the Kingdom of the Iron Hills, I thank you for allowing us to visit the enchanting land of our elven neighbors. I would just like to say that the move to create a proposed agreement has been started and I ask for permission to take the floor and discuss it."

The dwarven ambassador wore his stately robes and family insignia as did all the accompanying dwarves, but sported a fine mithril mace at his side. The fine weapon sat comfortably at his hip and seemed to capture the light from the magical lamps illuminating the chamber.

Seeing the looks on the faces of the human emissaries, Felastharn asked, "If the human ambassadors have anything that they wish to change or require elaboration please feel free to speak up. After all, this is a joint venture on all our parts."

The largest of the human emissaries stood up. The tall tan-skinned human responded to the king's offer quickly. "As nominated spokesman of the northern human settlements of Aragon, I, Jarot Nicks would like to offer my deepest thanks for the hospitality offered by the people of Elador. We look forward to hearing the trade proposal and will gladly offer our insights on the proposed agreements."

The human was a rough looking individual with short black hair and a large scar running along the side of his right cheek. The human was obviously a warrior by his appearance and his stance. The clothing he wore was reminiscent of a military dress, which many large settlements required their militia to wear. Unlike the other emissaries, though, this ambassador sported a fine broadsword hanging off his left hip. The worn scabbard demonstrated constant use by its cracked leather. Many of the elves sitting around the rangers dealt with the northern humans often and quietly expressed skepticism on their real motives for wanting the trade agreements.

A young noble by the name of Rathion leaned over towards the young ranger and sarcastically whispered, "I bet he'll offer insights. The word going around is that some of the humans want protection from their own people. This Jarot fellow is looking to control the largest human settlements in the area. I think he's looking to line his own pockets at our expense."

Nelfindal turned to the suspicious merchant and replied, "Some of the humans aren't so greedy for power. I don't know this Jarot Nicks fellow, but some are quite honorable. Give him a chance for now and listen to what he has to offer. Then we shall judge his honor."

"We'll see how he is during this meeting. I still bet he's expecting Darkwood and Elador to stand outside his city and protect it while his own forces move into the next towns. I also think he is going to trade mostly for elven and dwarven weapons and not finely crafted plow shares."

Nelfindal wasn't normally as pessimistic as the noble, but something about the muscular, dark-haired human just didn't seem right. Aside from the fact that the human reminded the eldar of a now-dead general. Instinctively, the eldar ranger agreed with the suspicious noble.

* * * * *

Garilin watched the two rangers from the far side of the council chambers with a wicked smile on his face. The two were representing Darkwood and were close enough to the floor to be addressed directly. The eldar merchant sat back thoughtfully, going over all the details of his elaborate scheme to disrupt the trust the people had in the rangers guild and to utterly destroy the young ranger's life in Elador. Thinking to himself, Garilin wondered, "If I do this right, the ranger will never be allowed in Elador again." The smile that formed on the elf's face would have sent chills down the spine of those who knew the devious noble.

* * * * *

After the formalities were dispensed with, the council got to the preliminary details of the trade agreement. The differing sides argued for over two hours until one elven merchant took the floor. The short eldar walked the length of the council chambers to get everybody's attention and finally spoke in a loud booming voice.

"I would like to introduce myself. My name is Garilin Silverbirch, trader, merchant and captain of the boat, White Swan. Many of you know me so I'll get to the point. We are all here to increase the amount of trade between our people. Correct?"

A half-hearted murmur of approval rippled through the crowd. It was followed by a comment from the human, Jarot Nicks. "We all know why we're here. We have been discussing the fact for over two hours. Get to the point," impatiently snapped the human.

"The point is that the ranger guild hasn't been entered into the discussion. Darkwood has the responsibility of keeping the lands safe for travellers and they should be charged with the protection of the caravans," The audience agreed much more fervently with the merchants statement this time.

Norin and Nelfindal looked at each other with a questioning side glance. Both were curious at what the trader was up to. Norin knew the eldar merchant was always attempting to embarrass the guild, but kept it from his younger friend. Garilin was after something. "But what?" thought Norin.

Looking over to the two rangers, Garilin added, "What have the rangers done lately to protect our borders?" The short merchant looked around challenging someone to offer an answer. When no response was forthcoming he continued, "Recently, a large army of orcs was discovered in the Black Hills. These monsters were planning to attack the peaceful nations of eastern Aragon. But where were the rangers of Darkwood?" Garilin let the question sit for a while before continuing his speech.

"There was no mention or forewarning of this growing evil only two week's march from the border of Elador. These rangers are supposed to be able to track an orc across bare rock and yet couldn't find an entire army of them?"

Norin uncomfortably shifted in his seat. The obvious affront at the rangers was getting more personal and the ranger captain looked about ready to kill the eldar merchant for the unjustified insults. Nelfindal felt himself flush at the unwarranted accusations. Even though the merchant attacked the honor of the guild, the young ranger maintained his composure. But the young eldar was unprepared with what was to follow.

After his last comment, Garilin turned sharply around and pointed at the young ranger and charged, "And here, we have a ranger who incites riots and social discontent in the elven homeland. Charging all of us with beating and killing our servants. He even accosted a fellow citizen in public, forcing himself into a temporary exile!"

The pain of the accusation was felt by the young eldar like a hot dagger thrusted into his heart. Nelfindal never meant any harm, but as a ranger he merely came to the aid of a defenseless servant. No amount of explaining would have calmed the heated uproar that flared up with the accusation. It took several minutes for the King to calm the attendants down. Even the human representatives were up charging the rangers with deceiving the people with lies of aid and assistance. The dwarven contingent, being long-time allies with Darkwood, only sat and watched, knowing that the rangers were an honorable group beyond dispute.

After the audience calmed down, King Felastharn spoke out in his authoritative voice. "We are not here to accuse the rangers of Darkwood or any other group for any possible past indiscretions. We are here to work out an agreement that will allow us to peacefully trade our goods with one another."

The short eldar, Garilin, slowly turned to the King and asked, "How can we peacefully trade with each other if there is no protection for our caravans? Without adequate defense our shipments will be attacked every time they set out!"

The audience rose up again in another round of loud roaring. Many defended the rangers' guild, but when one person defended the guild, they were quickly challenged by three others who agreed with the eldar merchant. It seemed only the dwarven representatives argued for the Darkwood rangers honor. The entire situation got so out of hand that the meeting was finally recessed until the argumentative attendants calmed down. Standing as one the entire royal family left the raucous council room to the quieter confines of their private chambers. Unseen by Nelfindal, the Princess Nickoleta walked out with a sad look in his direction.

* * * * *

The two rangers argued with the other council members until the royal guards began to force the attendants out of the chambers. Nelfindal followed the boisterous silvan to the lift as the older ranger swore out curses in the general direction of the other quarrelsome attendants. After leaving the meeting, Norin was in a foul mood. The two rangers walked quickly to the Oak Leaf Tavern. It wasn't until they arrived at the crowded establishment that Norin observed the seriously hurt expression on his companion's face.

"I'm really sorry about what that bastard-of-an-orc said to you. He had no grounds on which to accuse the guild of slacking in its duties. Let alone you, a respected member of the guild," bellowed the infuriated silvan.

Nelfindal looked at his angered friend and said, "I think there was more to all this than what appears. It is obvious that someone is trying to keep me out of Elador."

The reality of the young elf's observation caught Norin somewhat by surprise. "That may be possible. I knew Garilin was out for your father. It is possible that he is after you as well. Sure, and what better time to embarrass you and the guild," added Norin.

"What do you mean that he was out for my father? Did he have anything to do with his disappearance?" questioned the disturbed eldar.

"He and your father were enemies for as long as I can remember. That is why I kept you out of Elador for so long. I was afraid that he might have tried something against you," confessed Norin.

"Why hadn't you told me this before? You knew I have spent whatever time I had trying to learn of my father!" charged the enraged youth. "Why did you keep it to yourself for so long!?"

"I didn't realize it was anything at the time. I thought that you would be better off not knowing," calmly said the ranger captain realizing his error.

"Who said you knew what was good for me? I'm old enough to make judgments like that. Why? Didn't you trust in me?" cried the wounded youth.

Norin sat quietly without answering. He knew how easily hurt the young eldar could get on the subject of his father. No matter how he would have tried to explain, the older ranger had misjudged his younger friend. But it was too late to change that; the damage was done.

Nelfindal stared intensely at the older elf who appeared to age slightly at the eldar's accusations. Realizing the silvan was neither going to deny nor confirm his charges, the young ranger stood up and stormed out of the crowded tavern. The scene only quieted the festive customers for a brief moment.

Norin sat for many minutes before realizing exactly what had happened. Shortly after Nelfindal's dramatic departure, the silvan captain could only think of drinking himself into the biggest drunken stupor since word of Farifane Goldleaf's mysterious disappearance. And that phase in his life had lasted a very long time.

* * * * *

Darius and Raelin looked out from their tent at their company of elven warriors. The rough looking group of veteran soldiers were anxious for the expected appearance of the young eldar ranger. During the march to their present location, Raelin had moved casually, even confidently amongst the heavily armed warriors. The assassin tracker kept a close eye out for any signs of weakness in the assigned company. In most groups, the southern assassin would have easily found an inexperienced or incompetent soldier, but there were none in this company of hand-picked veterans. The range commander had chosen his elves well, thought Raelin.

Several minutes after camp was set, the two dozen southern elves made their way to the center tent of the campsite. The large tent had its front canvas flaps thrown down to close out the curious eyes of the awaiting warriors. When everyone was settled, the flaps were whipped back and the dark forms of the two silvan trackers appeared.

Darius stepped forward and stared intently at his company of formidable warriors making eye contact with every unwavering individual. "You are aware of our duty here. We are to capture the northern ranger known as Nelfindal Goldleaf. He is to be unharmed by orders of Range Commander Caric." The tracker leader looked around again to see the reaction of the group, but no one even blinked an eye. Good, thought Darius, they know their duty well.

"Anyone with the ranger may be disposed off in what ever manor you feel appropriate. But take care, those with him may be worth something as well," added the pacing tracker who looked over at his assassin companion.

Raelin stepped forward and announced the company in his dispassionate voice. "The plan is to lead the eldar to a glade one kilometer north of here. There, we will spring the trap," said the smirking assassin.

The look that Raelin saw on the faces of the listening soldiers was that of obvious revulsion. It was well known to the assassin that few enjoyed his presence and his reputation for being such an efficient killer created at least a sense of caution from his attentive audience.

"I will proceed with the plans and details of the ambush as we go along. If there are any questions, please ask," offered the sinister elf. Raelin knew full well that none would question his plans. Even Darius had to admit that the assassin tracker was unrivaled in his covert tactics.

* * * * *

After storming out of the Oak Leaf Tavern, Nelfindal strode off to the inn that he was staying at. The distant flet was much farther from the tavern than the one he had previous stayed at so it took some time to get there. Upon arriving at the White Goose Inn, the young ranger was met by four armed royal guards. The senior of the elite detachment greeted the tall ranger in his deep silvan tongue. "Your presence is required at the royal house immediately, sir. Your gear will be waiting for you there," ordered the soldier.

Nelfindal understood the summons and complied with it, even though he had no other choice. The walk back to the royal house was filled only with the noise associated with a typical urban area. The few stares received from curious onlookers were quickly dispatched by the icy stare of an elite guard. Many elven citizens learned early on that an armed escort meant trouble. They also learned that one should ignore one as best they could when it past by.

The trip to the royal residence was a long and frightening one for the young ranger. The last time Nelfindal remembered having such an escort was when he was commanded to leave Elador for his own safety. All these memories came back to the tall eldar in a disastrous wave threatening to overwhelm him, but the young ranger was used to such things and quickly suppressed the inappropriate emotions.

The group made their way to the lift that would take them to the royal chambers above. After stepping onto the magical device, the four armed silvans and their eldar guest were quickly and quietly transported up to the highest level of the tree complex. The lift stopped abruptly and the escort made its way onto the richly furnished level. Next to each door were two fully armored and heavily armed royal guards. The well disciplined warriors noticed everything, but made no move to look at the passing group.

At the end of a long and elaborately decorated hallway was a set of intricately carved wooden double doors with magical glyphs emblazoned on their surface. It would have taken an army of magicians to pass through the enchantments protecting the private inner chambers of the royal couple, thought the ranger. Even Elenar was shaken by the formidable power being used to defend the royal family. "This place gives me the chills," thought the bow to Nelfindal.

The young eldar ignored his empathic companion, because it was the last thing on his mind. The ranger wondered what was to happen to him now. While thinking of this, the magically protected doors opened slowly to allow entrance into the next chamber. The guards remained where they were when a feminine voice rang out to the waiting group.

"Guards, you may remain outside and see that we are not disturbed. Come in Nelfindal Goldleaf."

The command drew the ranger in with a pull he only felt a few times before. It was obvious that the queen was a very powerful enchantress as was demonstrated at that moment. There was no doubt in the young elf's mind that he must obey the summons. The steady long strides of the ranger quickly brought him into the center of the bright chambers. The room appeared to be a library of sorts with scrolls and books lining the high walls.

Seated in the center of the room in a pair of worn, plush chairs were the royal couple. King Felastharn stood up slowly to greet the bewildered young eldar. The king was even taller than the formidable height of Nelfindal and much broader as well, but his appearance was nothing compared to the presence he emanated. It took no thought for the Darkwood ranger to drop to his knees in humble respect. Seeing the honest display of loyalty, King Felastharn was moved, but his face hid his feelings.

"You show great respect to my house young Goldleaf. Long has your family honored the Royal House and the people of Elador. Please rise and sit beside us so we may speak with you," commanded the royal patron.

"It is my honor to serve all of Elador, your majesties," said the nervous ranger.

The confused youth stood up slowly and carefully walked to the offered seat. Allowing Felastharn to be seated first, Nelfindal slowly seated himself. The hand-made chair was well crafted and the tall eldar thought he could sit in the chair for hours without knowing it. The voice of the Queen disturbed the youth's dreamy thoughts.

"We know that we asked you to leave Elador many, many years ago and that you have only just returned." The Queen saw the hurt look on Nelfindal's face almost immediately after her statement, but quickly added, "but it was for your own good. It seems that the same force that sought to have you exiled last time is doing so again. We have an idea who is behind this and we need your help to flush them out."

Nelfindal thought about what the Queen was trying to say to him, but let her continue without interruption. He was also curious who was Garilin was working with in the latest political maneuvering.

Seeing that the young ranger wasn't going to comment, Queen Illidrais continued. "We believe that Garilin Silverbirch is involved in a plot, not the sole instigator of your persecution. He was an enemy of your father's for many decades and we think he is exacting vengeance out on you because of this. However, today's attack was to obvious to be his own doing. There are others who wish to do more harm to yourself and the guild."

"You don't agree with his accusations of the guild's failures?" asked the probing ranger.

"Not in the least. The dwarves don't believe him either, but there are many who are ignorant enough to believe in his persuasive speeches and that is why we summoned you," answered the King.

"After what you did for us and our daughter, we could not even begin to question the honor of the Darkwood guild or yourself," added the Queen.

The look the King gave his spouse after her statement at first looked as if tinged with some anger, but soon softened up as she returned the stare with one of unconcealed anguish. It was apparent to the young elf that the two never reconciled with each other on the recent covert rescue of their daughter. It was now known by many in Elador that the operation was performed behind the King's back, but its necessity was also understood. There were few people who didn't know of Felastharn's fiery temper. All agreed that the knowledge of his daughter's abduction would have led to disastrous consequences.

Breaking the sudden tension Nelfindal proudly remarked, "my duty as a ranger obligates me to protect all people from harm in the best way I can. With this commitment and my duty to the Royal House of Elador, it was only a matter of how quickly I could act. The last thing I would have allowed is one of the Royal House to fall to such a fate."

"Is that the only reason? Was there anything else that may have influenced you to do this?" inquired the king.

Nelfindal looked at the king. "That was my motivation at the time."

"What about now. Would you protect our rights to rule out of duty alone? Or is there anything that might motivate you otherwise?" persisted the elven leader.

Nelfindal was curious why the king was questioning him in such a strangely persistent way. "Monetary reward is of no concern to me. I have all that I need, the rest can be acquired from the mother forest."

The king quickly replied as if he knew how the young eldar would respond to the question. "An acceptable answer to your teachers, but that is not what I meant. I have heard from reliable sources that you may have an interest in my oldest daughter. Humm?"

The bluntness of the remark and the accusing looks the royal couple gave Nelfindal were enough to bring a deep flushness to his face and neck. The king and queen exchanged knowing looks as if their question was answered by the ranger's visible display of embarrassment.

Nelfindal felt foolish at his blushing, but was curious on how the two discovered his secret affection for the princess. The young ranger was an expert at stealth and subterfuge yet the two hosts apparently read him like an open book. He never told anyone of how he felt and only Norin could have been observant enough to tell.

The sympathetic voice of the queen broke the young eldar's distressful thoughts. "We understand your reasoning for keeping a relative distance from Niki. The current situation would have been even worse if it were known that the Royal House was in league with the rangers' guild. That is why we are sending you away."

The statement hung in the air for what seemed like an eternity. It was happening again, thought Nelfindal, they are ostracizing me from my homeland for my affiliation with my father and the guild. The heat of the thought again created a flushness in the young elf, but was soon quenched by the queen's offer.

"We are sending an emissary down to Terrilon to begin a series of peace agreements. We believe that a ranger would further increase its safety and success. The trip will be long and by then we will be able to locate the source of this latest dilemma and the reason for the latest assault on you and your guild. You will escort our daughter, the Princess Nickoleta, there personally with the usual escort and an extra company of elite guard."

The proposed plan was too much for the young ranger to turn down. The royal family was effectively giving its blessing to the two youths. Nelfindal wondered just how much Niki actually cared for him. He hoped the attraction was just as strong. Thinking of this, Nelfindal asked, "How does the Princess feel about this?"

Queen Illidrais smiled, a sight that took the breath away from the curious ranger and said, "you may ask her yourself. You will be leaving in two days and I think you should talk to her before you set out. In fact, she is waiting downstairs for us. We have other business to take care of so you may tell our daughter that we will talk with her before she leaves for the south. A servant is waiting to take you to her."

"Then with your permission, I shall leave to talk with your daughter," Nelfindal bowed low to the seated king and queen who returned the gesture with a slight nod of their heads. Nelfindal strode off out of the room with long, confident strides. After a storm comes the sun to shine on your day, once said an ancient elven philosopher. Nelfindal strongly believed that the sun was shining very brightly on his day.

* * * * *

Princess Nickoleta stood on an elaborate wooden balcony of the royal house, which also served as a private garden. Her platinum hair gently blew past her face masking a look of deep thought, which only enhanced her sculpted features. "How is it that my own parents know of every feeling or emotion I feel when I wish them not too? Yet, the one person I wish to know how I feel is shielded from those same feelings? Well Niki, you just may not be ready to let someone into your heart. Yes, that must be it." Niki immediately reprimanded herself for trying to rationalize her otherwise irrational emotions. It was a trait she had picked up from her indomitable parents.

Looking out across the golden treetops of the largest city in the elven homeland, the princess thought how complete her life would be if only she were able to share this same view with the one she truly loved.

"There you said it," thought the princess, "you are in love with him. Ever since that day you looked into his eyes atop that wretched tower. How wonderful his protective embrace felt!"

The young elfmaiden looked down at her clenched fists realizing the frustration she was putting herself through. She stood up staring out at the elven homeland for nearly an hour. It was while she waited for her parents that she realized the presence of another person on the balcony. Turning around expecting to see one of the royal couple, the princess was surprised to see the tall form of a finely dressed eldar.

* * * * *

Nelfindal strode purposefully to the awaiting princess. The servant guiding him down many flights of stairs and through countless hallways keeping the taller ranger moving at a fair pace. The young eldar wondered how the short silvan was able to move so quickly and yet so effortlessly. "It must be from serving the household of a demanding royal family," thought the smirking elf.

After what seemed like only a few minutes, the ranger and his guide stopped in front of a pair of open glass doors, which led out to a large terrace. The diminutive servant bowed low and backed off as the tall eldar passed him. The view from the main balcony of the royal house was breathtaking, but nothing the ranger ever saw compared to the view of the princess standing on the balcony.

Niki stood casually against the wood railing looking out across the quiet of Galadhon. She had since changed from her ceremonial robes to a fine silken gown of the palest mint green. Her long platinum hair cascaded softly down her back with a portion draped over her left shoulder. The golden beams of the late afternoon sun complimented the color of the royal daughter's long flowing hair.

As if on cue, the princess turned around and stared in confusion at her unexpected visitor. After several heartbeats, Niki broke the silence. "I thought that my parents had finally come to speak with me. What brings you here?"

Nelfindal found his voice in time to answer the question without appearing to be too much of a dotard. "Your parents, the King and Queen, had summoned me to talk about some important matters. They told me to inform you that they have other business to attend to and will talk with you latter before we set out for Terrilon."

A sudden excitement came to Niki at the mention of the 'we', referring to the long upcoming trip south. Barely maintaining her composure, the princess slowly asked, "Are you travelling with the escort as well?" The thought sent the young elfmaiden's heart racing at a wild rate.

Nelfindal walked slowly towards the tense form of the princess, never losing contact with her cool blue eyes. "Your parents thought it wise to send a ranger along with and to keep me out of the fire for a while. It seems that there are many people who do not like my presence here in Elador."

"Not everyone dislikes your presence in our homeland. Some actually enjoy your company," absently remarked Niki.

"Do you enjoy my company?" The question slipped out unconsciously, but Nelfindal was curious how the lady truly felt towards him.

"Yes, very much. Do you not share the same feelings?" the princess awkwardly inquired. She was somewhat worried about the answer she was going to receive, but needed to know.

The tall ranger stepped right up to the quivering form of the princess, their bodies only scant centimeters apart. Her nervous stance reminded Nelfindal of a frightened deer readying itself for flight from a potential predator. He hoped she wouldn't dart off from him now or ever for that matter.

Looking deeply into her sky blue eyes, Nelfindal responded, "I have always felt deeply moved by your presence since that first day. I just couldn't bring myself to say anything until today."

"Why is today so special?" asked Niki as she absently turned to look out over to the now lowering sun. The beams of light cast an infinite number of gold and red shadows across the treetops of the elven forest giving the illusion of a living inferno.

"It seems the king and queen took it upon themselves to act as counselors to an emotionally stubborn couple. They were rather insistent that I make my feelings known to you." Nelfindal took in a breath, which seemed to originate from deep inside his chest. He continued his narrative of the recent events and added, "I think the biggest reason is this recent assault on my honor and that of the Darkwood Guild. Someone is behind all this and the recent stirring in the caste system."

The princess shook her head in acknowledgement. "I heard rumors of someone being behind a move to disrupt our land, but couldn't imagine why they would do it."

"It always has to do with power. My guess is all this originated down south in Terrilon. I believe my father may have suspected something like this from them. The reason why I and the guild are being attacked so openly may be because everything is building to a climax. Another major controversy about the caste system and we will have a full blown civil war on our hands." The idea of elves killing elves repulsed the ranger especially when it meant fighting those he had no quarrel with.

"I hope we can get at the source of this before we get to that point. I don't wish for any of our people to be hurt. Somehow, my parents will handle the situation until the appropriate solution is found," replied the princess.

"Until things are worked out, you and I will be working closely together and we should be aware of each others feelings. I wasn't about to let you go south without your representative from the Darkwood Forest," Nelfindal smiled at the glowing expression on the princess' face.

"I was all ready to request you for an assignment as tracker and guide. Few people have been down south as much as you. Besides I need a bodyguard. As much as I enjoyed you rescuing me once, I don't wish to go through that again," admitted Niki.

Nelfindal took Niki into his broad arms and whispered softly into her small tender ear, "as long as I live, no harm will ever fall upon you. I will die before such a thing happens!"

The intensity of the declaration brought tears of indescribable joy to the princess's eyes like nothing she ever thought possible. The sudden expression of affection caught her by surprise but she waited too long to hear such words for them to catch her completely off-guard. Niki fell easily into the tall ranger's tight embrace.

The embracing couple stood silently on the balcony. The time passed slowly as each absorbed the love emanating from the other in a perfectly synergistic cycle. The memory of their first intense embrace would last well beyond even their own lengthy lives. The few kisses exchanged during that memorable embrace sparked a barely containable passion. If it weren't for the fact that neither wished to move for fear of breaking the bond, the two may have given into their passionate desires.

* * * * *

Brightly colored banners snapped in the light breeze of the late spring morning. The roar of cheering citizens was heard throughout the city of Galadhon as the long snaking column of a caravan rode out towards the front gates of the wondrous city. The announcement of the mission to their long alienated elven cousins brought many different reactions from the populace. Most of the average citizens knew of the southern realm, many contemplated the thought of reunification. However, only a few truly understood the difficulty of such a drastic step. The elven land of Ruithion was the most corrupt region in all of Aragon. The ruling council that resided in the capital city of Terrilon was a mixed bag of thieves, greedy merchants and secret representatives of the infamous southern guild of rangers.

Near the head of the column rode the platinum haired princess sitting straight backed on her snowy white mare as the caravan and its large escort passed through the city. Unlike many emissaries who chose to ride in the comfort of a coach, the Princess Nickoleta insisted on riding in a more visible fashion. Beside the enchanting figure of the eldest royal daughter rode the impressive figure of a Darkwood ranger in his shining mithril chain shirt and his forest green garments. The horse, which the tall eldar rode, was the same steed, which had carried him to and from the Black Hills only weeks prior.

Nelfindal looked into the crowd hoping to catch sight of his former master, but couldn't find the elusive silvan. Since their bitter argument, the two friends hadn't talked or even seen each other. The young ranger wondered how seriously he had hurt his mentor's feelings. Norin tended to be a callous even cold person, but even the sturdiest of creatures can be bruised from within and the older ranger was no different. The eldar thought about his merciless assault on the silvan many times since the fight in the tavern.

Nelfindal knew he was as much a son to his father, Farifane, as he was to Norin. The stinging words he used on his friend would fester long after the actual argument. And it was that argument which stayed in his memory every moment of the day. The glorious event of the parade was shadowed by the darkness enshrouding the young ranger's heart, but Nelfindal still exhibited a glowing smile for those crowded around the procession. The only other thought on his mind was the question of when he would see the irascible silvan again, if ever.

Niki looked over to her smiling companion and knew the exaggerated expression on his face was false. It wasn't a secret that the two renowned rangers had a falling out. When the princess first heard about the disagreement, knowing how the two were so close to each other, she thought of running to her lover and giving him comfort. Niki soon realized that such an act would have strained the already tenuous situation between the two old friends. It is something they have to work out together, she thought to herself.

The long caravan made its way through the main gates and out of the capital city of Elador. Picking up speed the column of elite guardsmen, mounted emissaries and an army of servants moved away from their beloved homeland. It would be many months before anyone would see their land again and the sound of many sighs could be heard as everybody expressed the same homesick thought.

Unobserved by the caravan and the searching eyes of the young ranger was a lone dark figure comfortably nestled in the embrace of a tall oak tree. The magical cloak wrapped about Norin's body shielded him from the perceptive sight of the scouts and the young eldar ranger. Even if the elves were looking, it was very unlikely they would have seen the virtually invisible form of the silvan ranger.

Norin thought to himself on how he could have let his young friend leave without so much as a farewell. It would be many months before the two would ever get a chance to see each other again, but the ranger captain knew that it would have been a dangerous situation for the two to meet. Ever since the disappearance of Farifane Goldleaf, Nelfindal became very touchy about anything that hinted to his mysterious father.

The tall elf lost his mother at birth, which left him only his distant father to care for him. Farifane knew then that there would be attempts on his son's life out of revenge from the elder Goldleaf's enemies. It was shortly after the then young Nelfindal was able to walk that he was taken away from Elador to Darkwood. It was there that the young elf began his training in the ways of the woodland. Occasionally, his estranged father would show up to check on his son's progress, but he usually stayed away. Only Norin knew how painful it was for Farifane to stay away from his only child.

Nelfindal constantly strived to be better than the rest, but always punished himself for not doing better. Norin knew that the young elf blamed himself for his father's estrangement. He wasn't told of the dangerous position his father played in the political scheme of Elador or even Darkwood for that matter. Few rangers knew the identity of the high ranger lords. The secretive circle of elders were the greatest of the guild and spent centuries mastering the ways of the woodland. Farifane was one of the most powerful elders and made the silvan ranger captain vow never to tell his son of his position. The older ranger lord thought to protect his son, but it more often than not caused much distress.

Since the day the younger ranger was brought to Darkwood, Norin was designated protector of the tall youth. After only a couple of years of training the young ranger, Norin began to sense the same talents and skills that made his father such a powerful leader. It was no wonder that Nelfindal was so well respected amongst his peers. After the story of his successful battle with the southern range commander his renown grew even more. It was unheard of for an apprentice to fight such an opponent let alone defeat an experienced ranger. If the older Farifane were alive, he would have truly been proud of his son.

When the silvan ranger thought about his life and how he had no children himself, the only remorse he had was that the tall eldar was not of his own blood. For if he had a child of his own, he would never have been more proud than the way he was in raising Nelfindal. Thinking of this Norin wondered how far his young student would get in the unpredictable future.

7 JOURNEY SOUTH

The sun hung low on the western horizon, the twinkle of the early evening stars could been faintly seen through the settling dust stirred up by the recent passage of the caravan. It had only been a week since the caravan had left the elven capital city and already the train of elven coaches and mounted guards were at the far western edge of the Black Hills. It took only a matter of minutes for the camp to settle in for the evening. Any army of servants quickly prepared a warm stew for the troops and individual meals for the escorted dignitaries.

Sitting in her tent playing absently with a scrap of venison, the princess thought deeply on the past few days. Niki tried to spend as much time as possible with Nelfindal, but the usual demands of the royal daughter limited the amount of her free time. Many hours were spent with the other ambassadors in the cramped confines of her couch going over the proposals being presented to the ruling council. The only time she was uninterrupted was in the late evening after dinner, which she always spent alone in her tent. At times Niki thought of going to the ranger's tent, but dismissed the idea. It isn't right for the royal daughter to go cavorting in public, she would always say to herself.

"However," Niki thought, "if I could secretly be with him without anyone seeing me. . ."

A mischievous smile crossed the princess's face as she thought of the surprised look on her love's face as she slipped into his tent unexpectedly. She knew how to be very quiet. There were many times she listened in on her parents or even her brothers when they were children catching little bits of their secret conversations, especially the princes who were always bragging about their romantic conquests of certain noble ladies.

Niki looked out of her tent and checked the positions of the guards standing outside. She knew they would rush at the slightest sound of a problem ever since her recent abduction. However, she also knew that they would not hear her slip out the back of the tent was unwatched. Even the sensitive ears of a ranger would be hard pressed to hear an intruder slip through the back of the tent. She knew that guards were not stationed towards the rear of the tent, because she used her own spells to notify her of intruders. And the presence of anyone other the her would activate the spells. The back way was the best, thought the princess. Now, it was only a matter of waiting for late nightfall.

On the other side of the camp, Nelfindal lay thinking about his beautiful princess. Her platinum hair shined in his mind's eye like a beacon summoning him forth. The thought of Niki's sweet smelling skin and her soft touch on his body brought a passionate burning to his already tense body. The young eldar thought to himself on how little he had really been with the princess since they had set out. The memory of their last time alone together on the balcony raised the ranger's passion to even greater heights.

Suddenly jumping up to his feet, Nelfindal surprised himself with the thoughts that raced through his mind. Pacing his tent, the ranger whispered to himself, "No, I couldn't. Yet, I could easily get passed the guards by her tent. And what ever spells she might have cast to protect her. Yes, that's it I'll sneak into her tent and surprise her!" The determination with which the statement was made only partially expressed the excitement that coursed through the young eldar's body.

After moving around the inside of his tent to locate the presence of the on-duty guards, Nelfindal moved to one of the canvas walls and slipped easily underneath it. Night had recently fallen and the only visible signs of life were centered around the campfires set up to illuminate the perimeter of the camp. The sound of laughter and outrageous boasts of personal prowess could be heard from the off-duty soldiers and relaxing servants resting around the area, but none of them noticed the silent form of the tall ranger. Nelfindal's dark form moved easily among the parked wagons and pitched tents that composed the center of the encampment. His long strides moving him quickly and effortlessly under the starry, moonless night.

A few royal guards walked passed the slinking body of the ranger, but never took notice of his passage. Nelfindal knew they would be unable to observe him. The skill of passing invisibly and silently through heavily guarded areas was the trademark of the Darkwood rangers. The best of the guild could pass in and out of a military encampment during the day with some difficulty, but at night a ranger was in his element.

The princess's tent was only a few meters away from the ranger's location; however, it took a full quarter hour to make it to the loose canvas of the back wall. The spells he detected were rather formidable and somewhat complex. The princess took no chances since her own abduction. After nullifying the detection spells temporarily, Nelfindal looked around quickly to see if he had alerted anyone. The guards were pre-occupied with a deep conversation on the best Eladorian wines, which caught the eldar's interest for a brief moment. The ranger waited to make sure they would continue their talk before slipping under the tent wall. Knowing their conversation would continue for some time, Nelfindal quietly moved under the canvas.

The inside of the tent was dark as was expected, but something felt somewhat out of place. Looking around, Nelfindal noticed the tent was unoccupied. Letting his eyesight adjust to the lack of light, the ranger looked to get a clue of Niki's whereabouts. He noticed that the dark cloak the lady often wore was missing, which indicated she must have been out for a walk. The tall ranger sat down roughly in disbelief and questioned his unfortunate luck. Feeling like a lovesick fool, Nelfindal quickly exited the tent and moved casually back to his own empty tent.

Niki silently made her way around the stables where the horses were munching on their oats and feed. She thought of taking the short cut through the center of camp where the wagons were kept, but didn't want to push her luck in being observed by a guard or servant. The horses were familiar with her presence and being a priestess of the White Tree developed a certain empathy with all animals. This didn't allow for true communication, but did give the priestesses a general impression of what the animals were thinking.

The princess gently rubbed the ear of the chestnut stallion the tall ranger rode. The strong animal sent many peaceful impressions back to the lady mixed with some desire of being with a few of the nearby mares. Niki laughed to herself thinking how ironic it was that even as advanced as the elves were they still shared the same basic feelings as the lesser creatures. Feeling more confident with her decision, Niki continued on her way to Nelfindal's tent.

The walk took longer than the princess had anticipated because a couple of drunken guards had stopped by the back of the ranger's tent to talk. The three soldiers swayed as they drunkenly slurred about an ongoing argument about what their southern brethren were like. Niki waited many minutes before the three soldiers moved on. The thought of sleep ended their discussion and drew them to their awaiting cots. The princess frowned at such an unprofessional display since they were in the wild and out of the protective confines of their homeland. Even though they were off-duty and not on watch, the group shouldn't be to comfortable with their surroundings. A point she would remember to take up with the company commander.

Seeing no other interruptions to her quest, Niki silently slipped into Nelfindal's tent under the unwatched side flap. Like her own canvas chambers, the tall eldar's were spacious yet lightly furnished. The princess looked around to determine where her lover had gone, but the dark loneliness of the empty tent gave no clue. She had looked forward to his shocked expression and his passionate embrace, but now sat in confusion at the sudden turn of events.

A cool breeze blew over Niki's neck from the side wall where she came in from. It was many moments before she realized that someone else was in the tent with her. Sensing the presence of the dark figure close behind her, the princess turned quickly on the unknown intruder. Niki slashed out with a small dagger that was hidden in her boot with blurring speed only to have her wrist caught in a vise-like grasp. The dark figure swung her frail form down onto the fur skins lining the tent floor.

Another firm hand landed quickly over her mouth as the intruder pinned her under his large frame.

Nelfindal easily caught the dagger wielding hand in his and pulled the princess down onto her back. Falling on top of her, the ranger whispered, "Do you love me so much as to take my life for yourself?"

Niki was shocked to hear her lover's voice and was utterly ashamed that she had struck out with her knife as she did. In a confused voice she asked, "What are you doing here?"

"I sleep here, remember? I should ask you the same question."

"I came here to surprise you. It has been so long since we have been together. I missed you," admitted the princess.

"Yes, it has been. But why try and cut my throat if you missed me so? Have you become bored of me so soon?" teased the grinning ranger in the darkness.

Niki caught the teasing tone in Nelfindal's voice and replied, "Didn't you know? I take the hearts of all my lovers."

Nelfindal sat up and opened up his shirt exposing his tanned chest and passionately offered, "then carve away my love for you'll never find a more willing victim. If you wish for my heart, it is yours forever."

Niki was deeply moved by the sincerity of the statement and moved close against the ranger's body. The faint light from the torches outside the tent sent small slivers of light through the front flaps highlighting her lovely face. Speaking in her most passionate voice, the princess replied, "since you have captured my heart, it would only be a fair trade. But if I am to have you then I must take all of you."

Nelfindal looked deep into her eyes, which reflected the same fire coursing through his own body. The passion was too much for the tall ranger to fight any longer. The young eldar gave in willfully to his emotions and passionately kissed the willing princess. Her sweet scented perfume brought out feelings he had never thought he had. Their lovemaking continued throughout the night releasing weeks of pent up emotions.

Just before dawn the royal daughter raised herself and quickly dressed. All the while she stared at how easy and peaceful he slept. Leaning over the still form of her ranger lover, Niki kissed his smooth forehead and moved to the rear of the tent and lifted the canvas to leave.

Before sliding under the tent wall she whispered, "sleep well my love and dream of the eternal bond we have sealed to our fate."

* * * * *

Darius stood out on a large tree limb, concealed from all except the most perceptive of his fellow observers. The tracker leader had gotten word only that morning of the caravan's sighting. As expected, the escort of armed elite royal guards stood back to allow the forward scouts some measure of independence. The northern scouts were led by a tall, darkly-clad figure, who evaded even some of Darius' most experienced trackers. It took the tracker leader some time to catch sight of Nelfindal, but the southerner knew what to look for.

Fortunately for Darius and his warriors, the northern scouts led by the ranger were only looking for the path that led past the Black Hills. The thought of an ambush in such a remote place was unheard of, except in this case. Darius turned slightly to get a better view of his quarry and to signal to Raelin who patiently waited some distance away.

The tall ranger made his way across a sparsely wooded area which afforded less cover for his stealthy moves. He was followed by only two royal scouts. The way they moved through the forest hinted to their inexperienced as woodsman, which explained why the northern ranger was with them. One of the following scouts looked about as if he had seen or heard something. The trap is almost set, thought Darius. Raelin was an excellent actor and his role as bait was well suited for him.

* * * * *

The caravan sat idly many kilometers away on the open plains as the forward scouts went ahead to locate the pass through the nearby hills. Nelfindal was always wary about the region, but wasn't overly worried about an attack. Turning to the scout behind him, Nelfindal whispered, "keep an eye out for orcs or trolls. There are still some in the area. Aside from that, I'm not too worried about much in this region. There aren't any signs of hostile creatures in this forest other than a stray bear or territorial pack of wolves."

The scout also appeared unconcerned about the chance of predators or orcs with an entire company of elite guards backing them. If anything tried to attack them, it would only take a quick dash to the open plains or a good blow on their war horn to bring the veteran warriors charging. Sharing this thought with the ranger the scout replied, "I would challenge anything to come and attack us. All it would take is a blow on our horn to bring a whole company of elite royal guards."

Nelfindal eyed his young sindar companion and grimaced. "I've seen people disappear with an entire army surrounding them without so much as a peep. There are powers you couldn't even imagine out here in the wilderness. Don't be too confident."

The statement caught the scout off-guard. He thought such existed in myth, but somehow this Darkwood ranger seemed to be convincing enough. The young elf had been with the ranger for only a few weeks and still the enigma of the Darkwood rangers shadowed his ever thought. The mysterious powers of the tall eldar were only exhibited once on the trip so far. A band of orcs tried to ambush the scouting party only a week ago. The resulting combat only lasted a few minutes, but in that time the tall ranger killed over half of the attackers. The rest were handled by the other four scouts who were ordered to follow along his protection. As if he needed protection, thought the scout.

It was while thinking about the strange talents of his companion that the young sindar noticed a shadowy figure pass in and then out of his vision behind him. The figure flitted amongst the trunks of some trees on the far side of the glen, which they had just passed. The young elf soon saw the shadowy image again; each time the inexperienced scout lost sight of it as it passed a tree.

"Sir, I just saw something in those trees of to the side," whispered the nervous elf. He thought himself a rather observant fellow, but he had never experienced such an elusive figure.

Nelfindal looked into the wooded glen and observed the cloaked shape of a human or elf moving from tree to tree. Their odd tracker was stealthy, but moved carelessly about in the lightly wooded area. The tall ranger motioned for the other scouts to follow his lead to give chase to the evading form.

The sound of crunching leaves caused by one of the scouts apparently alerted the character and it took off across a small glade in an attempt to lose its followers. Nelfindal almost laughed at such a foolish tactic. His legs were too long for anyone to out run him and his incredible endurance was enough to tire even a healthy deer out. After motioning the other scouts to spread out an pursue, Nelfindal ran after the escaping intruder. Although not entirely fast, their quarry was very nimble and ran around the many trees with ease.

By the time the tall ranger and his band of scouts were within an arms reach of the runner, they were in the center of the open glen. The trees hanging over the open grass suddenly came to life as the small band realized their foolishness. The whole chase was the bait for an obvious ambush, but the thought hadn't occurred to the trapped elves until too late.

Raelin moved quietly until he got in close to the ranger and his accompanying scouts. The assassin knew that he had to get the rear scout's attention first then draw the ranger's attention. The best way was to appear and disappear from tree to tree until he was seen. Apparently the trick worked, because one of the young scouts whispered something to the tall eldar. Seeing the attention of the scouting party focused on him, Raelin took off in a slow run so as not to lose the group. He was familiar with the speed the ranger was capable of. All he had to do was divert the eldar's attention long enough to get him into the center of the glade.

The diversion worked perfectly. The three northerners followed right behind the assassin and were about to catch him when they entered the clearing. The trees overhanging the small prairie were dense enough to cover the waiting elven warriors. Darius motioned for the company of soldiers to drop in on the unsuspecting victims. The ambush was performed with amazing speed.

Nelfindal summoned the magical bow, Elenar, to his hand and efficiently dropped an attacker before anyone could raise a sword. The young sindar scout beside the experienced ranger dropped to the ground with a crossbow bolt imbedded in his throat. The other member of the scouting party also dropped to the ground a few seconds later still clutching the hilt of his longknife, which contrasted to the sleek throwing knife sticking from his chest.

The tall ranger was about to summon the magical properties from a ring on his left hand when white smoke blew up all around him. The acrid smoke filled his lungs and burned his eyes distracting him from using the item. It was at that moment that Nelfindal realized his mistake in turning his back on the fleeing decoy. The instant he realized the error, the entire world exploded into darkness as the a sharp pain shot through his head. Nelfindal quickly fell to the soft grassy turf unconscious.

Raelin smiled at the ranger's foolishness at turning around to help his friends, which he knew the tall elf would do. He also knew of the eldar's talent for disappearing and then reappearing some distance away. So in an effort to nullify such a defense, the assassin threw down a poisoned smoke bomb. The smoke wasn't deadly, but it painfully blinded the victim for quite some time. Seeing his chance the assassin quickly knocked the northern ranger out with a simple blow to the back of his head.

Darius quickly made his way to the now immobile form of the tall ranger. The smiling face of Raelin was the first thing the tracker leader saw after looking down at the unconscious body.

Turning to two warriors beside him, Darius ordered, "Strip him of all jewelry, weapons, and armor. Leave him in only his undershirt and pants."

The two soldiers obediently went to work on the prone body. The articles were thrown into a large sack as they were removed. Raelin and Darius watched intently as the work was done. After a couple of minutes the rest of soldiers were standing over the body of the Darkwood ranger. After the mithril chain shirt was removed, a murmur of awe swept through the veteran company.

The reason for the commotion was the discovery of a single necklace hanging from the eldar's neck. The chain was made of mithril as much of the finest jewelry was. The amazing part was the medallion that hung from the small fine necklace. The pendant was no larger than the palm of a small child, but it was made from an almost diamond-like substance. No one in the awestruck group knew of any diamond being so large, yet the gem was just as hard. Even more fantastic was the glowing mithril star in the center of the twelve-sided jewel. The points of the star pointed to each side of the medallion which was also outlined in mithril. The entire piece was obviously crafted by a very ancient and magical craftsman. The power coursing through the magical item was like nothing the southerners had ever experienced before. Its power spoke of ancient enchantments, the secrets of which had long disappeared.

Darius forced himself to break free from the awe of the enchanted charm long enough to seize it from the searching warriors. Looking over to his companion, Darius said, "I think we had better hang on to this. Do you realize its value back at home? We will be very rich from this excursion!"

Raelin smiled in agreement. He had very greedy tendencies, but the value of such an item could be split evenly and still offer great reward. The rest of the items would be sold as well and the proceeds would go to the rest of the company. "Yes, this mission was well worth the trouble. This also puts a major feather in our caps. The capture of Nelfindal Goldleaf!" nearly shouted the assassin tracker.

Darius smiled to the soldiers around him and then said, "Let us be gone from here. The range commander wishes to meet us at the West Plains camp. And a hero's welcome awaits us in Terrilon!" A shout of excitement from the warriors mirrored the trackers announcement.

The southern company left behind the two dead scouts and one of their own dead who was unlucky enough to catch the ranger's arrow in the chest. As was expected, their corpses were thoroughly searched for valuables before the group moved out. The ranger's unconscious body was shackled to a pole and two burly warriors carried him off as the group set out. As the group made its way through the forest, Darius cast spells to cover the trail left behind by the awkward company of soldiers.

Raelin looked back at his companion and frowned at the need for such precautions. The assassin knew that if it weren't for the clumsy warriors, there would be no tracks to cover. The two trackers passed through the dense woodland without a trace and their footsteps never made a sound as they hiked through the dry leaves and stray branches laying on the forest floor; unlike the hard leather boots of the elven warriors, who followed the southern rangers.

Nelfindal regained consciousness after a few hours. His eyes and lungs still painfully burned from the noxious fumes of the gas bomb. The tall eldar's soft moaning drew the attention of his guards. Realizing that the ranger had regained consciousness, the two southern elves carrying the elf lowered his body to the ground and quickly untied the leather straps which held him to the pole. After the straps were removed, one of the dark elves slapped on a set of heavy iron shackles on the eldar. The cold metal felt strange to the tall youth. After the restraints were secured Nelfindal was dragged to his feet and forced to march with his abductors. For the first half hour of travel, the eldar felt sluggish repeatedly tripping over his own feet, after another hour he realized his pace was magically slowed forcing him to stumble.

The enchanted restraints were cast with not only a numbing spell of some sort, but an anti-magic spell as well. The usual link with his enchanted companion was blocked, forcing him to wonder where his talkative friend was. Nelfindal was so used to having Elenar around for support that the disconnection felt much like losing his own voice. After his captors realized that the eldar had regained his senses, they swiftly wrapped his head in a burlap bag to keep their destination a secret. This added inconvenience only exaggerated the problem of keeping up with the swift moving southerners. It appeared to the ranger that he stumbled and fell over every branch and rut in the forest. If it weren't for his less than careful bodyguards, the blundering elf would no doubt have suffered greater harm from sharp rocks and thorny brambles.

The painful burning from the gas bomb took two days to completely wear off. During that horrible time, the blindfolded Nelfindal was forced to march to a distant location where a herd of horses waited anxiously. The guards assigned the duty of watching the mistreated northerner threw him over the back of a unsaddled gelding who viciously snapped back at the unwanted rider. The putrid smell coming from the foul animal only hinted to its appearance as well as its ill-temper.

The nasty beast tossed, bumped and rudely jerked the ranger about to keep him from getting used to the discomfort of its exposed equine back. No doubt this horrible beast was picked especially for its rider. Never had the elf met a more malicious and evil animal. The shackles used to secure the tall elf closed about his wrists and ankles like savage, hungry jaws. Their cold steel cut deeply into the ranger's flesh with every bounce and sway of his mount. The beast seemed to exaggerate every movement in order to make the trip as least bearable as possible.

In those wretched days of hard riding, the mounted company of elves made great time with their valuable prize. The distance covered grew by the day as did the chances of escaping any rescue attempt. At ever step of the way the southern trackers left false trails, various traps and cast spells over their tracks to avoid any attempt of pursuit. Throughout the entire trip the tall eldar lay flat across the spine of the bareback horse. Sometimes the animal seemed to intentionally drive its body against trees and through thick bushes only to make the ride that much more insufferable.

After many uncountable days of painful travel, the still blindfolded Nelfindal and his determined escort arrived somewhere in the far western forests of Aragon. Here the exhausted group was greeted by another company of soldiers and several southern rangers. Nelfindal found it impossible to tell the exact number of warriors at the camp with the sack over his head. However, he could estimate from the number of voices quietly talking around him that over a dozen individuals marched with him. The eldar was able to deduce from fragments of various conversations that they had reached their destination.

A few minutes after entering the secret camp, Nelfindal noticed the conversations suddenly cut short. The silence hung in the air like a heavy blanket until a deep voice spoke out in a commanding tone to all those around. The apparent leader of the group gave out a series of orders. From the sound of the many quick moving feet, the leader was someone who held a position of some power. The blindfolded ranger continued to listen carefully to the leader and his vaguely familiar voice.

"Take the prisoner over to the pit and secure him to the wall. If he gives you any problems then do what ever is necessary to subdue him, but don't kill him," ordered the rough southern commander.

"I want two guards watching him at all times. If he escapes, those guards will be dealt with by me personally," the mysterious leader added vehemently.

The response to the order was immediately followed as the exhausted and soar Nelfindal was roughly dragged to a cold rock wall where he was rudely fastened in spread-eagle fashion. After everything was securely fastened the wrap about the young ranger's eyes was quickly stripped from his head. It took several minutes for his eyes to adjust to the bright light of the mid-afternoon sun.

After the glare became bearable, Nelfindal stared out at his still blurry audience. On each side of him where two very heavily armed southern rangers each one held a drawn broadsword towards his throat. Even though the position unnerved him, he hardly paid any attention to his rough looking bodyguards. What drew his attention was a very muscular silvan elf standing before him with his arms crossed over his chest. The dark brown-haired range commander looked sharply at the shackled ranger with his bright amber eyes and smiled broadly; a smile filled only with malice.

Nelfindal stared at the one person he thought he would never see again and wished he never would have to. He also knew that once again his life was in mortal peril. He felt the hatred emanating from the range commander, Caric. He also saw the madness that drove his abductor. The fire of insanity raged in his eyes like a blazing inferno.

The minutes of silence dragged on for what seemed an eternity until finally the range commander spoke in his gruff voice. "We meet again Nelfindal Goldleaf, ranger of Darkwood!" The words hissed dangerously through the air as the southerner spoke.

Nelfindal looked at the husky elf and threw back his shoulders in a crude display of insolence and replied, "Yes, Caric, we meet again. By what fortune brings us together? Surely you don't wish a rematch?" Many worrisome looks were exchanged between the others standing behind the silvan commander. No one truly knew what the two talked of, but many quivered at the thought of fighting the range commander.

Caric frowned back at the arrogant ranger and stepped within centimeters of the tall elf's face and said, "If this were for a chance at a rematch, then it would be your battle. For now, you are more valuable alive. For now, that is."

Nelfindal looked at the tension building in the powerful southern ranger as the veins in the silvan's neck stood out. The northern ranger realized that he was pushing the silvan beyond the limits of his sanity. Once Caric got what he wanted, his life would be immediately forfeit. Death was nothing new to the young eldar, but the realization of it happening so soon was a bit distasteful. Dying at the hands of this individual was a fate far worse than any other Nelfindal could dream of.

* * * * *

The caravan waited anxiously about two kilometers from the dense forests of the Western Black Hills. It was becoming apparent to the escorting guardsmen that the forward scouts led by the Darkwood ranger, Nelfindal, were becoming long overdue from their search of the surrounding area. Princess Nickoleta sat patiently on her snowy white elven mare as the escort's company commander rode up. The silver haired eldar warrior bowed quickly to the beautiful royal daughter showing signs of distress.

"I'm sorry to disturb you my lady, but I wish to send out a scout and a small detachment of guardsmen to check on the welfare of our forward scouts," requested the veteran commander.

"Is there a problem, Commander?" questioned Niki.

"This is the wilderness, your highness, and the scouts have been gone much longer than they should be. It is already midday and night comes quickly in this region near the dense woodland and the night is not a safe time to be traveling unguarded," advised the commander.

"If you think they might be in danger then rush to it. Send word back to us immediately after you find them," ordered the concerned lady.

With his orders the commander called out several names and sent a young scout and a group of a dozen warriors to track down the missing scouts. The riders quickly rode off south towards the last destination of the ranger and his two accompanying trackers.

The tracks made by the ranger and his fellow scouts were very hard to follow, but the leading scout of the search party managed to stay on the correct path. After a couple of hours the group made their way through the light woods near the clearing, which had been the site of the ambush. The young scout noticed the blood stained grass just before he saw the three dead bodies.

Realizing disaster had fallen upon the scouting party, the tracker ordered one of the warriors to ride back quickly and inform the caravan of the terrible situation. The guardsman rode off in a gallop without hesitation. The rest of the group fanned out to find some sign of the attackers, but only found the dead body of the one southern warrior. The charred remains of his body were still warm from the magical fire arrow, which had struck him in the chest sending his body aflame. Aside from the three corpses, only a few broken branches were found in the trees, but no footprints or other tracks. The young tracker scratched his head trying to figure out what had happened to the mysterious attackers.

The princess appeared to be sitting patiently awaiting word of her scouting party's whereabouts. Outwardly, the royal daughter looked calm, but her insides were in utter turmoil. She knew that Nelfindal could handle himself in most all situations, but something seemed to cry out to her for help. It wasn't actually a cry, but more like a strange sensation from the back of her mind. It was as if the distant forest screamed out in frustration at the loss of an ancient friend. Niki knew the priestesses of the White Tree could detect certain disharmonies in the wild, but this feeling was different. This intuitive sense grew by the hour as she waited for some message from the search party.

After several hours the distant cloud of dust, which announced the coming of a fast rider was seen along the open grassland. The young guardsman reigned in his horse only meters away from the company commander who intercepted him on his way to the caravan. The rider's mount was heavily lathered and the soldier himself looked extremely exhausted. It was apparent from were Niki was that something dreadful had happened.

After a few words with his commander, the young warrior dismounted to recover from his long ride and a servant took his mount to wash down the overheated horse. The frowning officer rode over to the waiting princess and slowly described the situation.

"Apparently, our forward scouts were ambushed and the preliminary report is that there are three dead bodies. Whether Lord Nelfindal is one of them, I am not sure," said the flushing soldier who could barely contain his anger.

The princess felt light headed, but quickly regained her composure. Her empathic horse read her feelings immediately and reared up and bolted. Niki at first tried to fight to regain control over her mount, but willingly gave in to the creature. The royal steed flew over the level ground like a white bolt of lightning. The commanding officer stared in shock for a brief moment before he kicked his own horse in pursuit. The amazing speed of the royal elven horses were unmatched by any normal living beast. Even the commander's own fast mount lost sight of the white streak of the princess's mount.

All Niki could think about was the slim chance that her lover had managed to escape the ambush. The only problem with her hopeful wishing was the announcement of three dead bodies. Were they all elven and if they were why didn't the soldier say whether Nelfindal was one of them unless his body wasn't there. Countless thoughts ran through the young princess's mind with alarming speed and clarity. Each new thought brought new hopes and yet new horrors. Finally, she concentrated on her powers of calming to keep her mind off the frightening thought of her lover's possible death.

The nagging feeling that something was definitely wrong continued its relentless pull, however. The closer the princess got to the site of the ambush the stronger her intuitive sense pulsed. It was as if something were calling for help from a distant place, but the closer she rode the stronger the calling got. It was like a beacon, which got brighter in the dark as you walked towards it.

After what seemed a lifetime of riding, the princess made it to the clearing. The speed of her mount caught the investigating warriors off-guard as she rode in just by the dead southern warrior. Dismounting in a fluid motion, Niki walked towards the impaled corpse of the southerner. As if the scorched arrow sensed her presence, it flared up in a brilliant blue flame that blinded everybody except the princess.

Niki stared into that flashing brilliance and for a brief moment she saw the ambush as it happened and the death of the two trackers. The picture wavered slightly as the vision of smoke erupting about Nelfindal flashed by and the sudden collapse of his body to the ground. The last image Niki saw was that of an evil looking southern elf standing above the still form of the eldar ranger.

After the flash of burning brilliance dissipated, the vision ceased and the once partly charred body was left to dust as well as the rest of the area around it. Amazingly enough the princess was completely unharmed as if the flame were an illusion. Niki absently stared out into the forest as her bewildered guardsmen stood in awe of the fiery display. No one moved or spoke until moments later the company commander rode up with a dozen more soldiers behind him.

All the princess could recall after the vision was the sound of distant voices begging that she return to the safety of the caravan. Niki followed the group willingly and remained silent until she bedded down for the evening. Once in the privacy of her own tent, the princess wept. Her mistresses were ordered to remain outside of her tent by the company commander who somehow knew she mourned the loss of the ranger.

The comforting sensation of her parents presence was felt late in the evening. The Queen's powerful magic closed the distance to give support to her grieving daughter. The mental impressions sent to the princess from her father shared her loss, but reminded her of her duty to the people of Elador. She was a princess above all else and she should only mourn the loss so long. The thoughts were harsh, but Niki realized the logic behind it. After a while, the royal daughter fell into a deep sleep with her mother's help.

* * * * *

The night seemed darker and colder than it actually was when Norin received word of the ambush. Somehow the ranger captain didn't entirely believe what he heard from the Queen. The news of Nelfindal's death was just not right. The description of the image seen by the princess and later shared with the Queen seemed incomplete. It was a well known problem with magical viewing that sometimes you see what you want or what you expect and not what really happened. Many soothsayers and other magical scryers knew that the interpretation of visions is a very inexact science. Even Illidrais admitted that she could be wrong, but the vision was very clear.

Shortly after the meeting with the royal lady, Norin left to inform the guild of the situation. If his young apprentice was captured by southern rangers, the possible threat to the guild could be incomprehensible. If Nelfindal were dead then the body would have to be recovered and properly taken care of.

Walking through the streets of Galadhon, the silvan ranger tried very hard to maintain his emotions. After thinking about the details of the vision he realized that the southern rangers would most likely kill the young eldar whether he gave them what they wanted or not. Either way the tall ranger was mostly likely dead and it was a fact the silvan captain could not accept. Tears welled up in his eyes as he recalled the day he heard of the death of Farifane. The death of his friend's son restored the pain he had felt that day.

* * * * *

A week had passed since the abduction of the Darkwood ranger. From across a vast lake made scarlet by the early morning rays the dark silhouette of the assassin, Raelin, quietly walked towards another figure who appeared deep in thought. The range commander contemplated a formal-looking parchment, which he held in one hand. All around the forest, the sounds of bustling activity could be heard as the camp came to life.

Turning around to face the assassin, Caric sounded a deep snarl, which seemed to originate from his feet. The assassin thought amusingly how much like a tall, beardless dwarf the commander looked at that moment. The red faced ranger glared hard at Raelin. "Word from guild headquarters," grunted Caric as he waved a piece of parchment. "They what me to deliver the ranger to Terrilon if our interrogations prove unsuccessful."

His words hung in the air for many moments before Raelin responded cautiously. "It is not our fault. The eldar's resistance to my drugs is incredible. I have given him doses large enough to kill a hephradon." The mystified silvan made reference to the six meter sloth indigenous to the southern forests as if to clarify his point.

"The letter orders us to bring him back so the magicians can work their spells of persuasion. I don't want someone else to get credit for his capture and the information he holds. I have waited far too long." The broad-shouldered commander slammed his fist against the tree he stood next to. The force of the mailed glove shot wood chips in all directions. Caric glared at the tree for a few seconds then turned around and stared out across the lake not speaking another word.

Seeing the conversation ended, the assassin left the infuriated range commander. On his way back to camp, Raelin thought hard about his next step. He agreed full heartedly with the silvan leader, but decided to stay out of the politics of the rangers guild. For the meantime, I'll stick to my job and get what I can from the northerner, Raelin thought to himself.

The golden beams of the mid-afternoon sun beat down on the barely conscious form of the northern ranger. Nelfindal remained shackled to the same cold stone wall he had been chained to since his arrival to the secret Farghest camp. His wrists were chaffed so badly that traces of dried blood were seen outlining his arms. As if the biting steel weren't bad enough, thought Nelfindal, the assassin had to visit every night to drug him in attempts at locating the secret location of the Darkwood guild. Fortunately, the tall elf's resistance to such things was beyond the norm of mortal men and even beyond that of other elves.

After regaining more control over himself, Nelfindal felt a faint tugging at the back of his mind. The sensation hadn't been felt for sometime, but its presence was a comfort. Ever since the interrogator who he learned to be an assassin named Raelin induced a mind nullifying drug into his body, he couldn't cast spells or call to his bow. Still sensing the silent but noticeable calling, Nelfindal concentrated on his enchanted weapon and only companion, Elenar.

The signs of strain from the link were apparent on his battered and bruised face as sweat beaded up on his brow. After many minutes of concentration, the cheerful voice rose up inside of the young ranger's mind.

"Well, we finally get to talk. Now that the link is established we can freely communicate to each other," commented Elenar.

"Yes, but how can we talk now and not before," questioned the dazed elf.

"You are free of the shackles they secured you with before and the spell nullifying drugs are wearing off."

"Where are you located? Are you close enough to come to me?" inquired the eldar.

"If we can talk then the answer is: yes. I think I am located in a bag somewhere near the camp. If you summon me to you, we can project your mind around the area to determine the exact location."

"I must wait until dark. My guards may question how I came in possession of you."

"Then until dark," responded the enchanted bow.

The thought of recovering his companion and the chance of escaping made the hot day much more bearable. For the remainder of the day, Nelfindal planned his escape attempt and the direction, which he would head in. The specifics couldn't be worked out because of his position, but the details would present themselves after he was freed.

* * * * *

The sun set low over the horizon extending the already long shadows across the forest floor. Darius walked about trying to collate his thoughts on his most recent dispatch from the guild headquarters. The letter was secreted to him behind the range commander's back with only the messenger knowing that he received anything. The coded message detailed his orders to return to the southern capital for a special assignment. A job of such magnitude that the success of it would alter the political structure of the entire southern realm.

Darius walked back and forth along the lake not far from where Caric had vented his frustrations many hours before. Its waves lapped casually against its sandy shores. The silvan enjoyed the sound, which helped to relax his many upsetting thoughts. Reflecting on his decision, the tracker leader heard the faint footfalls, which signaled his associate's approach.

Raelin walked towards the preoccupied Darius with a serious look on his face. Catching the tracker leader's attention, Raelin quickly asked, "It seems that today is a bad day for mail. Troubling message from home, friend?"

Darius turned to his fellow tracker and responded, "It seems there is never good news from Terrilon. Our prisoner is more valuable than we had first thought. It seems one of our spies from Elador has told us of a close relationship with our honored guest and a certain eldest daughter of the royal family. A chance to blackmail the young lady or an edge for you to use the information in your interrogations could change everything."

Raelin thought about the news and wondered why the range commander wasn't informed of the new information. The assassin began to smile at the thought of what was transpiring around him. He also thought of how the tall ranger's incredible resistance to physical tortures; however, even that now changed with this added bit of news. The assassin turned to look at Darius and said, "this is news I could have only dreamed of. The ranger will do anything we ask. The chink in his armor, so to say."

"As for me, I have many duties to perform before I set off for Terrilon."

Startled by the announcement, Raelin looked hard at his ranger companion. "You return to the capital? There is much that you have not told me. Something's up, I can tell." Regaining from his initial surprise, the assassin considered all the news together and added, "good luck with your promotion."

Darius was shocked by the statement and responded, "how do you know I have been promoted? I didn't say anything about that."

"I knew it was coming. Besides, no one gets called back to Terrilon from the wild lands unless it is of the greatest importance. And such things require the special handling of range commanders. Caric is not fit for this. He will not remain in his position for long."

"You have noticed his madness as well? It worsens by the day. I fear he will have the eldar killed before we can use him.

Getting him away will be very difficult," whispered the silvan tracker.

"A task, which I would offer my services to you for a small price," offered the grinning assassin.

"You will have it, if we can do it without incriminating ourselves," agreed Darius.

"No worry. Tonight is as good as any night to do it. I will notify you of the details later. For now, I bid you good day." The conversation ended, Raelin turned and left disappearing into the dark forest.

Darius turned away from the departing figure and walked towards the camp. The tracker leader planned his next steps to leave the secreted southern outpost and return to Terrilon unnoticed.

* * * * *

Night fell quickly upon the small glade where the tall elf was imprisoned. Nelfindal's guards fell into a silent conversation about some obscure subject. Even if he could hear what they were saying he wasn't paying much attention. He was preoccupied with concentrating on his location and the direction of his bow's presence. After a few moments, a small reddish flash of light flickered from one of the ranger's fingers. The spark was followed by a pale blue flame which engulfed the shackles around his wrists and ankles. The intensity of the magical fire left small scorch marks on the elf's skin, but otherwise left him unharmed. However, the heat did effect the iron shackles fastened to him. The soft metal flowed away as it was completely melted much like wax from a lit candle. The small magical display went unnoticed by the preoccupied silvan warriors as their discussion began to become more intense.

Seeing his chance to escape, the ranger quietly climbed up one of the tall maple trees surrounding the small glade which acted as his prison for over a week. The old tree offered a good silent climb as its large branches moved little under the light weight of the eldar's body. The tree branches rose up over the rock overhang which he was previously fastened to. Taking a deep breath and giving a small prayer to the forest mother for silence, Nelfindal leaped from the broad bough onto the rocky overhang with barely a sound.

Moving with the speed and silence born to him, Nelfindal made his way across the top of the ridge to a small cave not far from the camp. Recalling the direction and general lay of the surrounding terrain, the ranger found his way to the dark entrance. The cave was guarded by an armed warrior who appeared less than alert probably feeling comfortable with the relative secrecy of his location. Taking a good hard branch, the eldar snuck up to the drowsy elf from behind and dropped the hard wood heavily on the southerner's exposed skull. The large elf slid of his stool and lay unmoving as the eldar entered the cave.

Earlier, just before sunset, the ranger had magically investigated the area with the aid of his enchanted weapon. Remembering the location of his gear and the identity of the remaining items, Nelfindal quickly found a large burlap sack containing most of his confiscated possessions. The bag was emptied and the ranger quickly replaced his stolen items. As was expected, certain valuable items were missing, but his armor, weapons and clothing were left untouched. Like the rest of the valuable items, the fabulous medallion was nowhere to be found. The revelation of the fact made his heart sink. The priceless artifact was the only gift Nelfindal had ever received from his father.

Sitting in a comfortable position, the tall elf focused on summoning the unique powers of his bow once again. Concentrating, Nelfindal let his consciousness free itself from his body. He felt himself move freely without hinderance, though his physical form remained in the cave. The unique form of travel was very dangerous, but the risk was necessary in finding the healing charm. Feeling himself float through trees and rocks was strange, but the ranger ignored the odd sensations and concentrated only on the location of the priceless relic. After a few minutes of blurring travel, the location of the item was determined. The shock of its whereabouts nearly forced the ranger to lose control over himself. The medallion hung around the neck of a southern ranger; one of those who had captured him. Marking the location, the eldar returned to his body.

Quickly readying himself, the tall ranger left the cave entrance and took off in an easterly direction. After only a few moments of slowly sneaking about the camp looking for the southern elf, the cry of alarm was sounded. "The prisoner has escaped" was heard throughout the area. Hearing the discovery of his escape, Nelfindal quietly ran towards the shore of the nearby lake.

It wasn't until then that the young ranger realized how weakened he truly was from his ordeal with his silvan interrogator. The short trek towards the water seemed to last for millennia. Every step took its toll on the eldar's body as the effect of the drugs returned. Finally reaching the sloshing edge of the lake, Nelfindal slowly slid into the dark water. The exertion of the dangerous spellcasting and the week of tortures and drugs was forcing the tough ranger to unconsciousness. It was only through a primitive drive to survive that continually saved him. Seeing a floating log pass by in the dark night, Nelfindal managed to swim a few extra meters to it and grab on before slipping under the cool surface of the water.

The shouts of command were only faintly heard as the flowing water carried the driftwood and its sole passenger down stream. The young ranger never heard the death cries of the two guards assigned to watch him. He never saw their faces as the range commander punished them for their carelessness. And Nelfindal never saw the incredible loathing, which flared in Caric's eyes. For if he had, he would have willed his clumsy raft to move much faster.

* * * * *

Fever racked the body of the tall elf as he drifted in and out of consciousness. The log which the ranger clung to floated for many days along the murky waterway. The river carried the flotsam into a large region of swamp known by the few local inhabitants as the Dire Marsh. The desolate region earned its name for its many deadly hazards; many natural and many not so natural. The stagnant pools of stagnant water were excellent breeding grounds for many disease carrying insects and other unseen killers. The barren marshlands were also home to many vile creatures no less deadly than their smaller counterparts.

As Nelfindal floated his way into the marsh, he was slowly nudged towards the shore by the weakening current. The gelatinous feeling of the muddy silt slowly brought the youth to a fevered consciousness. Realizing that his ride had ended, the eldar slowly pulled himself off the log and half-crawled, half-swam his way towards higher, more solid ground. Only meters away from the wet and delirious ranger grew a clump of skeletal, stunted trees firmly rooted into the submerged loam.

By grabbing hold of the elaborate network of raised roots, Nelfindal managed to pull himself onto the elevated mass of dry brush. A jolt of incredible pain shot through his head as he looked through blurry eyes at his new surroundings. The excruciating pangs almost pushed the ranger back into unconsciousness, but he fought back with what little will power he had left. The recurring pain appeared to be a side effect of the drugs used on him in his interrogations.

The incessant throbbing had kept him awake for the better part of the trip. Fortunately, it also saved him from slipping into the peaceful embrace of the dark waters. Several times during his journey, the rush of pain had cleared his head long enough for him to realize he had slipped under the surface of the water. Even though the cool darkness beckoned to him with its peacefulness, the ranger refused to allow himself to give up.

Since the unusual side effects of the assassin's drugs had first appeared, they had begun to worsen. The thought of the magnifying pain forced the tall ranger to look for anything that could ease the incessant throb. Taking a deep breath, Nelfindal summoned his enchanted companion. Once again, the mental presence was felt clearly in his mind as strong as ever.

"Help me search the nearby area for healing herbs. I don't have the time or the energy to walk around in search myself," ordered the desperate ranger.

Using his waning will power, Nelfindal was mentally carried around the small raised landmass in search of roots or herbs he could use to ease his torment. As luck and the blessing of the gods would have it, a small bush grew nearby that the eldar recognized. The rare and expensive plant was known as an ellenberry bush. The greatest contribution from the thorny vegetation was its yellowish sap which was reputed to have the ability to completely heal the body. The only side effects from the powerful drug were strong hallucinations that were known to often leave the patient mad with insanity.

Nelfindal knew he had no other choice. It was an all or nothing shot and he proceeded to take it. Slowly pulling himself towards the small bush, the ranger scrapped and bruised himself amongst the many unforgiving roots. Welts developed along the young elf's arms and legs as he clumsily moved across the floating mass. The entire journey appeared to take an eternity; Every bit of progress took its toll on his already battered body.

After pulling himself to the base of the thorny bush, the battered elf carefully drew one of his sharp blades and cut a long gash across the main root. The sticky fluid slowly coursed out of the severed plant. Nelfindal quickly leaned over and sucked on the bitter fluid with a vengeance knowing full well that his life was depending on it. After several minutes of imbibing the thick sap, Nelfindal moved himself to a small depression on the floating island and slipped into a deep sleep.

After many hours of exhausted sleep, the eldar was awakened by the sound of grunting and snarling. The vision of a large voracious rat came crawling towards him. The only defense the weakened elf could muster was to lamely raise his enchanted dagger to the creature. Waving the knife in the air didn't seem to scare the beast. The slime covered rodent jumped on top of the ranger clawing and biting his unprotected flesh. Just as the ranger thought he was dead, the image vanished and he was left strangling the sack carrying his rations. For several uncountable days after, many different hallucinations tormented the eldar. Each vision became more vivid and real than the next, and each time the elf would collapse into a wave of exhaustion.

The last three nights had been the most hellish of all. The hallucinations were incredibly strong and dangerously realistic. At one time, the exhausted elf thought a swamp troll was stalking him. All the young ranger could do was summon a dome of flame about his small island. The fury of the blaze singed and scored the entire area within a fifteen meter radius. Not one sign of vegetation showed within that area. Even the usual aquatic flora was burned away just under the surface of the murky swamp water.

Resting after the days of fighting the hallucinatory monsters, Nelfindal raised himself unsteadily to his feet. Confident that the visions had disappeared and the pain had stopped, Nelfindal began to gather himself together and move on. The spongy earth of the floating land mass resisted his weight only shortly before giving way to the sucking mud underneath.

Before long the tall ranger was slowly moving through knee deep muck. The slurping sounded each time he moved a shaky step forward. After traveling only a few kilometers, the pains of hunger developed and grew with increasing persistence. Thanking all the gods within earshot that his stomach was the only sensation of pain he felt. Since the hallucinations ended, the weary elf noticed the pain had ceased.

Feeling a sense of urgency to move on and a need to feed his nearly healed body, Nelfindal foraged for anything sustaining. The swamp appeared to be rather desolate at first, but it was actually teaming with life underneath the brown and decaying layer of reeds and dead saplings. The roots and tubers of many indigenous plants were tough yet edible, even palatable to the famished elf.

After a few unsuccessful attempts, the eldar was able to capture a few small lobe-finned fish, which clung to the roots supporting the many floating islands. Having had enough of the tough skinned amphibious fish, Nelfindal continued on in a easterly direction. The ranger knew well enough that the swamp had to end in dry land eventually. However, the swamp appeared to continue indefinitely as each step seemed to take him deeper into the savage wilderness.

* * * * *

The lightly clad group of elven trackers looked upon the burned out ring of vegetation where the ranger had rested only days earlier. The trail to the scorched island was difficult to find. If not for the assistance of magical detections, the eldar would have been long gone. The small group quickly searched the area for a hint as to the direction the northern ranger went. After some speculation the leader spoke out.

"He will be heading towards the west plains of the Everhighs. He must expect that Caric would send scouts south to block his passage to Terrilon. Send word to Caric that we shall head due east and have him rendezvous with us at the foothills," ordered Raelin to a tall silvan tracker.

The rest of the group moved on continuing east through the murky, dank waters of the marsh. Heading off in a different direction was the young tracker sent by Raelin, he moved quickly south to intercept the fast moving range commander and his party.

After a couple of days of slow passage through the swamps, the search party stopped to rest their waterlogged mounts on the green meadows of the west plains. The two remaining trackers sat away from the quiet and thoughtful Raelin. Since their departure from the secreted camp, the assassin kept to himself. Aside from giving occasional orders he remained quiet. This forced solitude even unnerved the experienced southern rangers.

Sitting by himself, Raelin contemplated the recent turn of events and the power play going on in the southern capital city. Once his mission was over he would return to Terrilon and see what had transpired in his absence. One thing for sure, thought Raelin, the eldar won't be coming back with me.

With the horses refreshed and the riders dried off, the group mounted up and headed after the fleeing prisoner at a fast pace. Raelin had no care for the dumb beasts and pushed them to their limits everyday. By the fourth day, the first horse collapsed. The poor animal bled profusely from its mouth and nose from the strain. Its massive heart had exploded under the cruel hard riding.

Leaving the unmounted ranger behind with orders to catch up as soon as possible, Raelin and his other mounted tracker moved on. After several more hours, the other two horses dropped, dead. Moving on foot the two elves continued until they reached the first signs of the massive mountains. The large outcroppings of granite rock thrust upward as miniature imitations of the Everhighs which lay just beyond.

* * * * *

It was almost three weeks since his escape from the Farghest ranger camp. Nelfindal made his way across the wide open plains, which he knew led to the vast mountain range known as the Everhighs. Since reaching the wide open grasslands at the foot of the mountains, the eldar sensed that he was indeed being followed. After stopping to rest for the night in a shallow gully,

Nelfindal prepared to use his enchanted bow to locate his unseen trackers.

The dark moonless sky blanketed the great grasslands in darkness. No predators were out that night because of the impenetrable blackness. Here, under the cloudy and starless night, the young ranger sent forth his essence across the astral plane like he had some many times recently. The speed of travel was too fast to equate in normal, mundane terms. The blurring speed demonstrated how fast the elf's presence was moving, but the sensation seemed to go on for much longer. It was an unusual way to travel, but it covered far more distance than normal tracking could ever do.

After what seemed like hours of searching, the small band of elven trackers was sensed close by. Focusing his attention on the details of the group, Nelfindal recognized the slim and dark form of his interrogator. The dark shape of the assassin sat just outside the perimeter of a small camp fire completely invisible to the elven eye. Another pair of silhouettes sat close to the comforting warmth of the blaze apparently needing its companionship. The trackers were more sensed than seen, but it was enough to know where the search party was and its number.

After returning to his cool body, Nelfindal realized that he had been gone for only a few minutes. The southern trackers were roughly four days march behind, but had swift mounts and would catch up in little more than a day. Fortunately, the foothills were less than a day ahead. After reaching the mountains, the horses would be unable to climb the rocky slopes.

The following morning just before sunrise, Nelfindal was off and loping towards the rocky base of the mountains. The early morning mist hung just above the waist high grass even as the reddish sun rose over the horizon. The fleet footed ranger moved through the misty ocean causing swirls to ripple away from his body like the wakes of some great warship. The trip took less time than previously figured as the foothills came within sight of the long-legged elf. The first outcroppings of rock were visible only an hour or so after the midday break. Thinking quickly, Nelfindal began to set up several traps to slow his quick moving pursuers. After an hour of hard work, the traps were completed and the ranger continued up the first rocky mountain slope.

* * * * *

The accompanying tracker took the point position with the tracker leader closely behind. With caution the two passed the sharp rocky edges of the welcoming formations. After another fifty meters up a steep slope the leading tracker observed a poorly concealed snare and moved to avoid the trap. The silvan tracker never looked past the obvious ruse, instead he fell victim to an unseen trip wire. The result shocked the southern elf as the sound of a couple of falling rocks was heard from above. The tracker stopped and looked quickly around expecting disaster, but none came.

The two trackers climbed a few more meters when a loud rumbling could be heard as if the mountain revolted at their passage. Looking around the two silvans tried to determine where the sound came from. After a few moments, they had their answer. Thousands of tons of rock and stone came tumbling directly at the two startled rangers. Raelin looked quickly to escape but could only dive behind a small upthrust of bedrock. The rock slide seemed to go on for hours as countless boulders, some as big as huts, crashed all around the barely concealed assassin. Occasionally fragmented rocks no larger than a small fist careened off their larger brothers only to find an unlucky target.

After the dust settled, Raelin could see that the entire face of the slope had been changed from the rock slide. The quick thinking tracker leader was cut and bruised in many places, but suffered no broken bones or severe trauma. However, the sand covered hand of the other tracker was found many meters away down the slope. The mangled appendage was the only visible sign of the broken elven body buried below under tons of the loose stone.

The sight of the dead tracker filled Raelin with rage and a deep sense of caution. "There is much to this eldar that should be respected," mumbled the assassin to himself.

After looking out over the still dusty mountain slope, the assassin tracker turned and continued much more cautiously after the elusive and resourceful Darkwood ranger. With each step the silvan became more enraged by the elusiveness of the eldar ranger, but grew to appreciate the cunning of his opponent. "A truly worthy adversary," mumbled Raelin as he wiped the sweat from his brow after reaching the top of the now shattered mountainside.

8 SOUTHERN POLITICS

The princess Nickoleta stood on an ivy covered balcony overlooking the twinkling lamp lights of the city of Terrilon. She was dressed in a fine gown of powder blue silk embroidered with small diamonds marking her family's station. She wore soft slippers of the same palest of blues, which only partially protected her feet from the hot rock floors. The daytime sun had been hot to the barest of tolerable levels. Every step on the searing stone of the balcony demonstrated to her how terrible the day actually felt to those living in the city below.

Unused to the scalding rays, the young elven lady stayed indoors for the better part of the day trying to remain cool. The head councilman's residence was strategically built into the side of a small hill. The coolness of the earth around the underground rooms made the property highly valued in the blistering summer, but even the coolness of the building's design could not battle the unrelenting heat of the day. Niki waited patiently to escape from the musty and uncomfortable man-made dwelling. Until now, there was no chance to enjoy the fresh outside air. After a few

223

deep breathes the lady felt somewhat refreshed. The cooler air helped to relax her mind as she recalled the past few weeks.

The vast cosmos hung easily over the princess as she looked thoughtfully at the twinkling stars. Thinking to herself, Niki wondered if her lover could see the same flashing eyes of light. The eldar princess thought hard on the news delivered in a recent dispatch from Elador. Her parents had sent word that a rescue party had been mounted in search of the abducted ranger. The Darkwood Guild was very concerned with the possibility of information being leaked out to the abductors, assumed to be members of the Farghest Guild.

Deep in her heart Niki knew that Nelfindal would fight to retain all he knew. She knew all too well of his self-control. The same control, which concealed his feelings for her until her parents had intervened. Niki loved the tall ranger, but felt uncertain as to whether she would ever see him again. The southern guild was infamous for killing its prisoners unmercifully after using them.

A booming voice called out to the princess from behind her dismissing further thought on the painful subject. A brown haired human walked purposefully towards the taller princess. The pudgy aristocrat stopped very close to the questioning stare of the elven lady. "My lady, I have been looking all over for you," said the human.

"My Lord Gyron, please forgive me, I am not use to being confined indoors for very long," replied the smiling princess.

"No need. I realize the elven need to remain close to the outdoors. It is something of which I enjoy myself. I was a successful farmer for many years before I became Head Councilman," boasted the leering noble.

The penetrating look received from the beady-eyed human made the princess shiver with revulsion, which she attributed to the cool air. Ever since she arrived in the southern capital, the obnoxious and persistent nobleman never left her alone. The mornings were filled with the trying negotiations with the greedy, self-interested council members which persisted until no one could stand the midday heat. Then, the evenings continued with many flamboyant and even gaudy costume parties hosted by the irritating council leaders.

How their society remained successfully intact was a mystery to the civilized elfmaiden. The most trying aspect of this diplomatic trip was the daily court intrigue. It was like playing several games of chess all at the same time. The only difference was the lack of rules. It wasn't uncommon to be asked, in an indiscrete manner, if the princess was interested in taking on a southern consort or even just a lover for the duration of her visit. All done publicly in a vain attempt to gain an advantage in the great game.

Gyron sensed the princess' distracted thoughts and inquired, "are you troubled my dear?"

Niki looked at the councilman and nodded her head. "You'll have to forgive me. Much has been going on and I must admit that your court politics have me a little mystified," exaggerated the eldar princess.

"Do you not have such political maneuvering in your homeland?" asked the pudgy human.

"Yes, but not to such a degree. We pride ourselves on our determination to get things accomplished. Such distractions are not conducive to effective governing," answered the princess.

"We pride ourselves on our political games. You see, we do not have a monarchy such as yourselves. Our government is based on who can persuade the majority that they can benefit from certain ventures. This way everybody has a say in the matter," proudly boasted the human.

"You do have a point. I think I understand your system much better with that thought in mind. Thank you for the clarification."

"Any time. For a demonstration, you can accompany my son, Garin, to the DuBastro's party this evening. He is a fine fellow with a charming personality that I think you might find very entertaining."

Niki wondered how long it would take the sneaky council leader to reveal his real motives behind his friendliness and persistent presence. Not wanting to create an enemy with the powerful noble, the princess responded, "I think a good demonstration of your court's scheming would help me in my negotiations. Are you sure it is fair that your son should go. He can't be more that twenty years old?"

"Forgive my bluntness, my lady. But at twenty, my son is already a man who should be establishing a family and running his own business. I believe your people wait until their hundredth day of ascension to be considered adult. By then most humans are long dead."

"Forgive me again, I forget that human children mature quicker than our own offspring. I will regard your son as the fine and mature noble he takes after," apologized the princess.

"Thank you my lady. You will learn much from us as well as we from you. I understand that few humans have ever visited your kingdom and little is known of my race by your people."

"As you said before, we are learning. It was only recently that we opened up to the other races. We fear stagnation more than we fear our sense of racial purity," added Niki.

"And yet there are many elves in my kingdom. How is that?" inquired Gyron.

"The dark elves, as we describe them, broke off from my people many millennia ago because of the same need of racial purity. Many fell in love with humans who lived and traded near our borders. This resulted in many short-lived, half-breeds who were considered bastard by my people. This schism forced many to move out of the elven capital and establish communities elsewhere. The number of these renegades was very large and the exodus left our society weak."

"Is that when you're people nearly fell to the Dark Beast?" questioned the enraptured nobleman.

"Yes, the wealth of Elador was impressive back then. The people who left our land took only what they could carry. Much unguarded treasure was left behind with only a small armed force of loyal guards to protect the land." Niki fell silent for a moment recalling how the deadly invasion must have appeared to the remaining elves.

"Well, after a while, the Dark Beast appeared with an army of orc warriors and armed black trolls. The annihilation of the elven people was almost complete except for the unexpected appearance of the mysterious rangers' guild and a young heroic eldar nobleman by the name of Delfius."

"Wasn't Delfius the one who slayed the beast?" inquired the councilman.

"The same. However, he died from the festered wounds received from the vile demon. His valiant action and the incredible number of orcs which fell to the rangers changed the tide of the battle. Where thousands of orcs once stood before the battle, only a few hundred escaped unscathed. The forces of Darkwood, then at its peak numbered only some eight hundred to a thousand."

The thought of the rangers invoked the painful memory of Nelfindal to Niki's mind. The image lasted only a few scant seconds before she thrust it deep into her heart barring any visible sign of sorrow in front of the human leader. The only hint or trace of the memory of her missing lover was a watery glazing of her sky blue eyes.

Gyron stood awed by the historical narrative and the demonstration of the northern elves' might. He knew of the Darkwood guild and its loyalties to the elven nation, but the incredible efficiency with which the rangers fought was thought to be only the stuff of legends. Such an overt display of power must have sent shock waves throughout the land, thought the council leader. The magical talents of the rangers were well-known even to the most isolated humans.

Calming herself as she was taught by her priestess tutors, Niki explained the current mood of her people. "Since that dreadful time, our people have closed themselves off to only a few outsiders. Now, we wish to reestablish relations with all our neighbors and learn how to be a more accepting people. The royal family wishes for the old ways to be turned aside. They see the stagnation and the internal weaknesses of our society that can only be healed by other races and kingdoms."

"A fascinating story, my dear, but why did you come to our land? We are a distant nation that is mostly excluded from northern politics and has little to offer the great nation of Elador," asked the curious human.

"You are as much a kingdom of Aragon as the rest and we wish an alliance of power and trade that will benefit us all," offered the lady.

"I see. If you put it that way to the council, you may get much more support. Remember what I said, we are dealing with a group of self-interested individuals. Each one wants something out of every deal," explained the councilman.

"Interesting point. I will keep that idea in mind tomorrow at the council meeting."

"If you will excuse me, my lady, I must go now. I will send my son to escort you to the party later this evening at Narmisis' zenith. Until tomorrow." Gyron took the lady's hand and left, leaving the princess on the balcony recollected all she learned of the human and his fellow council members.

* * * * *

Gyron left the elven princess and walked purposefully down the long stone corridor of his castle. After passing a few alcoves, the head councilman stopped and waited a few moments to see if he was being followed. Seeing no one around, the short noble reached towards a loose stone in one of the many alcoves lining the dark hallway. Feeling the stone move freely, Gyron pushed the hidden lever forward. The click of the secret door was barely audible, but Gyron expected the familiar sound. He quickly pushed the freed section of the wall and entered the blackness of the secret passage. After closing the hidden portal, the councilman felt his way forward down the lightless passage until it opened up into a small faintly lit chamber.

The only light came from a short stout candle, which burned slowly on a small wooden table in the middle of the room. The illumination was only bright enough to leave a modest globe of light around the table. A set of slender calloused hands were visible in the yellowish glow of the candle, but their owner was deep in shadow. Seeing the other seated, Gyron quickly took the only other chair directly across from the dark guest.

"You are late, Gyron," hissed the disembodied voice.

"I was with the Princess. I cannot rush my plans with her," answered the unsettled human.

"You mean `our' plans, councilman?" replied the same cool voice.

"Yes, I meant `our' plans. Either way, this is delicate business. She is far brighter than she appears. She uses her beauty well. The stir she has created among the noble ladies in the capital will be felt months after she leaves."

"Word from the north is not good. It seems the ranger, Nelfindal Goldleaf, has escaped his imprisonment. He is very lucky, but he is not in good shape for travel. If he cannot be recaptured, he may arrive on your doorstep to ruin your plans."

Gyron thought about the possible situation and added, "Then I will have to watch my words more carefully. How are your superiors taking all this?"

"They are patient. The eldar's condition is poor and my leaders are true elves. Time is of little importance for those of such long life," remarked the calm informant.

"Then the ranger will be found? Before he gets here?" asked the nervous human.

"He may. He may not. Prepare for either," offered the dark voice.

"I will. You have helped me greatly, thank you."

"Gratitude is cheap, councilman. Information is not," replied the figure.

Taking a bag out from under his courtly robes, Gyron jingled it once then tossed it into the shadows behind the hands.

With the speed born of an experienced warrior, the hands disappeared into the shadows. No sound came from the bag as it was caught. The only response was a satisfied sigh.

"There is enough in there for your troubles," said Gyron.

"If there wasn't, you wouldn't be still talking, councilman."

Gyron knew the threat to be valid. He had dealt with the shadowy figure and knew no one lived long after crossing him.

"Until later then," added the human uncertainly.

The only response was the faint cool breeze signaling the meeting had already ended. Raising himself quietly, Gyron left the still burning candle behind and made his way to his private bedchamber. The secret passages led to almost every room in the large castle, but unless someone was familiar with their layout they would easily get lost. After only a few moments, the councilman was in his room locking the secret door behind him to leave out any possible assassins who also knew of the secret maze.

* * * * *

Darius walked cautiously out of the secret passage near the large gardens surrounding the castle of the head councilman, Gyron Vardonos. Even though Darius had secretly served the greedy human for many years, he still didn't trust the portly weasel. The human noble achieved his status more by eliminating the competition than by business skill alone.

The small bag of gold from Gyron weighed heavily in his right breast pocket. It contained the usual hundred pieces of gold for the information plus another hundred or so for `his troubles'. The risk in giving the information was minimal. The real treasure hung about the southern ranger's neck. The same medallion, which was taken from the eldar, Nelfindal Goldleaf, would finance a comfortable living for Darius to the end of his long life. The councilman was the only real buyer for the magical artifact and the price would be very high.

Darius made his way carefully across the dark streets of the business district and continued on towards the docks where a small, dark tavern warmly called to him. Before the silvan made it to the docks, a faint whisper reached his ears. Turning quickly about with his sword in hand, the elf faced off against several other darkly clad and almost equally quiet figures. All were well armed and stood confidently around the ranger in a small semi-circle.

"`Tis a dark night to be walking about alone, eh friend?" inquired one of the figures.

"Darkness suites me fine, friend stalker," replied Darius in the response to the thief's question.

"You are familiar with our guild. What are you known by so that we may curse your name over your corpse?"

"I'm known by many as Darius of the Farghest," replied the silvan.

"Forgive us friend. We had not realized you were one of our fellow associates in the great game," replied the dark figure.

"Many play the game, but prefer to be anonymous."

"True. We, however, do not. Remember well, our role in the game," replied the figure.

With a signal from the leader, the stalkers left the ranger sheathing his sword. The great game was played by everyone in Terrilon, but only the stalkers were known to live by and for the game. They were involved in every deception, assassination, or other devious play of the game. Next to the stalkers only the council board members played the game to such a complex level. And as all knew, the two were constantly using each other to the final end of total supreme power.

Thinking to himself as he entered the Wayfarer's Inn, Darius wondered how such an end could be achieve with so many players looking out for themselves. It was utter chaos, yet it seemed to create a loose sense of order where order could never be. The lithe silvan walked over to a comfortable booth and sat down. After sitting down a sweaty human limped over wiping his hands absently on a dirty apron.

"What can I getch ya'?" inquired the barkeeper.

"Just get me a grog," ordered the ranger.

After getting the silvan's order the barkeeper moved off to get the dark, foamy ale. As the human stepped behind the bar, a few grungy sailors walked into the bar. Their loud voices boomed over the din of the crowded room. The human returned to the small common room with a few mugs in his meaty hands and placed one in front of the relaxing elf.

The southern ranger leaned back comfortably in his dark booth and sipped on his mug of stout. The bitter flavored beverage tasted good on the silvan's pallet. Darius had too much of the northerners' ale and wine. The strong liquor of the south made most people of Aragon cringe, but local inhabitants could never get enough. The drink was also reputed to have a mild narcotic used in its processing. The tracker leader mused at the idea of how so many patrons had died from overindulgence.

* * * * *

The passage through the mountains was very slow going for Nelfindal who like many of his fellow rangers was considered a veteran trail blazer. The varying terrain of the Everhighs, as this massive series of peaks and valleys was called by the humans, tested the conviction and stamina of the hardiest souls. If it were not for the group of Farghest rangers who still followed him, the young eldar would have turned around long before. However, this adventure was no normal excursion into the unknown wilds of Aragon. The tall ranger's life depended on how much more determined he was than his pursuers.

After hearing the distant rumbling of the landslide which signaled the southern followers progress, Nelfindal once again took the chance at sending his presence across time and space to the steep mountainside. It was during his magical snooping that the eldar located the assassin making his way up the hill. As well as a small group of more distant trackers many hours behind. The tracks left behind by the young ranger would be easily followed by the experienced southern rangers who tirelessly pursued him.

Realizing the closeness of his pursuers, Nelfindal moved on with new found determination. Thinking to himself, the eldar realized that if he were to stop or slow down for any reason it would be to his demise. With this still in mind the ranger moved on down through a steep and overgrown gully. Sliding down the sides of the rutted dirt wall, Nelfindal found himself in a dark and unusually quiet glade of small white birches. From above, the small valley looked to be heavily wooded with tall stands of trees, but once inside the appearance changed some. The deep foliage was mostly due to the dense growth of vines grown over many uprooted trees.

Walking carefully across the quiet forest floor, the experienced ranger heard no wind, no birds, not even the usual humm, which identified the presence of insects. It was as if a sudden deafness had come to the tall elf's ears. Never before had such an absolute silence been observed in such an apparently rich forest. Moving with almost exaggerated stealth, Nelfindal made his way across the picturesque scene. The lack of sound made the elf feel as if he had walked into a painting. Each of his footsteps, quiet as they were, sounded like a herd of charging horses.

The silence went on for many hours as the young ranger made his way through the mute forest. It was at dusk when the silence was shattered by a large crashing sound. The concussion of the sound was amplified by the prior absence of noise, but nonetheless would have been considered loud even in a city's market district during the day. The source of the sound was a large scaly leg dropping only meters away from the cloaked figure of the resting Darkwood ranger. The scaled leg alone was nearly a meter in diameter and following the leg up to the body, Nelfindal froze in his place.

Only meters away from him stood the largest dragon the elf had ever seen. He had not seen many dragons, but enough to figure that this one was a grandfather of dragons. The wingless land dragon moved at a very slow pace for one of its size. The unintelligent worm passed right over the elf who would have been considered a tasty morsel by the huge behemoth. Luckily, the creature was either not hungry or had some other agenda in mind.

After several moments of standing still looking around the valley floor, the great lumbering beast passed by without incident. Nelfindal allowed himself a long sigh to relieve the tension from his close call with the ancient creature. It hadn't occurred to him that he had stumbled upon a great worm's hunting grounds. Such territories were rare now that the civilized races took it upon themselves to eliminate such voracious creatures. Making his way quickly across the valley floor, Nelfindal found a steep path, which use to serve as a game trail for a herd of goats or deer. All of which now probably sat digesting in the belly of the resident dragon.

Several times after passing the dragon's territory, Nelfindal found himself back tracking from unpassable terrain. Certain regions in the mountainous area were so overgrown with brambles that nothing larger than a small rodent could move through. These delays in his forward progress began to worry the anxious eldar. With a small host of southern trackers intent on catching him, the tall ranger wanted to waste no time with the great forest mother's diversions.

It was after a little over a week into the mountains when the eldar caught sight of his nearest pursuer. The dark figure moved out of the dense forest behind him and moved with great agility towards the surprised youth. Nelfindal thought it would be at least another day or two before the southern tracker would catch up. Instead the determined assassin stood armed only meters away from the now sword armed eldar.

A pair of longknives rested comfortably in the silvan's hands as he and the eldar circled each other on the uneven rocky ground. The younger elf was concerned about his silvan opponent, because of his obvious superiority in swordsmanship. Very few warriors had the talent or the confidence to wield two blades.

Raelin looked seriously at Nelfindal then broke into a big grin, which contrasted sharply to the pair of silver blades he held. "Well, I found you at last. I must admit you almost had me back there on the western slope. That trap you set killed one of my trackers, but I managed to avoid such carelessness."

"I would have been surprised if you had fallen for so simple a trap. It doesn't say much for the Farghest when one of their own falls victim to the most basic of traps," boldly admitted the eldar.

"True enough. I for one care little for the guilds. I only work with the Farghest because it serves my purpose for now," conceded the silvan.

"I thought you were one of those mercenary types."

"I'm hardly one of such limited vision. I play the great game more than anyone except that I am much more patient."

"The Great Game of the south. No one could ever achieve its goal yet you fool yourself with its ideal. No one can reach it," said Nelfindal.

"I am not the only one who works towards the fabulous prize. However, I do not wish the power myself and there are others who are working for the One to achieve the power."

"Who is this One that all of you are helping to get the power for? And what exactly is this power?" questioned Nelfindal remembering a distant conversation with another southern elf on the topic.

"The identity of the One is secret. As for the power, it is the essence of Shri-La. The total embodiment of all that was he will be achieved when the one has control over the three great talisman which are held by the representatives of the other players. The stalkers, the ruling council, and the Farghest are these three players. With the three talisman together Shri-La will again command," bellowed the proud assassin.

Nelfindal was awestruck at the mention of Shri-La, a mythical figure who supposedly ruled the world by his will alone. The creature was known to have demi-godlike powers. Stories of how the tyrannical beast had destroyed cities with a mere thought was believed to have been child bedtime stories. Many of the tales were supported by some fact and many still believed the tales to have been completely true.

"Shri-La would bring chaos to all that there is. How could you work for such destruction?" questioned the eldar.

"He will reward his servants as he did in the past. As for those who go against him. . ." Raelin left the sentence hang for only a few moments while he stared at the taller elf with malice. In a blur of motion the twin blades were filling the air with there musical whistle as they cut through the space separating the two elves.

Nelfindal reacted just quickly enough to parry the lightning fast barrage of twirling steel. The young ranger was hard pressed to defend against the deadly knives as one went low then the other high. Each strike came closer and closer to its mark as the eldar backed away. Seeing no immediate opportunity to escape, the desperate youth began to establish his own offensive moves. His light elven broadsword slashed forward forcing the assassin into a defensive posture. However, the attacks surprised the southern elf for only a short time.

The shorter silvan used his extra blade to his advantage as he dodged the slower broadsword and moved in for a double attack. The unexpected maneuver forced the taller elf to move treacherously on the uneven ground. After a couple more aggressive moves Raelin managed to make the youth stumble and fall back onto the rough ground. Exposed skin and rock contacted causing a rush of pain and fear to shoot through the eldar's body. Not unaccustomed to pain Nelfindal recovered quickly and rolled away from a downward strike from his opponent. The southerner's silvery blades dug into the earth were his chest had been only seconds before.

Rolling to his right Nelfindal managed to regain a defensive posture and prepare for the southerner's next attack. As expected another wave of blurring strikes came at the younger eldar. The veteran silvan used his extensive battle experience to land a few skillful strikes on his taller opponent leaving him bleeding in many places, but with no real major wounds.

After many minutes of unsuccessful strikes an opening appeared, which the quick witted assassin took advantage of. The result was a long deep gash down the eldar's forearm. The pain and the loss of much blood in his right arm caused the tall youth to drop his sword, which skittered across the rocky incline the two fought on. In a vain attempt Nelfindal dropped to his knees to grab at the weapon as it fell far out of reach. A look of utter defeat crossed over the northern ranger's face as his weapon slid down the rough slope behind the sneering tracker.

"Well, youth. It seems that you have lost your sword," mocked Raelin confidently.

Nelfindal stared back at the silvan and his mood changed. The primal instincts inherent in all creatures began to surface in the young ranger. Still on his knees, the eldar began to distract his adversary as he slipped his hand towards one of the dwarven daggers, which rested in his boot.

"You may kill me, but I will not give you any satisfaction in doing it. My soul will be returned to the Forest Mother in eternal peace. What will you have? Shri-La? That path can only lead you to destruction." The youth felt the cool touch of the hidden weapon just inside his left boot.

"I will enjoy killing you, ranger. And after I parade through the guild with your head, I will resume my quest. Fear not for my eternal soul. I have greater rewards awaiting me than you could ever imagine," replied the silvan as he moved towards the wounded eldar. "Now, you will die the fool that you are."

As Raelin lifted his blades for a final blow, Nelfindal quickly slipped the finely crafted dagger from his boot. In one fluid motion the blade slipped from its sheath an across the short distance into the assassin's chest were it cut through the treated leather armor like vellum paper. A small glow appeared on the handle of the knife as it sank into the silvan's heart.

The southern elf stood in utter dismay as the blade dug into his chest. It seemed like minutes went by as he looked out into space. Then slowly Raelin looked down at the glowing rune etched into the elaborate handle of the weapon taking his life. A small trickle of blood ran down from the small incision in the leather breastplate. Not long after the first drop had touched to the ground, the assassin fell forward, dead.

Nelfindal observed the scene in a distracted sort of way. It was as if he was no longer a participant, but just an observer of the battle. It took a while to realize his enemy had been defeated.

With a last surge of energy, the young ranger lifted himself from his crouching position and left the scene of the conflict. Pushing himself to get as far away as possible from the site. As he moved on he vaguely remembered to bind his wounded arm and cast a healing spell over it to stop the flow of blood.

The quick departure of the sun over the horizon left the slopes covered in shadow as Caric and his two trackers followed the faint tracks left behind by the northern ranger and his unseen escort. Caric bent down low almost touching the ground with his chin to get a better look in the failing light. The rocky ground didn't leave much sign of the two elves recent passage, but enough scratches were made to hint of rapid movement.

A few hundred meters farther up the slope, the cold form of the dead assassin welcomed the three approaching southerners. The silvan's corpse remained untouched by the wildlife, but the weather had taken its toll on the decaying figure. The dwarven dagger still protruded out of Raelin's body as a grim reminder of the deadly battle only a week before. As if to make a point of the assassin's failure, Caric walked right passed his still form as if the body were just another feature of the landscape. The two trackers looked hard at the withered elf and developed an increasing respect for the northern ranger who they were sent after.

The range commander stopped only meters away from the ghastly site when he turned around and looked thoughtfully at the body. Then as if decided on a new plan, the husky silvan pulled a chain from his neck unceremoniously. Hanging from the silver necklace was a smoky crystal of quartz, Caric placed the crystal on top of the dead elf and began to chant a complex series of archaic commands. The volume of the summons increased as the intricate spell casting went on. After a quarter of an hour of the strange litany, the chanting stopped abruptly.

The next few minutes were the scene of unusual activity as the crystal slowly melted away. Shortly after the pendant disappeared, a grayish fog began to swirl about the body. The ever increasing mist spun rapidly in a small maelstrom of excitement until a shadowy form began to coalesce above the ground. The two trackers stared in horror as they realized what was being done; a shryker had been summoned. The hellish creature was a tall non-corporeal creature with odd wing-like protrusions jutting out from its back.

The demonic beast looked out towards the range commander with its two pairs of red glowing eyes. Each of those fiery orbs exhibited all the vile wickedness inherent in its kind. The silence permeating the area was unbearable, but the gravelike voice which followed sent shivers done their spines.

"Who has dared to summon me from my domain?" growled the abhoration.

"I have, beast! I command the power to control you and you will do as I say," fervently replied Caric.

"Then get on with it, mortal. What petty deed do you require?" inquired the shadowy figure.

"The creature that killed my servant is still alive. I want him dead. You may have this body and the one that slayed him as well as his priceless soul," offered the elf.

"I smell the scent of the elf who slew your dead servant upon the weapon. It has the smell of a noble elf. I agree to the terms, but beware! You shall never summon me again or the price will be your life!"

As if to reassure the silvan of its promise, the shryker turned and struck out at one of the two quiet trackers. The unfortunate elf never saw the shadowy appendage coming and fell to the ground dead; his body shriveled up like a dry husk. The demon's eyes appeared to flame even brighter for a brief second then returned to there same crimson glow. After appearing to sniff the air the beast flew off into the night sky with the speed born of its kind.

The night sounds normally heard in the wild were muted throughout the entire encounter. Even after the shadowy apparition left the area, the forest remained quiet for some time.

Caric looked down at his dead tracker and measured the price of his endeavor. The silvan shook his head once then accepted the cost as the price of doing business with other worldly entities.

The surviving tracker couldn't appraise the situation in quite the same way. His first thought was to express his opinion, but quickly thought better of it when he felt the cold stare of his superior on him. Trying to appear unmoved the tracker inquired, "What do we do now, sir?"

Caric merely replied, "We move on after the eldar. If the shryker gets him then we will find his dried carcass. If not then we will have to finish the job ourselves."

* * * * *

Nelfindal had been traveling over the rugged mountain slopes for a week and still the treacherous range seemed to go on. Every time the tall elf crested one peak, another stood in mockery of him barring his way to the great forests beyond. Whether there were forests beyond or not was a matter of speculation. The veteran ranger knew of no one who had ever passed the expanse of the Everhighs. It was not something a sane individual cared to do willingly.

While resting comfortably on a shelf of exposed bedrock warmed by the summer sun, Nelfindal thought about the princess and her mission to the southern capital city of Terrilon. "I wonder if she thinks I'm dead?" mumbled the elf to himself.

High overhead a lone hawk soared through the sky. Using the updrafts common in the vast mountain range, the golden predator glided effortlessly in large circles. The sight of the relaxing ranger seemed to have attracted the bird's curiosity. Not long after it had completed a full pass around the valley, the broad wings furrowed and the hawk swooped down to a nearby tree limb. The branch was a good size, being close to a human's arm in diameter and yet it stilled bowed under the bird's weight. From so high up the massive bird appeared much like a common hawk, but upon a closer inspection the bird's real size came into perspective. The observing avian was a good two meters high and twice that long in the wings.

For a moment, the young ranger thought the bird was considering him as prey. Even as big as the creature was, the tall elf was far to big a catch for it. Somehow though, the bird seemed to be watching the eldar intently as if looking for something. After a few minutes of observation with its keen eyes, the hawk launched itself from the tree and flapped once, then twice to gain altitude until the updrafts supported its large frame. The bird circled once more around the valley gaining height then flew north away from the confused Nelfindal.

Lifting himself from the warm stone, the eldar continued his arduous hike up the steep cliffside. After taking one look back over the valley and the direction the strange bird had taken, Nelfindal resumed his quest to escape the embrace of the Everhighs. Cresting the ridge with care Nelfindal looked down the opposite side where a vast forested valley lay hidden in the embrace of the Everhigh Mountains. The deep green vegetation extended for many kilometers in all directions outlined by the surrounding mountain peaks. A powerful sense of antiquity could be felt as the tall ranger moved down into the isolated woodland.

Unlike many trapped valleys, this region was teaming with life. The forest ceiling was alive with many different varieties of birds. Most no larger than a common sparrow, but as varied in color as a rainbow with many bright greens, yellows, reds and every other combination of the three. The cacophony of the flitting inhabitants could be heard throughout the valley floor.

As the eldar walked under the broad boughs of the ancient trees he felt a feeling of complete peace. A feeling he had not felt for sometime. The moist ground was lightly covered with decaying leaves giving a spring to every step. Nelfindal began to get intoxicated by the feeling of life, which embraced him more and more with each stride of his long legs. As the young elf moved deeper into the ancient greenland, larger forms of life could be seen. Small herds of deer grazed on the lush vegetation which grew everywhere even under the shade of the massive oaks and birches. Red and grey foxes could be seen chasing after a plethora of rodents.

Following a herd of young bucks, Nelfindal realized that he was sprinting along with the nimble footed deer. The bachelor herd seemed to enjoy the ranger's company as he moved in among them and shared in their carefree run over the soft ground and past the broad tree trunks. The young stags accompanied by their newest member loped over fallen trees larger than a man's height and across small creeks without worry until the juvenile band reached a small river. Unable to cross the waterway in one jump the herd stopped to take a long drink. Following his new friends' example, Nelfindal bent over close to the water's edge and took a long draw himself.

The cool flowing water quenched his parched mouth almost immediately and eliminated his now growing exhaustion. Looking up through a break in the trees, Nelfindal realized he had been running with his free spirited friends for well over an hour. The sense of timelessness brought back century old memories of apprenticing in the vast forest of Darkwood. It was a time for work mixed with play as the experienced elven ranger recalled his days with the other youths practicing their arts of forest survival.

Nelfindal rested comfortably on the edge of the swirling creek as his new found friends foraged amongst the weeds sprouting alongside the water's bank. With a tender shoot in his mouth, looking much like a lounging human teenager, the young elf leaned back on a large fallen log covered with a blanket of moss. The soft greenery felt more comfortable than any bed the wandering eldar had ever experienced in his decades of traveling. The reclining elf closed his eyes to feel the life force about him and decided to rest a while before continuing as the sun set low behind the horizon.

A cool late afternoon breeze blew gently through the high treetops causing the many countless branches and leaves to sway in a gentle rhythmic motion. The faces of the leaves twitched back an forth from the deep green of their faces to the silver grey of their bottoms. The gentle currents of air awakened the smaller nocturnal inhabitants of the trees bringing a burst of new life to the quieting forest. The combination of the swaying trees and the chorus of millions of chittering insects created a symphony of sound and motion, which gave the entire forest the appearance of some grand opera. Unknowingly adding to the mixed harmonies was the soft resonance of a snoring elf, who could be faintly heard over the other forest sounds.

As Ryor approached its zenith, the forest symphony ceased. The sudden silence alerted the slumbering elf, but he remained immobile and apparently asleep. Without opening his half-lidded eyes, Nelfindal listened intently, but could only hear the gurgling of the nearby stream and the wind high overhead rustling the many countless leaves shielding the stars from sight. After a few minutes of sampling the smells and sounds of the area, Nelfindal slowly opened his eyes.

About a meter away, next to the ranger sat a dark silhouette staring intently at his relaxed posture. Immediately the eldar jumped to his feet only to find himself tripping over a very large cat resting on the ground below him. The elf caught himself just before falling face first into the cool stream water. The only response from the black and brown feline was a low groan and a sleepy look at the stumbling ranger. The golden orbs blinked a few times then disappeared again as the lazy cat went back to its peaceful rest.

Waiting for the young elf to steady himself and regain his composure, the dark figure said, "I apologize for my companion. He likes to nap far too much and always decides to do so in the worst of spots." The only response to the stranger's comment was a soft rhythmic rumble from the large pile of fur.

Nelfindal regained his balance and walked towards the odd pair noticing the herd of deer had departed sometime ago. "I. . uh .. I .. didn't know anyone was here. You caught me off guard," stuttered the eldar.

"Well, yes. I suppose you wouldn't expect us here," replied the dark visitor oddly. "My friend and I came here to greet you to our domain. A wonderful little forest when you get to know it. The trees tell us stories of the past that are so very fascinating. Though they tend to talk way to slow and they usually talk about past seasons and weather, which we don't care much about. I knew you were coming, but it was difficult finding you. However, my friend here, when he is motivated, mind you, has a peculiar talent for finding things."

"Who are you," questioned the confused youth.

"Forgive me, I get so carried away. I do so much enjoy visitors and it has been such a long time. One of our forest friends said that you were coming and that we should expect you anytime," continued the odd figure.

As Nelfindal approached the rambling figure, he noticed it was a worn looking middle-aged human. The little man had a long, braided pony tail extending from the back of his head all the way down his back were it ended just above his knees. His clothes were in disarray as one shirt tail stuck out of his trousers. From the looks of his soiled vest, it had been sometime since he had washed his clothes though it looked like he kept himself properly bathed.

The tall ranger looked at the stranger and asked again, "Who are you?"

"Didn't I say? Well, I guess I should. I am known by many people. then again nobody does really know me. Where was I?" inquired the human as he scratched at his rough collar.

"Your name," quickly replied the elf.

"Oh yes. My name is Gabriel Sebastion Alexander Nimbleleg. Or as my friends call me, Gabby. And this lazy fellow, here, is Armis," announced the boisterous hermit.

"I am pleased to meet you, sir. My name is Nelfindal."

"Oh a noble name, indeed! It is an honor to meet you, Nelf."

"It has been a long time since anybody has come to visit my fair forest, but it tends to be well too isolated for most travellers. What brings you here, my friend?" inquired the human as he absently scratched at some soiled clothing.

"A long story," wryly answered the elf.

"I so love stories. Please tell it to me," begged the scruffy hermit.

Nelfindal's recounting of the past few months continued into the late evening as the forest darkened dramatically from the long absent sun. After the young elf was finished the human broke in with a series of fantastic tales himself. The little man seemed to never tire of his own voice. Even when the blue moon, Ryor, had also set the woodsman continued on with his endless narratives. On many occasions, Nelfindal caught the rambling storyteller repeating the same tall tales.

It was quite apparent that the odd hermit enjoyed his own voice more than his stories. Even when the loud rumblings of the hungry elf's stomach were heard, the garrulous human continued on. It took the combined rumblings of the ranger and the big cat to shake the hermit from his monologue and admit to his own growing hunger. Gabby apologized for another quarter of an hour until finally Armis growled a very intimidating snarl of hunger.

Realizing that his friend and companion was beginning to look at him a little too closely, the human moved on in search of food. With the big cat and the tall ranger in tow close behind, Gabby walked away from the water's edge to a dense stand of short willows. The thick leafy branches moved aside with one graceful sweep of the human's extended arm exposing a clearing larger than a good size house. The young eldar was startled to discover such a large and well concealed space in the old forest. It was also well known that trees fought for space to embrace the sun's bountiful light. Nearly every forest in Aragon was constantly expanding.

The odd break in the forest opened up to the sky like a great window. Countless stars twinkled in the black sky, more than the traveled ranger had ever seen. It was as if every star that had ever existed could be seen no matter how distant or faint. The sight was absolutely wondrous and yet somehow discomforting. Such a display could only be through the use of strong magic, strong enough to hold nature itself at bay.

Gabby and his furry counterpart walked over to a large flat stone, which appeared like a table more suited for some emperor. The red granite stone was covered with ripe fruits and clay pitchers full of sweet nectar and cool spring water.

Gabby offered the tall ranger a clay cup and some fruit and began to dig into his own food. Armis decided to move off and find his own supper seeing the others involved in there own meals. With one great leap the giant cat disappeared into the depths of the forest. Seeing with eyes accustomed to night travel. The eldar and his odd host continued with their meals in relative peace.

The absence of the ivory orb in the night sky left the forest in an impenetrable blanket of black ink except for the occasional flash of a firefly. The deep darkness played games with the keen elven eyes which stared out into the noisy darkness. Even though, the young elf couldn't see the raucous forest life, he could here them keenly. Ever since entering the dense woodland, the forest never remained quiet. During the day the countless thousands of birds sang their enchanting tunes and during the night the symphony was continued by a nocturnal chorus.

The night continued on in its own peaceful way surfacing thoughts of Niki. The painful feelings burned at the core of his heart. It hadn't been very long since he had last thought of her sculpted complexion, her fragrant body or her lady-like laugh. All the traits that made Nelfindal love the princess coelesced in his mind creating the illusion that she was standing right next to him.

It was during his dreaming that the young ranger realized the potency of the nectar beverage which he had consumed. Already the effects began to take their toll on the now swaying eldar. Thinking to himself, Nelfindal wished that his friend, Norin, was around to sample the tasty beverage. But he had walked out on his best friend after an exchange of painful words. Disturbed by the thought of his friend, Nelfindal drained the rest of his cup and gently eased himself against a comfortable bend in a tree and fell quickly asleep.

The onset of morning brought more than sunshine to the young elf. The fierce pounding of a hangover reverberated against the sides of his seemingly oversized head. From the tolling of the invisible bell, Nelfindal concluded that the drink was far stronger than anything he had ever imbibed. Unfortunately, there was no available medicinal relief for the never ending pain.

Before the sun completely rose above the elevated horizon, the odd little human returned from some recent excursion into the old forest. The hermit was followed closely by the huge cat like some trained domestic. The huge feline stopped to lick its massive paws and yawn, taking a most impressive snap of air that would have sent most anybody running for their lives.

Gabby carried a large mutton leg freshly killed from the smell of it. As Nelfindal made his way slowly towards the scruffy pair, a sense of incredible hunger nagged him. Feeling foolish and somehow childish, the tall eldar remarked, "It feels like I've been sleeping for days. What was in that drink?"

"Hee, Hee! You have been sleeping for days. Two days, in fact. I forgot to warn you about the effects of the drink I gave you. It is very potent especially when consumed at night under the starry sky."

"What does a starry night have to do with how strong a drink is?"

"The nectar of the Starfire Blossom is best served during starry nights were it gets its magic from. And a strong magic it is! Oh yes, very strong magic. Once I consumed a whole bottle on a night like the night before last and I slept for a whole week without so much as raising an eyelid!" recollected the short human as he carved the fresh meat into long thin strips.

Nelfindal assisted the old man by building a quick fire with the help of his enchanted bow. Soon a small, hot fire was burning and the strips of meat were stuck on long, sharpened reeds for cooking. After a few minutes the catch was cooked and eaten in swift order. The ranger ate a great deal of meat, but less than he normally would have after sleeping for two straight days. With every bite of the succulent meat, Nelfindal observed the golden stare of Armis. The giant cat looked longingly at the ranger's ministrations much like one of the many large dogs he had seen in keeps housing human nobles.

Feeling guilty, the elf threw several of the larger chunks towards the cat. Faster than the eldar could follow, Armis snapped the slices out of the air.

"Armis! I told you, it isn't nice to beg. You already had your portion of the meal. Now go off and keep yourself busy. Can't you see that this youth needs his nourishment?" reprimanded the hermit.

The cat replied by curling up into a ball and quickly falling asleep. The resounding purrs could be heard throughout the area as the satiated feline slept soundly. Several times the twitch of a leg or the reflex movement of a stray muscle could be seen as the cat dreamed of wonderful hunts.

Nelfindal asked, "Gabby, you say it has been a long time since you had seen anybody around here, how long has it been?"

Still munching on a slice of the roasted mutton, Gabby spit out, "Weh, ith been many, many yearth since I met anotha human." Various sized chunks of meat flew out of the human's mouth some landing on his grungy lap only to be returned to the toothy maw.

Nelfindal stared in disbelief at the utter lack of eating habits, but realized it to be the habit of a recluse. Trying to avoid being hit himself the elf kept the questions down to a minimum as he probed his odd host for information. After several unsuccessful attempts at keeping his questions simple, Nelfindal relaxed himself and kept his mouth shut. Even without provocation, Gabby managed to talk about something spreading particles of half-eaten food in all directions.

After everybody had their fill, the unlikely group packed up and made their way out of the clearing. Nelfindal found himself impressed with the strange little human and his feline companion. As the three moved through the forest growth, not once did a creature stir as they passed. Occasionally, a young buck or small rabbit would dart away only after the hermit and the cat came within arms reach of them. Their footfalls never made any noise even over dried leaves and branches. Nelfindal found himself flushing at the amount of racket he made. And many fellow rangers thought he was one of the best in the shadow walk, the silent step of the rangers.

By the end of the day the three had crossed a small fraction of the large valley. When night came Armis disappeared to do what ever nocturnal creatures do. This left Nelfindal and Gabby alone to sit back along a creek and listen to the murmur of the flowing water as it passed them. The same oddness which plagued the elf when he first came into the forest began to build once more. Feeling oddly curious about the feeling he asked his human friend, "Ever since I came into this forest, I have felt an odd sort of feeling as if something was trying to talk to me."

Since meeting the whimsical hermit for the first time, Nelfindal had never seen him serious until he asked the question. For a strange moment the eldar thought he saw a faint look of longing. Gabby quickly shed the expression and solemnly replied, "That my friend is the mourning of the land. Here you find it more pronounced because this forest is so ancient. More ancient than even your home forests in Elador or Darkwood."

"Why do they mourn?"

"They still mourn from the time of the Evil One. When he devastated the land north of here and warped the life that exists today. When the Evil One first appeared there were no trolls or orcs or any other creatures which terrorize this world except for the dragons who have always been around. He created these abhorations and many more others to serve him. As his power grew so did the pain and suffering of the land," recounted the human.

"I don't remember ever hearing of this Evil One. Is this the same creature that my people call the Great Beast?"

"The creature which you refer to was only a servant of the Evil One. And the reason you never heard about the Evil One is because until recently no one was safe enough to speak his name aloud."

"What happened to the beast? Was it destroyed with its master?"

"I wish it had. The Evil One was banished from this world long before his servants developed enough courage to even confront those who cast their master away, namely the elven mages of Elador and the human alchemists of Ci Aates."

"Strange how the elven records never spoke of such things. I thought I had learned all the history of my people."

"This was before the common elves learned to record history. Only the royal family and their loyal magicians new enough to record the events. Even then they had little time for such things since they were more concerned with their own survival."

"Yes, I can see were that may play a part in the omissions. How is it that you know so much? For a hermit you seem well versed in the goings on of other races and nations," inquired the suspicious elf.

"I wasn't a hermit all my life you know. I was once a great mage you know!" boasted the scruffy human.

"Nelfindal looked at the hermit as he thrust his chest out in a ridiculously silly display of strength. The sight so amused the ranger that his bellowing laughter rang out over the sounds of the rippling creek. Gabby simply straightened his uncharacteristic posture and stuck out his tongue at the hysterical eldar. The gesture only increased the elf's mirth who fell against a tree trying to maintain his balance as the laughter continued unabated.

After resting for a small time, the ranger and his unlikely guide continued on there trip across the valley floor to the far side of the range. After a full day of traveling the two travelers decided to stop and rest in a small clearing suitable for a campsite. After traveling through the ancient forest, Nelfindal realized that there were very few meadows.

This open grassland was by far an exception what was usually considered the rule in the northern regions where forest and grasslands were equally common. The break in the trees offered a refreshing glimpse of the open sky. The clouds floated majestically across the blue tapestry of the sky with no apparent direction or destination. The sun set quickly in this part of the world and the first signs were demonstrated by the golden glow frosting the cottony puffs.

Even at dusk the large feline, Armis, had not reappeared. Gabby saw the elf's eyes searching the forest shadows and responded, "He hunts for some time. He has a great mass to fill and when he is finished, he is usually to full to move."

Nelfindal smiled at the thought of the cat sleeping lazily after eating his fill. It never really occurred to the ranger that the big furrball would ever harm anything, but even the most gentle creatures need to eat. Comfortable with the fact that the cat was somewhere sleeping off a filling meal, the ranger fell into a deep sleep. His dreams were filled with large, furry cats chasing each other with careless abandon in the bright moonlight and sleeping lazily under the hot golden rays of the sun.

It was about an hour past midnight when the strange dreams invaded the young ranger's sleep. After a few brief glimpses of strange and unexplainable horrors the eldar awakened abruptly. Clearing the foggy sensation which permeated that brief moment after sleep, Nelfindal sensed the bone chilling sensation of demon spore. The realization so confused the elf that he froze in his spot, paralyzed by fear.

After a few moments, two pairs of red glowing orbs appeared in the glade. The tiny specks of fiery light grew quickly as their owner homed in on its victim. After a few minutes of utter terror the strange feeling of control tore through the fear-filled shroud covering the cowering ranger. Nelfindal couldn't explain the sudden change of mind, but didn't spend much time on the topic. Seeing the dark apparition approach his position was enough to gather his wits in time to move into action.

As the shryker approached its prey, the demonic beast slowly savored the scent of noble blood; it was rare to sense such a strong sensation. Walking towards the fearful elf the evil predator sensed more than saw the change in the eldar ranger. The tall form of the elf stood up quickly and prepared to engage the silent assassin.

As Nelfindal moved towards the silhouette of blackness, he maintained a sense of control which he had never sensed before. It was as if another person was running his body and he was only an observer. This sensation continued as he drew his fine blade from its sheath. The action caught the attention of the invader, because shortly after the sword was drawn the demon attacked. The exchange was vicious and ended quickly as the clawed appendage of the beast struck out and barely caught the ranger just under the jaw. The maneuver still sent the young elf flying against the hardened trunk of an old oak. The jarring impact sent waves of pain and dizziness through the ranger's mind.

After impacting with the tree, the shryker moved confidently towards the stunned and nearly unconscious eldar. After getting within a few meters of the still form the dark blurry shape of Armis came flying out of the forest. The giant cat struck the demon stalker hard in the side knocking it across the open grass. A heart-stopping shriek emanated from the creature more out of shock than pain as it hit the ground. Nelfindal was awed by the cat's courage to fight something so powerful, but somehow the ranger felt more than understood that the odds were strongly in the feline's favor.

The shryker's cry awakened the previously sonorous hermit who jumped at the sound of the demon's rage. Seeing his private domain invaded by an uninvited visitor, Gabby changed dramatically and began to enchant the complex language of magic which Nelfindal could not decipher. As the words rolled of the scruffy human's lips, the air itself took on an alien feeling. The sensation didn't go unnoticed as the shryker hissed at the spellcasting human. After the last syllable was spoken the human screamed out, "Begone!"

That one simple word apparently carried much weight as the smell of burnt embers permeated the forest. Followed by a blast of searing cold which left the stunned Nelfindal shivering intensely. While the eldar shook uncontrollably he realized the pair of fiery eyes were gone. In fact, there was no sign of the creature or that it had ever been present. The only indication of an encounter was the brief silence of the nocturnal symphony which eventually resumed its persistent thrum minutes after the confrontation.

Recovering from the attack, Nelfindal turned towards the human and asked, "what was that?"

Gabby seriously replied, "it seems someone sent a shryker after you. However, the beast has been dismissed back to its own plane."

"I don't know how you did this, but thank you."

"I was merely protecting my home. Please, let us get some sleep. This evening has been an exhausting one," begged the human as he rolled up into a ball below the spreading limbs of a willow tree and continued his rhythmic ministrations.

Nelfindal looked over at the surprisingly resourceful human and wondered to himself on how his fortune had turned to the better. The reclusive hermit had turned out to be a powerful sorcerer with the rare ability to dispel demons; a quality that deserved much respect. The ranger refused to question his fortune, but the nagging feeling that he was directed towards the ancient forest permeated his thoughts. Many people believed in chance, Nelfindal was not one of them.

He had encountered magicians before, but never had he met a mage powerful enough to command a demon away with a simple word of command. Thinking of the past day's events only tired the exhausted elf. Soon the rhythmic sound of the eldar's breathing could be heard, which was echoed by the strange hermit. Armis stood watch over the two with an alertness that surpassed any normal cat's senses. The rest of the night proceeded without incident and if anything had interrupted the peaceful slumber, Armis was ready to deal with it.

Nelfindal woke up with a start the following morning as the sun rose out over the eastern mountain peaks. Looking across the small meadow the elf realized that the hermit and his companion were nowhere in sight. Wondering were the reclusive and whimsical human had wandered off to, the eldar began a thorough search for any signs of their location. After a good hour of an intensive scouring of the area, Nelfindal came up empty. Throughout his investigation not one bent blade of grass or broken branch was found. It was if the entire episode the prior evening were one bad dream.

Feeling the same oddness that had been plaguing him since first entering the ancient forest, Nelfindal somehow sensed that his stay had worn out. For the rest of the morning the eldar contemplated his next steps. The need to get to the southern capital was becoming more apparent as the tall ranger remembered his recent escape from the Farghest.

Realizing that he was just wasting time sitting around, Nelfindal moved on in hopes of escaping the grip of the Everhighs.

* * * * *

The eastern side of the Everhighs ended in sheer cliffs dropping hundreds of meters to deadly piles of fragmented boulders. The winds blowing off the plains below created dangerous gusts capable of blowing even the heaviest of objects from the cliff's edge. Oddly enough, small bushes clung precariously to the dramatically sloping mountain sides. Their tough roots drove deeply into the rocky ground securing the unusually hardy vegetation to the stone face.

Nelfindal maintained great distance from the cliff's edge as he approached it. He felt the faint touch of the incredible winds which pulled everything down to the grasslands below. The tall ranger carefully approached the crest of a large ridge were the thunderous sound of crashing water could be heard. The eldar stepped cautiously over the top of the ridge only to happen upon a marvelous sight. The ridge was actually the bank of a wide, fast flowing river.

The white froth cascaded breathtakingly over the mountain's lip falling nearly fifty meters to a massive swirling pool of deep blue-green water. The turbulent waters continued into another waterfall and continued on through three other smaller flows; all of which being less impressive than the first, but nonetheless awesome in their display. The crashing falls created a fine mist which drifted upwards eventually landing kilometers away on the vast green lands just east of the range. The delicate spray covered the region in a odd halo of reflected light causing many colorful rainbows to appear.

As enticing a view as it was; however, the ranger continued his hike past the edge towards a narrower strip for crossing. As he passed a small outcropping of rock, the faint shadow of a humanoid could be seen just before the flash of a steel sword. The golden haired elf dogged the attack only to be sprayed by stone chips as the falling blade dug into the rock close to his head. Rolling out of his maneuver, the eldar again had to dodge another series of deadly blows as sparks and splintered rock shot in all different directions.

The dark elf didn't give the ranger much time to recover from the surprise as he swung once then again. Each time the sword fell, it came closer and closer to hitting its mark. Eventually, Nelfindal managed to get to his feet and draw his sword in time to block an arm numbing blow against the hilt. The shock shot forth up through the eldar's arm forcing him to drop his weapon. The attacker maintained his onslaught as Nelfindal dodged each strike and thrust. Often, the dark elf managed a close scrape leaving the tall eldar bleeding from several places.

Worsening matters, the young elf saw the dark form of another Farghest quickly making his way towards him. But nothing could compare to the terror developing from the sight of the broad chested range commander. The fear grew with each passing glimpse of the rage filled face of the range commander, Caric. So distracted with the presence of Caric, Nelfindal failed to block his adversary's low sword thrust. The blade sank deeply into his leg cutting through the tough leather greave protecting his left thigh. Somehow the Darkwood ranger managed to stand long enough to ward off another blow aimed at his head. The rush of pain coursed through his body, but subsided slightly after hearing a faint calling. It was the voice of his enchanted bow.

"Call upon me! Engulf yourself in flame like you did before!" shouted Elenar telepathically. "Do it, now!"

Unable to comprehend the repercussion of summoning the fire, Nelfindal called upon his will to command his weapon. Within the blink of an eye the entire region about the eldar was enveloped in a blinding burst of brilliant fire. The attacking elf could do nothing, but helplessly thrash on the ground as the magical fire consumed his body. The fiery shield slowly radiated out away from the tall ranger destroying everything it touched.

Caric saw the golden-haired elf drop to the ground as he approached. A thought flashed into the husky silvan's head unconsciously guiding him off the path and towards a calm portion of the river. Diving head first into the swirling waters, the range commander felt the unimaginable heat scorching his exposed skin as he hit the water. From the river bottom Caric could see the steam lifting away from the surface in a vast cloud of vapor. The flowing river was all that protected him from the horrible death awaiting less than a meter away.

Like so many times before, a strange and unexpected premonition had saved his life. The dark elf knew it came from his sword, but wasted no time on pondering how it was possible. Instead, the range commander concerned himself with how long the fire would rage on. He had great confidence in his ability to hold his breath, but was impatient to eliminate the tiresome eldar. The Farghest moved away from the odd twilight effect created from the steam above and swam towards a clear spot bordered by a large group of rocks.

When Caric thrusted his head from the cool water, the fire had ceased, leaving only a barren region of ashes where his tracker had once stood. The northern ranger knelt close to the ground smoldering slightly, but otherwise unharmed by the summoned magic. The vicious sword wound inflicted by the incinerated elf was apparently slowed by a healing spell. The pale look on the weakened youth showed the amount of blood lost was considerable. Quietly slipping out of the water, Caric carefully made his way towards the eldar raising his sword for a killing blow.

Nelfindal knew of the southern elf's approach, but chose to remain still concentrating on the healing spell he remembered from his days with the healers of Darkwood. The flow of blood slowed then stopped completely as the eldar strained to will the tissue together. Just before Caric was able to deal his deadly thrust, Nelfindal rolled away from him. The momentum of the move was more than the youth had expected causing him to slide towards the water.

Caric was taken off guard by the Darkwood ranger's maneuver, but didn't loose track of his target. Caric managed to slash across the leather armor of the eldar as he rolled away, but the enchanted armor resisted the grazing of his blade. Nelfindal finally stopped his rolling just as he hit the watery edge where he was able to summon his bow. The faint flash of magic was all the dark elf could see before the hard wood of a longbow crashed into his stomach. Nelfindal heard the resounding thud and the groan that followed indicating a successful hit. Standing up quickly, the wounded ranger swiftly loaded his bow and fired an unaimed shot at the recovering southerner.

Caric ran at the drawn bow without a thought and swung at the deep brown wood. The poorly nocked arrow careened of the stone several meters to the side of the attacking range commander. The oddly sounding clunk of steel on wood was heard, but was soon followed by the flash of combating enchantments and a loud percussion. The power of the magical confrontation threw both fighters in opposite directions both weapons flying out of their grasp.

Minutes went by as neither one moved, finally Caric raised himself with intense agony as both his hands and his face showed signs of serious burning. Raising himself to a kneeling position Caric looked towards the still form of Nelfindal. With a strange sense of weariness, the dark elf approached the golden haired ranger. Standing over the motionless form for a brief moment, Caric drew a dagger and bent over to insure that the eldar never breathed again. The range commander grabbed the sweat soaked head and slid his dagger towards the exposed throat of the tall northerner for the final slash.

As the eldar's head moved upwards the startlingly vibrant hazel eyes flashed. Caric felt the sudden sensation of cold steel as the realization of the eldar's trickery became evident. The young ranger duped his anxious attacker into letting down his defenses for the easy kill. The ruse would have been complete if the short-bladed hunting knife had driven deep enough in the southerner's ribs. The ploy did give Nelfindal time to move away from his comprising position and find safe ground to fight from.

Caric recovered from the painful attack quick enough to chase after the fleeing eldar. The pursuit led the two elves over slick moss covered rocks and through the shallow waters bordering the deeper regions of the river. The pursuit lasted only a few moments with the recent injury to the eldar's leg, but in that short time the two managed to cover nearly half a kilometer.

Nelfindal finally stopped only meters from the edge of the mist shrouded waterfall; his thigh going numb from the loss of blood which continued to run down his leg.

The close proximity of the drop-off made the youth's position even more precarious as Caric approached him through the shallow waters along the bank. Standing in a defensive position, Nelfindal gathered himself enough to speak to his long-time enemy, "So, you finally caught up to me."

Caric slowed as he walked towards the tall elf keeping a wary eye on him. "Your resourcefulness has lasted longer than I anticipated. However, the only thing keeping you alive now is my wish to see you suffer. You destroyed my life that day we met. I have waited too long to return the favor," seethed the dark elf.

"How did I humiliate you so much that you have sought to persecute me for so long?" questioned Nelfindal.

"You remember that day long ago? Do you remember the fight and the elf you killed? Do you? Well, I'll tell you what really happened. That elf was my brother. That is why I wish to see you die. And now, you shall!" With blurring speed Caric charged towards the tall eldar and struck out with his longknife.

Nelfindal expected the attack, but not the speed of the silvan's assault. The younger elf managed to block the onslaught with his shorter knife, but was thrown of balance and slipped into the deep, fast moving water. Thrashing around in the strong current of the river, he managed to grab a hold of a large rock and pull himself into shallower water. The tall youth looked across the flow at Caric. The range commander bounded from boulder to boulder making his way towards the waiting eldar.

Not wanting to wait for the silvan's attack, Nelfindal charged his adversary with a series of weak thrusts and slashes.

The attack didn't affect the southern elf a bit. Each pass of the hunting knife was met by the fine bladed longknife. The ring of steel on steel sang out faintly over the deafening roar of the falls below.

Each parry was followed by a promise of a slow death by the range commander as he toyed with the ever weakening ranger. After several exchanges realized he had lost too much blood to continue for very long. The wound received from his earlier battle was slowly taxing his strength.

Stepping back from a violent and dizzying series of thrusts, Nelfindal discovered that he was dangerously close to falling into the swirling waters of the lower falls.

Caric noticed the eldar's dire position and responded, "See, you have no escape. No one can help you and I will make sure you don't escape."

With a few more feints, Caric managed to get the tall ranger right up to the edge. Aware of the eldar's precarious position, Caric took one final lunge to finish off his defeated opponent. So confident with the sure kill, the range commander didn't pay much attention to his own situation. Nor did he watch his footing on the slippery rocks under the shallow waters. With a sudden move the dark elf dove in for the attack, but slipped on a slimy patch of moss.

Time seemed to slow as seconds became minutes as the silvan slowly drifted over the falls and into the mist below. Nelfindal's last memory of Caric was the look of insane denial as fate dealt out another little twist. Caric's flailing body disappeared into the misty vapor of the vast falls.

Slowly recovering from the image, the weakened eldar moved towards the shore slipping occasionally on the countless moss covered rocks. Slumping roughly against a small boulder, Nelfindal clumsily wrapped his wounded leg and cast another healing spell over it. He slid off the rock and onto the rough ground slowly closing his eyes to rest. The crashing of the waterfalls was the last sound Nelfindal heard before darkness consumed his consciousness.

ABOUT THE AUTHOR

Richard B. Crowley was born on the south side of Chicago, but subsequently grew up in the western suburbs of the Chicagoland area. Richard has always had a love for reading science fiction and fantasy with J.R.R. Tolkien, R.A. Salvatore, Raymond Feist and Piers Anthony being his greatest influences. This novel, his first written work, evolved in his last year of undergraduate study in accounting, but left incomplete for nearly 20 years before taken up again. It was his need for escape from the mundane world and the desire to free himself from the conventions of reality that evolved into this work.

Richard shares his living fantasy with his wife Debbie, their dogs Rags and Charlie along with the menagarie of exotic creatures unfortunately none of which breath fire.

Made in the USA
Lexington, KY
09 July 2018